PENGUIN BOOKS

THE ASH HOUSE

Audrey Chin is a Singaporean writer whose mission is to tell the Southeast Asian story from the point-of-view of a multicultural Peranakan woman. She is a Fellow of the 2017 University of Iowa International Writing Program.

Her books include *Learning to Fly* (1998), *As the Heart Bones Break* (2013), *Nine Cuts* (2015) and *When Heart Meets Spirit* (2016). She is contributing co-editor of *Singapore Women Re-presented* (2004), a social history of the lives of women in Singapore. Her short-stories, essays, poetry and translations have been published in the US, UK, Singapore and regionally.

Audrey is sensitive to the atmosphere of spaces and believes in 'the imponderables'; love, ghosts and God included.

You can find out more about her and her work at www.audreychin.com

CW00550154

Enjoy

2021

PRAISE FOR *THE ASH HOUSE*

'*The Ash House* is everything I love about a gothic ghost story: intimate, familiar, yet deeply unsettling. I am so tempted to draw comparisons with Shirley Jackson, but Audrey Chin's novel is an inimitable beast of its own, seething behind some gorgeous imagery of post-colonial Southeast Asia. It is an enchanting whisper in the dark, a shadowy, sensuous call to revisit the demons that reside within the crevices of our ancestral memories.'

—SUFFIAN HAKIM
author of #1 Straits Times Bestseller
Harris Potter and the Stoned Philosopher
and *The Minorities*

'In *The Ash House*, Audrey Chin weaves an intricate, startling matrix that does away with the gaps between the visible and invisible life forces influencing human choices. The story is a riveting and sensuous voyage into drama and duality, love and betrayal, dreams and delusions, family and belonging. Reader, prepare to be deliciously unsettled.'

—YVONNE ADHIAMBO OWUOR
award winning author of *The Dragonfly Sea*,
Dust and *Weight of Whispers*

'*The Ash House* is an elegant and original addition to the literature of subversion, alchemically blending the traditional Asian ghost story with the European gothic tradition. It's intelligent, politically aware, sexy and, above all, spooky. This is a book to be read with the lights on, and with a lot of free time because you won't be able to put it down.'

—STEPHEN CARVER
author of *Shark Alley: The Memoirs of a Penny-A-Liner*

'Spectral and haunting, *The Ash House* spirits you deep within the Tjoa household. Encountering the pain, turmoil and deep longing experienced by three generations, you must continue reading till the last page to fully comprehend the lasting impact of a buried family secret.'

'Compelled by sexual desire and the emptiness of unrequited love, the characters of Audrey Chin's *Ash House* reside in 21st century South-East Asia and in the landscapes of our own souls. Who will deliver them from the hollow within, the ruse of hungry ancestral spirits and the devious wiles of evil? The *Ash House* is cleverly crafted; a bold, intriguing, and eminently readable narrative of social domination, the eternal thirst of the soul, and of our ultimate equality before the pull of evil.'

'*The Ash House* blew me away – An intelligent and imaginative ghost story, yet so much more as it opens our eyes to all the beings in South East Asian cities we often simply don't see. Not just ghosts like the pipa-player Bing Fa, but also flesh and blood humans like Girl, a migrant worker from Indonesia. Chin spins a web that entangles the reader as much as the vivid and fascinating characters whose lives and dreams are thwarted by forces bigger than themselves. I love it!'

The Ash House

Audrey Chin

PENGUIN BOOKS

An imprint of Penguin Random House

PENGUIN BOOKS

USA | Canada | UK | Ireland | Australia
New Zealand | India | South Africa | China | Southeast Asia

Penguin Books is part of the Penguin Random House group of companies
whose addresses can be found at global.penguinrandomhouse.com

Published by Penguin Random House SEA Pte Ltd
9, Changi South Street 3, Level 08-01,
Singapore 486361

First published in Penguin Books by Penguin Random House SEA 2021

ISBN 9789814954273

Typeset in Adobe Garamond Pro by Manipal Technologies Limited, Manipal
Printed at Markono Print Media Pte Ltd, Singapore

www.penguin.sg

For the shelter at HOME
(Humanitarian Organization for Migration Economics)
that it continues to be a place of refuge and support
for vulnerable domestic workers here
in our city state.

'I have been woman
for a long time
beware my smile
I am treacherous with old magic
and the noon's new fury
with all your wide futures
promised
. . .'

A Woman Speaks by Audre Lorde

1

Like every Catholic child in Kota Cahaya, the City of Light, the one who became Sister Mary Michael Chan had been warned about Ghost Month sacrifices. Who knew what lingered around the smouldering piles of Hell Money and pyramids of sticky buns on the five-foot ways outside Chinatown's ash houses? Who could predict what might latch on to her if she stopped to stare? Whom she might unwittingly invite home?

But Mary Chan was the daughter of a strict Peranakan mother who only ever said 'no' and 'don't' and 'stop'. She'd been emptied so thoroughly of want she was a hollow who couldn't help but echo when the voices from the white ashes called. It had surprised no one when the Sisters of Succour asked her to join them on her sixteenth birthday. What other vocation could she have?

She has been at it now for sixty years, offering her hollows to the whatnots still lingering in her sparkling-clean twenty-first century city-state. And on this very early Friday morning in yet another Ghost month, there it is again, another voice calling for her.

The dawn light is reaching through the stained glass of the chapel windows and the nun is on her knees praying 'no' and 'don't' and 'stop' to the pain thorning through her bones when she hears it—a woman's voice singing.

'望穿秋水 . . . gazing into . . . water, 不见伊人的情影 . . . my beloved . . . lost, . . . 依旧是当年的情景 . . . only . . . remaining . . .'

The voice, which seems to come from everywhere and nowhere, is as soft and inviting and suggestive of the closest intimacies as that of a natural mother. And the lyrics of her song—which the nun only partially understands—suggest an emptiness only a child's love can fill. But Sister Mary Michael has long abandoned her childhood and the need for a blood warm natural mother. She isn't deceived.

'Oh, stop it, you slave of that father of lies,' she says into the half-dark. 'If it's salvation you want, just say so.'

The voice chuckles.

'Life, death, love, salvation, especially salvation . . . It's all an illusion you know, Sister. I know better than to hanker after any of that.'

'That can't be true if you've come to me,' the nun replies.

'You, the one on her knees because her medicine's failing and she needs a miracle to mend her brittle bones! Whose need is so great, even I heard it! You, who can't raise a peep from your god! What can you and your lot do for me?'

Sister Mary Michael ignores the comments about her God's silence. 'Our Lord and His Church can do a lot for you, and you know it. Just tell me who you are and what you need me to do.'

She hears a trill of notes running across pipa strings, like water rippling down a stone bank.

A pipa player, she thinks.

'Perhaps,' the voice says, as if its owner has heard the nun speaking aloud. 'And then perhaps not.'

There are more tinkling notes, this time plucked rather than strummed.

'I could be playing a pipa. Or maybe a liuqin. Or a guzheng. You can't tell, can you? And I'm not telling,' the voice teases. 'Not until you set me free. If you can . . .'

'There's no "if" in that,' the nun replies. 'It's easily done. The only "if" is whether freedom is what you really want. Is it?'

There is no answer to the nun's question.

Sister Mary Michael stares up at the shadows clinging to the chapel's vaulted ceiling. The spirit is gone. It will be hours till the mynahs announce sunrise and Morning Office. But as surely as the sun will flood through the red glass of the St Michael window above the altar, there'll be another encounter with this spirit. For, whether the spirit admits it or not, she's just like all the others who make their way to the nun. She wants her freedom and time is running out. Sister Mary Michael, so open to the voices of the netherworld yet so close to the divine, is her last resort.

Sister Mary Michael slides out of the pew and creaks her way back to her cubicle to retrieve her overnight bag and the wooden case she keeps on her private altar. The pre-packed bag contains a change of clothes, toiletries, her spare breviary and a rosary. The wooden case—her tool kit—holds a crucifix and rosary, containers of Holy Water, Blessed Salt and Holy Oil, a pair of candles, the Sister of Succour's prayer book, and three laminated sets of the Roman Rite of Exorcism.

The nun checks to make sure the candles are fresh and the containers topped up. Then she clicks the wooden case shut, places it onto a trolley along with her bag and sits down on her bed to wait. She's as ready as she'll ever be. All she needs now is the Bishop's phone call to send her to her next assignment. To the owner of that voice. And her song.

* * *

The Bishop's secretary calls shortly after Morning Office.

'He wants you to beard another whatnot,' the secretary tells the nun. 'In the Tjoa ash house, up on Green Hill. You're to come to the Residence right away.'

'And who's the afflicted?' the nun asks.

'Someone from the Tjoa family, that's all I know,' the secretary replies. 'You'll have to wait and find out from the man himself.'

'It's Arno Tjoa Jia Hao, the Tjoa family heir,' the Bishop tells the nun, forty minutes later, after he shuts the door of his private office and Sister Mary Michael has settled her bones as comfortably as she can in the oversoft chair facing his desk.

'The family cook found him in his grandmother's old bedroom this morning, enacting a scene suggesting malign influences.'

He pulls a stack of printouts from his in-tray and slides them across his desk.

'The cook who found him took these pictures on her phone and sent them to the boy's aunt, Madam Irene Tjoa. Irene's the de-facto head of the family now as the boy's grandmother has passed on and his father's near death in a hospice. She thought the content warranted my attention.'

The nun takes in the photographs showing a re-enactment of six hangings; one adult Barbie doll and five smaller ones, all stark naked and strung by their hair to the top frames of a series of sliding doors.

'Not nice,' she says.

The Bishop nods.

'I'm told he's still in the room, backed up against a wall under a table. His aunts are divided as to what the appropriate response should be. Some are for an institution, but from the pictures, Irene Tjoa suspects it could be something else. And she wants us to help her make the assessment.'

'Which requires me observing him and ruling out psychological or psychiatric issues?'

'And also doing whatever you can for him, as you think fit,' the Bishop adds.

'Total discretion?' the nun asks.

This isn't standard procedure. In all her years as a Sister of Succour, she has only been given total discretion one other time.

In reply, the Bishop turns the screen of his monitor around towards her and clicks a file open. It contains scans of two documents. The first is an extract from the minutes of a trust meeting recording a unanimous vote to sell a house on Green Hill as soon as practicable and to set aside half the proceeds to fund the living expenses of two beneficiaries and to donate the other half to the church. The second is a more recent court order affirming Arno Tjoa Jia Hao's right to live in the selfsame house for his lifetime unless he chooses otherwise.

'It's an easy way out for the trustees if the boy's committed. He'll be out of the house and they'll have a free hand to do whatever they want with the property,' the Bishop says.

'But a psychiatrist can decide whether to commit him or not. Why call us?'

'Two possibilities,' the Bishop replies. 'One, Irene Tjoa has a genuine concern about spiritual affliction. Two, she and her sisters think we can be bought.' He clicks the file shut. 'If it's the latter, they're sadly wrong,' he says. 'And we've to make sure anyone else who hears about the matter understands that. We can't be seen to be a party to a family putsch, especially since we've an interest in the outcome.'

'But what if there's nothing wrong spiritually? Nothing we can deliver him from?' she asks.

The Bishop is an undeniably good man but he's being put in a hard place. If she can't determine that the Tjoa heir is spiritually afflicted, it will become a psychiatric issue and the boy will be put out of the house and into an institution. And then, whether the Bishop likes it or not, the Church will be left holding half the thirty pieces of silver. Does he mean for her to come up with a foregone conclusion, the nun wonders?

The Bishop sets his elbows on his desk, joins his palms together and brings them up to his lips, then closes his eyes.

'Have I ever sent you on a wild goose chase, Sister?' he asks.

2

What the Bishop sends Sister Mary Michael to is a house looking so disappointingly drab the nun can't help but feel let down after the macabre drama of the photographs.

She has been conveyed to the ash house in a Mercedes, in the company of the cook who'd come upon Arno Tjoa in his grandmother's room. The cook is silent on the journey and the nun does not try to engage her in conversation. The heavyset woman smelling of garlic, turmeric and cooking oil is no doubt still traumatized by the scene she'd encountered earlier in the day, the nun supposes. There will be nothing to be gotten out of her just yet. Instead, the nun shifts her spine to align it against the back of the Mercedes' leather bench, flips open the Sisters of Succour handbook and begins to pray, 'St Michael the Archangel . . . Be our defense against the wickedness and snares of the Devil . . . O Prince of the heavenly hosts, by the power of God . . .'

It is sunset and the nun has said all the prayers in her handbook when the Mercedes exits the freeway and climbs to the top of Green Hill to stop at the most faded façade on the street.

So, this is it, she thinks, staring up at the eroded plastering of ribbons and flowers decorating the front of the house. This is the home of the Tjoa sisters she'd idolized as a child, the six stylish, confident girls who'd been everything she—the young Mary Chan—was not. *It* . . . a house with none of the Tjoa girls' joie de vivre. *Her* . . . a grand old lady down on her luck trying to keep up appearances despite her troubles.

Of course, as the Bishop has briefed Sister Mary Michael, there have been a heap of recent troubles. There was the death of the third Mrs Tjoa Ek Kia sixteen months ago, followed by the foreign domestic worker who jumped from a tree in the back garden and the Labour Department's investigation of Arno Tjoa and his father B.K. Tjoa's roles in that tragedy. In the midst of that, the alcoholic B.K. Tjoa's end-stage liver disease had come to a head. Then, most recently, the family had become embroiled in a very public quarrel over the Tjoa estate and the disposal of their ash house.

Still . . . The nun looks at the house's drooping lintels and sagging roof. It can't be just recent troubles weighing the house down. And yet, according to the Land Office archives, until the last few years, nothing but good fortune and prosperity had visited the builder of the house.

Tjoa Ek Kia, the founder of the Tjoa family, had built the house for his boss Towkay Ong. However, the Towkay, who had intended to use the building for ancestral tablets, his ashes and those of his descendants, never moved into the house. Instead, he had gifted the purported ash house to Tjoa Ek Kia in 1925, the year he made the young man his partner.

Tjoa Ek Kia and his first wife had moved into the house shortly after and made it their primary home. When Tjoa Ek Kia's third wife gave birth to B.K. Tjoa, his only son, the founder and his first wife had transferred the house into a trust for the use and benefit of all Tjoa Ek Kia's descendants. Through it all,

Tjoa Ek Kia's business had prospered, his daughters had married well and his grandchildren had attained the highest academic honours. So . . . no, the nun sighs. There is nothing in these dry bone archival facts to explain the tired desperate state of the house.

She examines the building from top to bottom again.

Something in its walls seems determined to pull it down. Something that wants to escape—to set itself free.

Her breath catches in her throat. Of course. It is her dawn visitor, the trapped spirit who wouldn't admit to needing freedom, the owner of that beautiful seductive voice. Whom she'll meet. Now.

She steps over the threshold.

It is not a voice but three glowering countenances that greet her in the shadowy foyer. Not manifestations, she realizes, as the cook following behind her turns on the lights. Rather, what she's seeing are three faces in an almost life-sized painting of old-style Chinese musicians: two blowing on flutes, and a central figure holding a pipa.

Courtesans, the word comes to the nun.

She leans in to examine the painted faces more closely. The eyes of the two flautists are modestly downcast and focused on the bamboo pipes brought up to their lips. The central pipa player, however, looks straight out from the painting, as if she's independent of the fingers she's raised to strike the strings of her instrument. 'Stop me if you dare,' her eyes seem to be telling the world. She, this diva, is the one asking to be freed, the nun is certain.

'I'm here to help,' she says silently to the woman in the picture.

3

Technically, Sister Mary Michael has fudged the truth. The Bishop, who knows nothing of her dawn visitation, has not sent her to the ash house to deliver anyone other than the Tjoa heir Arno. And remembering this, she turns to the cook to ask, 'Where is he? Arno?'

The cook, still silent, leads her into a corridor lined on one side by wooden panels and slides one of them open.

'The Young Sir's in there,' she says.

The Young Sir, Arno Tjoa, proves to be an enormously fat boy standing inside a scene that can only have been created by a madman or someone possessed. The nun has seen some of it in the photographs, of course: The naked dolls hanging by their hair from the door frames of what had once clearly been a sick old woman's room with a wooden armoire pushed against the wall; a TV monitor hung high beside the armoire; and the slightly stained outline of a since removed hospital bed on the opposite wall. But there is also the unexpected—what the Cook had not taken pictures of: Ribbon ends and petals scattered on the ice-white marble floor; a black-topped table covered partially by a red carpet strewn with roses; a flower-lined aisle crossing the carpet and leading to a doll house which seems to be a replica of the house the nun has just entered; a teenage Barbie doll dressed like a bride standing in front of the house; and next to that bride doll, a scarlet clad duenna doll with an arm protectively placed on the younger doll's shoulder and a pipa slung across her chest.

Arno Tjoa is standing behind the bride and duenna dolls, humming a melancholy little tune. His eyes are set on the marble floor somewhere near Sister Mary Michael's feet.

The nun lowers her sit bones carefully into one of the blackwood chairs pushed against the side of the room and hunches down until she's directly in Arno's line of sight. Smiling blandly into his pale round face, she says, 'Hello, I'm Sister Mary Michael Chan.'

He returns her smile with a slow upward curve of his lips.

'Hello,' he replies in a low gruff rumble.

'Well . . .' The nun looks around the room and exhales. 'This is certainly something.'

The boy's smile widens. He nods. 'Yes. Magical, isn't it?'

Diabolical would have been a better word, the nun thinks. But she doesn't say that. Instead, she points to the dolls hanging from the tops of the sliding door frames and asks, 'Why?'

Arno's eyes follow the nun's pointing finger.

'They're m-my aunts,' he stutters, his forehead furrowing, as if he's as puzzled as she is to see the dolls and the state they're in.

'Did you hang them up there?' she asks.

The boy frowns even harder. Then, unwilling or unable to confront the if and how and why he's strung the dolls up, he closes his eyes and begins to hum again.

Sister Mary Michael waits. She's used to waiting. Soon enough, the boy or whatever is working through him will manifest itself. It isn't often someone like her comes along, a not quite 'holier-than-thou' open to everything and willing to receive anything. They can't resist her, the lost creatures she baits. She knows that for a fact. She closes her eyes and invites whatever is behind Arno Tjoa's humming to speak to her.

There's something familiar about the tune the fat boy is humming. She's heard it before and recently but she simply can't remember where or when. That's one of the problems with being seventy-six and so hollow, she thinks wryly. She receives so many impressions, it's hard to place where each comes from any more.

But patience, she tells herself. It will come to her, unbidden, by and by.

Sister Mary Michael's morning medication is beginning to wear off and she's still no nearer to recovering the when and where of Arno's music when Cook re-appears in the room.

'I thought you might need this,' she says, placing a jar of water and a glass on the black-topped table. 'Also, Ma'am Irene phoned and said you'll be staying the night and I need to ask you about arrangements for sleeping and for meals.'

Sister Mary Michael gives Cook the Sisters of Succour's standard request. 'Plain water, plain rice porridge with vegetables followed by a little fruit, a sleeping pallet in Arno's bedroom, and someone to take over from me if necessary.'

'That will be me, Ma'am Irene says,' Cook replies in response to the last request on the nun's list. And then, looking disbelieving, she asks, 'As for the food . . . just vegetarian porridge and fruit, nothing else?'

'That's right.'

'And what time will you eat?'

Food and feeding times are of no import to a Sister of Succour on assignment, especially when she's waiting for a sign to manifest, the nun would like to tell Cook. What's important is silence and an absence of distraction. But she doesn't suppose Cook will understand.

'I'll wait till he's ready,' she says to the Cook instead, tilting her chin at Arno Tjoa, who's still standing in the far corner of the room with his palsied body listing to the left.

'And when might that be?' Cook asks.

'It all depends,' the nun replies. 'We'll have to play it by ear.'

'And eat cold food?'

The nun shrugs.

Cook rolls her eyes. 'Not likely when I'm in charge.'

She turns to the boy and says, 'Arno Young Sir, this Sister is here to help you. You tell her what she needs to know, OK? Otherwise, it'll be no dinner for you too.'

Something in the way the woman speaks to Arno, as if she's his mother or at least someone who has loved him as a child, demands obedience. Arno opens his eyes and begins to speak again before Cook is even out of the room.

'Why?' he throws the nun's first question back at her. 'Why does anything have to have a reason?' The look he flashes her is perplexed, childlike. 'I'm unhappy because I haven't got what I want.' He points to the teenage Barbie. 'Her. This bride. I haven't got her. That's why.'

'That's why this . . .' The nun indicates the carpeted and flower-strewn tabletop.

The boy nods.

'If Girl let me have her. If my pipa diva, Bing Fa, was entirely honest. Well, there'd be no "why" then. I'd have gotten what I wanted. You'd be attending a wedding. Girl's and mine. Girl . . . a pensive bride on the way to her new name. A little blue because of all that's happened. But only a little. Not crying.

Not like her sisters. Because it is what she wanted. To be married into wealth and to be married to me.'

The nun's waiting has paid off. The boy's tongue has loosened.

'And me,' he continues, 'I'd be as proud a groom as the best. Even if my looks are . . . well . . . you know . . . I'd be the kindest of bridegrooms. Beyond a doubt. Me, Arno Tjoa Jia Hao. I'd have orchestrated a wedding for her, a mere girl, a second maid. A wedding, despite everything. A wedding like this.'

He points to the tableau he's created for the doll and beams, then picks the doll up and kisses it.

The doll does not respond, and the nun sees reality take its hold on the boy again.

'But we don't have a wedding, do we? She's lying unconscious in that nursing home and won't say yes to me. And you've interrupted my wedding by proxy. That's the answer to your question. That's why.'

'But there's got to be more,' Sister Mary Michael says. And then, looking up at the naked dolls hanging on the door frames, she asks, 'What about those? What have they to do with the wedding?'

'More? More what? More reasons? More names?' the boy asks, agitated.

'More of anything you want to share with me.'

The boy considers the hanging dolls then gives the nun a sly smile. 'It's people that are the reasons, no? So, I'll give you names then. More than one. Because . . .' He pauses here and another mischievous grin crosses his face. He leans towards the nun. 'Because, we're legion, many names in one,' he tells her.

The nun stiffens as if the boy has pushed a red-hot iron up her crumbling spine.

'Yes, legion,' the boy repeats, chuckling. He taps his fat-cushioned chest and says slowly, enunciating every syllable, 'First, me, Arno Tjoa Jia Hao. The number one, the Tjoa heir with his left side stricken, one palsied hand and no social skills to speak of. A disappointment. Next, number two, my father B.K. Tjoa, the arsehole son of the rubber trader Tjoa Ek Kia. That's three names. Then we have another three, Tjoa Ek Kia's three wives: Big Mother, Bing Fa and Gran, known as Mrs Tjoa Ek Kia number one, number two and number three because their real names have been swallowed up by marriage. After which, we have Big Mother's daughters, six of them, double threes. Irene the oldest, Eileen her rival, then the four others, no names needed. And finally, Girl. And oh yes, that Buffalo Boy, who's the reason why Girl won't marry me. That's all the who, with all their small reasons why. Everything and everyone, connected. Do you see?'

The nun does not. But she nods anyway.

'Do you? We wonder . . .' the boy says.

The nun waits, on the alert for whatever the 'we' that represents 'legion' might unleash on her.

All that happens though is the boy giggles.

'It's a joke. A joke, that's all,' he says. 'I didn't mean to scare you. I'm sorry.'

He does not appear the least sorry. And looking up at the strung-up dolls, Sister Mary Michael cannot help but wonder again who is acting and speaking through the enormous pallid-skinned body belonging to Arno Tjoa. But it's far too soon for that question. Instead, she asks, 'What were you doing earlier today, before I arrived?'

And, oh! Out it comes. Like a deluge.

4

Irene Tjoa had called Arno that Thursday night, Arno tells the nun. She'd informed him that the Labour Ministry was done with its investigation into Girl's fall. After fifteen and a half months, both he and his father had been absolved. Girl was no longer a subject of investigative interest. She could be released from protective custody. The family was now free to send Girl home. Within the week, Irene had said, brooking no argument and refusing to entertain Arno's pleas to bring Girl back to the ash house and under his care. At some point in their conversation, he reports to Sister Mary Michael, she'd hung up on him.

Arno can't remember exactly what happened after that. When he came to, it was morning and he was squatting in the shadows underneath his Gran's table, with his forearms wrapped around his knees and his Girl doll, the teenage Barbie, clutched in his hands.

His aunt Irene's high arched feet in their impeccably shined shoes were pointing straight at him. The shoes' one-inch heels were ground into the white marble. They'd been standing there for at least a quarter of an hour, their double bows weighted down flat by heavy gold buckles. It was clear to Arno the feet and shoes weren't planning on going anywhere. But then, neither was he.

He'd pulled his arms tighter against his knees, pushed the Girl doll deeper into the folds of his body and tilted his head up and back into the wall.

'I'm not coming out,' he'd said to the underside of the table.

In reply, he'd heard his aunt Irene's nails tap-tap against the tabletop.

He hadn't seen his aunt's fingernails, he tells the nun, but he could imagine them. They'd be a deep cherry red and as smooth and hard as the red varnish lacquered on the back door of the kitchen. The same red he'd painted on the fingertips of a geisha Barbie he sold quite recently, he adds in a sudden digression. Red against white and red against black, had been the colour scheme for that Barbie, he shares. Just like the colours of his aunt's nails against the black tabletop.

'And why is it important for me to know about this doll?' the nun asks.

Because the doll was meant to be a representation of Irene. Red lips just like hers against a white doll face painted so thick all its wrinkles were blotted out. Stiffly coiffed hair dyed an artificial black with a single pulled out lock left white. And the clothes in the colours she liked too. An outer kimono of black silk with a white underskirt in the softest velvet. The obi embroidered with cherry red roses past their prime and half-stripped of their petals. The whole thing pointing to a fading old crone trying to disguise her years with her powders and paints.

'Not quite the Irene Tjoa in the society pages then,' the nun comments.

Arno grimaces.

'Well, there's me looking at her. And then there's other people. Like what happened to the doll,' he says. 'Hardly anyone saw what I expected.'

He'd posted the doll's picture on his website and asked his fans to give her get-up a name, he explains to the nun. He'd even offered a free Arno Tjoa costume Barbie for the most apt one and was looking forward to the insults that would flow in. To his surprise, 'witch' was the worst he got out of the hundreds of submissions. His most ardent fan had sent in 'Windblown Flower' and followed that with a row of red hearts. 'Kissed all night by a storm' someone had commented to that. A third had submitted 'Raped Rose' together with an offer to buy the doll for however much Arno demanded. That had started a bidding war which closed at slightly less than $3,000, far more than he'd expected. Later, the doll had gotten $7,000 in an on-sale, and he's since seen it trading online for nearly five figures.

'My attempted dig at my aunt became a collector's item,' he tells the nun. He shakes his head, bewildered. 'Anyway, that was what I was thinking about when her nails were tap-tap-tapping against the black table. How she'd become the objects of certain doll collectors' twisted fantasies.'

If she'd known, Arno had thought as he sat under the table, she'd have melted with mortification onto the marble floor like one of those witches in *The Wiz*. But she hadn't known, which was why she was still standing there at the end of the table, as whole and as hard as those tap-tap-tapping nails of hers.

For all Arno cared, his aunt Irene could go on tap-tapping on the table forever. But she wouldn't. She liked completions. And so, he'd waited and counted off the taps as he stroked his Girl doll's lovely sticky plastic hair.

'I'm too old for this Arno,' Irene had said after twenty-eight taps. 'Have a bit of consideration. If not for me, then for the fact you're the Tjoa heir. Come out from under there. Please.'

Never a raised voice, always polite, that was his aunt Irene, he tells Sister Mary Michael. And why not? She'd always been the queen bee, no one objecting to anything she reached out for—not his grandfather, nor Big Mother, nor any of his other aunts except maybe Eileen, just a little. Neither Arno's own Gran nor his arsehole of a father B.K. Tjoa nor Cook, who ruled the roost in the house, had ever said no to Irene either. No one could. Indeed, Arno hadn't even thought that was in the realm of possibility. Not until Girl had arrived.

'No,' he'd said again to Irene. 'I know what the court decided. I've a right of residence. You can't make me come out and you can't make me leave. I need to want to, they said. And I don't.'

The heels of Irene's pumps had risen a hair's breadth. She was pulling herself up straighter and getting ready to stand on her dignity, Arno realized.

'Well, if you won't be sensible,' she said.

Hah! Arno had bared his teeth at the underside of the table and mimed a growl. So now she was threatening consequences? But what could she do even if he was acting like a madman? The court had made a final and definitive declaration about his rights. As for the investigation, it was over, as Irene had told him. Misadventure, that had been the Labour Ministry's conclusion. He'd been cleared of wrongdoing. He couldn't be sent to jail. And he wasn't dying of a pickled liver like his father B.K. There was no question of the hospice for him. His aunts could not get him out of the house, or for that matter from under the table.

He wouldn't say anything more to Irene, he decided. He was twenty-five. His aunt, Irene, was nearly eighty. There was a value to being patient. To being like Girl, mute and motionless in her cot at the nursing home.

It was almost noon. Arno could hear the blender whining in the kitchen at the other end of the house as it ground the spices Cook had dumped into it. Cook was making lunch for him. Even if his aunt wasn't making an issue of it, it was time for him to crawl out from under the table. But he wasn't hungry. Not yet. He had a cushion. He could starve for a week and there'd still be excess fat on him. He could wait. Not his slim elegant aunt Irene though. Oh no! He stretched his legs out under the table. In a wait-out, he would win, every time.

Sure enough, by and by, the one-inch heels of Irene's shoes had swiveled. And then, they'd gone tap-tap-tap towards the sliding door panels of Gran's room and into the corridor beside the air well.

The receding tap-taps stopped in the entry foyer. There was a soft thump. Irene had sat herself down in one of the two over-upholstered armchairs there, under the painting of the old-time Chinese musicians. She was scheduling appointments, oblivious to the disparaging looks the three painted divas were casting at her.

He heard her call her driver, then one of the other aunts. She said something about consulting the Bishop and getting someone to come do an assessment. An assessor for the rental value of the house, he had imagined. And because he hadn't known it would be Sister Mary Michael from the Sisters of Succour who was being summoned to assess the state of his soul, he'd simply sat and waited for Irene's shoes to make their way out of the house.

When they did, he'd barely noticed they were now followed by the slip-slide of Cook's sandals. The only thing that lodged in his consciousness was the taps stopping for a moment after crossing the five-foot way. Irene was pausing to evaluate the fading pastels of the façade and considering the impact on the price if she put the house up for sale, he'd thought.

'But she's jumping the gun,' he told his Girl doll. 'We're never leaving, you and me. Never. She's the one who'll have to leave first.'

And as if Irene had heard Arno, the sound of a car door clicking open and then thudding shut came through the front windows of the house. A car engine started. Irene was gone. He had outwaited her after all. As he would outwait them all, he thought. His other aunts, his father, and Girl too.

'You'll see,' he said, bringing the Girl doll's face to his, and kissing her on the lips. 'You'll see,' he repeated.

* * *

Feeling falsely secure, Arno had continued to sit under the table with his Girl doll and allowed time to eddy around him and pass on.

He wasn't hungry. He'd not been hungry since Girl's accident. He ate only because Cook set meals in front of him. He'd spent a lifetime stuffing himself. It was no great shakes for him to plough through the pyramids of rice Cook coloured with turmeric or sprinkled with poppy seeds, or to dig furrows into the accompanying plates of shredded tofu and chicken, chopped salted eggs and deep-fried sticks of fermented beans, or to polish off the side-dishes of sambal and acar. He could put everything spoonful by spoonful into his mouth, and chew on it as if he was truly enjoying it all without the least effort. It cost him nothing to do it. And it made Cook happy.

Feeding Arno had become the be all and end all of Cook's existence. That was why she dutifully called him to his four daily meals: breakfast and dinner at exactly seven a.m. and seven p.m. respectively, lunch on the dot at noon, and tea at three. She'd done it every day like clockwork since Girl had fallen from the tree.

'Every day except today,' he tells Sister Mary Michael.

There hadn't been a call for lunch earlier in the day. Nor did Cook come into Gran's room with his tea. And at some point in the afternoon when time had settled itself around him again, Arno had realized how strange this was.

Tucking his Girl doll into the waistband of his trousers, he'd crawled to the end of the table, stuck his head out, and called, 'Cook! Are you there Cook?'

Since Gran had died and his aunts had sent his father to the hospice, Cook had begun spending large parts of her afternoons in the basement, in the room she once shared with Girl. That afternoon though Arno had not found Cook there watching TV serials on her phone or counting the zeroes she was accumulating in her bank book. There was only her smell in her quarters, the oil-laden kitchen smell Arno had sucked in greedily from her apron before he discovered the vastly more attractive rose and jasmine of the diva's perfume and the sweet plasticky fragrance coming off his dolls.

The empty room tempted Arno to do something he'd always wanted to but had never had the opportunity to attempt. He lowered himself onto the bed opposite Cook's, Girl's bed, and stretched out on it. Then he sat his Girl doll on the cushion of his chest for a pillow talk.

He began tentatively.

'I used to visit Cook a lot down here when I was little and we used to have really good talks,' he said to the doll. 'But I've never been down here with you. I wonder why?'

The doll hadn't said anything in reply. But her silence was defiantly strident. He was such a fool, didn't he know he'd been a full-grown man for quite some time now and it just was not done, her side-long glance seemed to scold.

'You're so unforgiving,' he said to the doll, whose gaze remained fixed sideward, as if she was staring at a spot above his right ear.

'Regardless, I miss you and I miss our chats,' he told her. 'So, talk to me, please . . .'

Arno knew very well that the real Girl was lying motionless and voiceless in the nursing home, no longer even living her back-of-house life wiping up sick, cleaning shit and administering slop. The eyes that wouldn't meet his weren't hers. They belonged to a 1998 edition teenage Barbie doll made of plastic. He knew this. Yet, he still pleaded against all logic, 'You could say yes. You could agree to marry me.'

She wouldn't, that's why she'd left his room and gone to hide up that tree she'd fallen from. Arno knew this in his heart of hearts. She'd decided all she wanted was that simpleton childhood lover of hers, Buffalo Boy. And she'd demonstrated that she wasn't going to change her mind. But that afternoon, Arno wasn't going to take no for an answer.

He'd turned the Girl doll's head 30 degrees around so he could look directly into her eyes. Then, he'd told her, 'We can have it all if only you'll say yes. After all, you did say yes before, when you made that promise.'

The doll's head seemed to swivel away, back to how it had been. It was a passing thought, the doll appeared to be saying. She hadn't meant it, that promise.

Arno understood. Girl had wanted a rich husband but had never really thought of him as the one. He had been an option, her last option. She hadn't expected him to be her only way out.

'But I am,' he said to the doll. 'You and I, we're each other's only way out.'

Still, the doll had remained silent.

They had so little time, Arno had thought desperately. With the Labour Ministry's investigation done, his aunt would be flying Girl home a.s.a.p. Girl had to say 'yes', or they would both be trapped by the promises they'd exchanged with Bing Fa. One way or another, he had to marry Girl, even if it meant a crazy ghost marriage like the one his grandfather reportedly forced on Bing Fa, the diva.

A ghost marriage. Of course! Arno leapt from Girl's bed at the thought. Not a ghost marriage like Tjoa Ek Kia's to Bing Fa, since Girl wasn't dead. More a ceremony with himself as groom and his Girl doll as a proxy. That was it! That was what he'd do.

Arno believed life had a grudge against him. The evidence was all there, from his misshapen body to his runaway mother, his wretched father and that cabal of aunts pulled one way then another by that squabbling pair, Irene and Eileen. And now life was threatening to take Girl from him too. His aunt Irene, in ascendance and in cahoots with the authorities, would surely be sending Girl home if she didn't wake. And if Girl went . . . He was not certain he could hold on to anything then. He'd be put out of the house on some excuse or other for sure. Life would take everything.

He would marry Girl by proxy, he decided. Before the end of the day.

'That anyway, had been the idea, before you came and put a stop to it,' he says to Sister Mary Michael.

5

Arno shows the nun the Girl doll's wedding costume he'd spent the afternoon labouring over. It's a beautifully fashioned kebaya the colour of green apples, bordered with red rose buds and jade green leaves matched with a sarong made from a scrap of Pekalongan batik printed with full-blown roses.

'See. No puckered seams, no hanging threads, and the reds of the roses on the kebaya and sarong match perfectly,' he says to the nun. 'Isn't it a wonder?'

'It is indeed,' Sister Mary Michael agrees. She points to the roses. 'I particularly like the flowers. They're quite different from the phoenixes and dragons one usually sees on Peranakan wedding clothes.'

'It wasn't my idea,' the boy shares. 'I get all these commissions for Peranakan wedding sets and usually I just give them phoenixes and dragons and double happiness motifs. But I was fed up with the same old same old, so I asked Girl for something new. She was the one who came up with that rose bud pattern. It was the first costume we worked on together and somehow . . .' He flushes a deep red before saying, 'Somehow, it seems fitting to use the pattern again for my own wedding.'

'A proxy wedding,' the nun reminds him.

He shrugs and then pointing to the doll's face, says, 'Look at her expression, it's different too. Not like your usual run-of-the-mill Peranakan bride expression, is it?'

The doll's lips are curved slightly upwards in a shy secret smile, the nun observes. It's an impression Arno has affected with an eyeliner brush, beige face contour and soft pink nail varnish.

'You know how doleful those brides in the vintage photographs look? But I didn't want a tight-lipped teary bride at my own wedding,' he explains. 'I wanted a happier one. One who understands marrying me is the best thing for the both for us.'

'But does the real Girl herself understand?' the nun asks.

'I did try to convince her as I was getting her dressed,' Arno replies. 'I told her we had to free Bing Fa because we'd promised. We'd made our wishes and promised. It was said and sealed with Girl's hair as a good faith deposit. And most importantly, Bing Fa had made good on those wishes. Girl wanted a rich husband and I wanted to marry her. Bing Fa set everything up for that to happen and the only reason we weren't getting what we wished for was because she, Girl, tried to run away at the last moment.'

He looks piteously at the nun and shakes his head. 'It's hard for Girl to understand, you know, coming from a village and all. I'd to explain it over and over to her, how it wasn't like in her village and how she couldn't back out without consequences after putting down a deposit. There're penalties, I told her. That's why all this shit is happening to us, my aunts trying to kick me out of the house and her trapped inside her body. I told her that's why I was going to do this proxy wedding. It was for our good. The wedding would fulfill Bing Fa's part of the bargain. What the lawyers call pre-conditions met. And once that happened, I said, we could deliver on our side of the deal. We could burn the things in the doll house and free Bing Fa. Quid pro quo. Girl and I would have received what Bing Fa promised. I would give Bing Fa what we promised. And maybe, Girl might even wake up.'

Bing Fa, ice-blossom. An intriguing name. And so many mentions of her suddenly, as a pipa diva and as the Tjoa founder's second wife. The nun is tempted to learn more from Arno. But she holds back.

'What did Girl say to all those points you raised?' she asks instead.

'Nothing,' Arno admits despondently. 'But I was past caring. I dressed her and brought her down anyway and set up the wedding. This one.'

The nun watches as Arno takes a step back from the table to admire the tableau he's created on the tabletop. There's the carpet, half of a cut-off Tientsin that might have been used for a tea-ceremony at a wedding in China 100 years ago, its red silk shining like fire under the light of the two flex-lamps the girl would have used to check the old grandmother's skin for bedsores. Arno has arranged the carpet cleverly, tucking the cut-off edge behind the far end of the table so no one can see, and leaving the fringed end hanging in the front like a waterfall. The rug's dragon and phoenix patterns have been covered over with strategically placed rosettes. Across the carpet, he has outlined a rose-filled walkway leading to a rosebud-wrapped arch.

'We used to put my grandmother's therapy stuff on this table. But look what I've done to it? A more fitting way to end Girl's and my journey don't you think, the two of us walking across a bridge of roses spanning a fiery lake full of floating rosebuds?' he says to the nun after he has his fill of the scene.

When the nun doesn't answer, he picks up his Girl doll and tells the nun, 'I'll be shrinking myself down to her size now.' And then tucking the doll's tiny hand into the fleshy crook of his elbow, he begins to hum again.

Sister Mary Michael sits and watches, praying her Rosary as the fat boy sways to his own music and circles the black table.

She does not have the full story and no matter how strange things are getting, it is not time to intervene yet.

Arno walks around the table three times before stopping in front of the nun.

'Why are you praying? God has never answered any of my prayers,' he says to her.

'But he does answer mine,' the nun replies.

He frowns at that. 'Well, if that's all you're relying on, Girl and I are surely sunk.'

'You'll be better off with God,' the nun insists. 'It's really only God who can do anything in cases like this.'

'Have it your way,' Arno says, unconvinced, before walking over to the other end of the table and setting the Girl doll back on its stand beside the scarlet clad pipa diva doll and in front of the doll house.

'Don't worry,' he says to the Girl doll, smiling a faraway smile. 'We'll do it ourselves. We'll get married and set my diva free and everything will be fine.'

'And how would all that happen?' the nun asks.

Arno wrinkles his brow. 'I'm not sure,' he allows. 'But it will. My diva will help. After all that Girl and I have been through, I'm certain of it. Because she's real you know, my diva. We couldn't both have imagined it, that beautiful voice we both heard.'

'A beautiful voice?' the nun echoes.

'Yes. The most beautiful, seductive, mesmerizing, enchanting voice ever.'

'Like a mother's?'

'No. Definitely not.' Arno shakes his head for emphasis. 'Like a diva. Or maybe a very good actress. One who can make you believe she's whoever she's playing.' He pauses to think, then adds. 'But maybe I have that idea because the person behind the voice had already come to me in lots of ways before I heard her in my head. Her personality had already shone out from my diva doll. And she'd given me those stories about her life and let me know how she liked to look and smell through the laces and batiks and silks and perfume bottles that would appear in the attic.' He shrugs. 'She's come to me in so many ways. How can I tell you what the voice is like in just one word? That's impossible. All I can say is, she's real.'

'And does she have a name?' Sister Mary Michael asks tentatively, in expectation.

Without hesitation, the boy gives the nun the name she's been expecting. 'Bing Fa, the diva whom my grandfather Tjoa Ek Kia trapped in a ghost marriage. Bing Fa, that's what my Gran called her. What Girl and I call her.'

He picks up the diva doll dressed in the red qi-pao with the pipa slung across her back.

'This is Bing Fa, the diva,' he tells the nun.

'A Barbie doll?'

'Well, she was that originally. But now, she's Bing Fa,' Arno replies. He tries to explain, 'When I discovered her in a corner of the attic, she was dressed in one of those black-and-white striped swimsuits that the first 1959 Barbies wore. But everything about her—curled bangs and black lined eyes, scarlet lips and those little feet in their open-toe high heels—everything screamed

Shanghainese diva. So that's how I costumed her. And then . . .' he adds, 'I found, or Bing Fa led me to, a pipa under another pile of stuff.' He strokes the pipa on the doll absentmindedly. 'It's the final enlivening element, don't you think?'

Enlivening. Sister Mary Michael shudders at the word for she senses the pipa has indeed fulfilled its purpose and given some form of life to the doll.

The boy, however, does not notice her discomfort.

'Of course, as you can see, her skin's a little dulled because I've kept her in her crocodile-skin trunk in the dark for months, ever since Girl's fall . . .' he rambles on. 'But she's still quite a personality, don't you think Sister?'

The nun nods. While the doll is not quite as evocative of her dawn visitor's voice as the painted pipa diva in the ash house foyer, still she has no doubt who the doll is meant to represent.

'But what does this diva doll have to do with you marrying Girl?' she asks. 'And the doll house? What's that about?'

'Bing Fa brought Girl and me together,' the boy says. 'It's only fitting she's present at the final tying of the knot, even if it's just in the form of my diva doll. As for the doll house . . .' He hesitates and turns to look at the doll house on the black table. 'It's hard to explain. It's like the voice in my head. One thing and then another. I'm not sure I'm clear what all it might be.'

'Well, give me some words. Any words. Like a toy perhaps? Or your diva's home?' Sister Mary Michael dangles the possibilities like bait.

'Like a toy, yes,' Arno echoes. 'Something custom made for my aunts, obviously, since it's a replica of our house. An appropriate girl thing to play housekeeping with, I suppose. But that's not the whole story. Because, see . . .' He points to the letterbox by the door with its tiny slot through which coins might be deposited, and the tiny front door with its very real keyhole. 'It's a safety box too. And in fact, that's what my Grandpa's first wife, Big Mother, and my own Gran used it for. And others as well. Myself too. We used the house as a box, to safekeep our stuff.'

'Stuff? Like?' Sister Mary Michael prompts.

'Stuff,' Arno says shortly. 'But you won't understand unless I tell you this story . . .' And that is when the nun first learns about Tjoa Ek Kia and the diva Bing Fa, Tjoa Ek Kia's reluctant second wife.

6

Tjoa Ek Kia had come in a dream to give Arno the story, the nun is told. He'd appeared to Arno as his fourteen-year-old self, an apprentice newly arrived from China and bound to Towkay Ong, the rubber trader. It was just before the Great War, at the start of the boom in natural rubber. Towkay Ong had needed trusted kin to help in his expanding business. For six years of Tjoa Ek Kia's life, he'd undertaken to feed and house him, teach him to figure on the abacus, enter the accounting numbers in the ledgers (both the ones for the revenue officers and the real ones), keep an eagle eye on his inventory of smoked latex sheets and read and write in English.

A future in Kota Cahaya, the City of Light! It was an opportunity Tjoa Ek Kia's widowed mother could not refuse.

Towkay Ong, Tjoa Ek Kia's employer, was a lover of music and women. The times gave him the means to indulge his passions, indulgences he hid from his principal wife. After his evenings out, he would always wash himself and change before going home, leaving his play-stained clothing in a laundry basket under his desk. In addition to his accounting duties, the young Tjoa Ek Kia was tasked with emptying the basket and bundling the clothes up for the Indian washerman.

Towkay Ong had enjoyed many bodies and the perfumes fermenting on the clothes in the Towkay's laundry basket were

Tjoa Ek Kia's first introduction to woman flesh, Tjoa Ek Kia told his grandson. He had passed many a titillating hour imagining the different bodies from which the smells emanated. Young bodies scented like shy orchids and green leaves. Experienced bodies who disguised their age with sandalwood and gardenias. Even a few sharp orange scented shrews. Sniffing the Towkay's clothes became an addiction. Tjoa Ek Kia had not stopped even when, at the height of the war, he pulled out a shirt reeking of fear and the iron of blood. Indeed, that had been strangely arousing, and for weeks after, he had found himself trying to recreate the circumstances of the encounter.

Shortly after the war's end, as Tjoa Ek Kia himself had begun visiting the city's cheaper sing-song rooms, he realized Towkay Ong had begun to patronize only one entertainer. This woman was of such singularity, Tjoa Ek Kia had seen her whole the moment he ingested her scent. She was an unadorned pipa player with lips coloured very simply by plum wine. The fingertips of her hands glinted with only the cold jade stone of her plucking shields and her body was covered with the merest dusting of rice powder. She was almost scentless but for the perfume she released when the trader encountered her deepest regions. There, she had smelt like freshly risen bread, soft and white and yielding. Tjoa Ek Kia had been overwhelmed, he whispered in his grandson's dream.

This same woman later began leaving the fragrance of winter snow, spring and summer flowers, and autumn desire on the Towkay's clothes. It was the imprint of a perfume the Towkay had brought back from his first business trip to Europe in 1921. Although entirely different from the fragrance Tjoa Ek Kia had fallen in love with, still he knew it was her. And when finally, he met her in 1925, at the party the rubber trader threw to celebrate his becoming partner, Tjoa Ek Kia had recognized her immediately. She was the pipa diva Bing Fa, the ice-blossom. The woman Tjoa Ek Kia had loved forever and would love forever. And despite all her protests, he had made sure to marry her.

The diva had redeemed her contract and never wanted to be owned again, Tjoa Ek Kia told his grandson in the dream. She had died. But still Tjoa Ek Kia had tied her to him in a ghost marriage.

'Love makes one selfish. If you ever love someone, be generous,' he said to Arno. 'Don't be as stupid as I was,' he'd warned, before adding, 'But what could I do? There was the baby to think of.' And then, he'd thumped his only grandson on the shoulder and asked for the favour.

The favour is why Arno is sure it was really his grandfather who visited, he explains to Sister Mary Michael near the end of his retelling. After all, the dead never come calling unless they want something.

And what was it that Arno's grandfather, Tjoa Ek Kia, wanted?

To let go of his burden of regret and guilt in the same way those alive want to let go of theirs, Sister Mary Michael is not surprised to find out. And if he could not do it, then surely, it was something his heir could, he intimated to Arno.

'It would be nice if you can free her,' he said to his grandson.

'From what?' Arno asked.

'The consequences of my loving her, of course,' the old man replied. 'And all the longing that came after,' he'd added. 'She'll tell you how. She's in the doll house. All you have to do is open it, and she'll tell you what to do next.' After which, he'd blown on Arno's face and disappeared.

And despite being dead asleep, Arno had promised.

Which was when the trouble began, the nun realizes. The trouble she's here to fix after nearly 100 years.

She is making progress. She knows now the owner of the dawn voice is trapped in the doll house on the table. She also knows the name of that voice's owner—Bing Fa, the pipa diva.

'Well, that's a start,' she says to Arno. 'Now we know who we're dealing with and where she's trapped.'

Arno grimaces.

'No, it's not just one person. Sure, Bing Fa is tied up in the doll house. But like I said, there's other stuff too. Stuff that connects Big Mother, my Gran, my parents, and Girl and me to her. We're trapped together. All of us.'

Legion then, as the boy had said. A heavy weight indeed. No wonder, the sag in the house.

'And how does it all work?' she asks.

She doesn't really expect the whole answer. But Arno gives her enough.

'It's a string. Well, two strings now. And they tie all the stuff together,' Arno says. 'Stuff people used as deposits or payments for favours Bing Fa promised to grant. Or had already granted. And Bing Fa's trapped spirit too. Although . . .'

It seems to the nun as if Arno's voice is fading. As if it is being muffled by another sound, not yet present, but approaching inexorably. 'Although . . .' she hears him saying again, 'I'm not sure Bing Fa is as trapped as she makes out. Or . . .'

She blinks.

Now, it is not only Arno's voice that is fading but the fat boy himself.

'Or as you think,' she manages to hear him say before something else fills the room entirely.

It is her, Bing Fa, the owner of the voice that reached out to Sister Mary Michael at dawn. Finally come. Introducing her presence with the soft twangs of a pipa and the fragrance of a long-gone scent of faded jasmine and roses and something chemical.

7

'There are so many ways to be trapped,' Sister Mary Michael hears the voice of the diva Bing Fa saying. 'There's being locked between four walls and being held inside a yearning. There's staying to wait on the right time and the next time after that. And being too late because times have changed. There's lingering because one still has hope and lingering because of the comfort of the familiar. There's refusing to leave out of sheer bloody mindedness. And then there's attachment . . .'

The nun feels the diva looking down at her from a liminal not-space beyond the ceiling of the grandmother's room, pondering what next to say.

'Attachment is a trap. Once you're caught by it there's no getting away,' Bing Fa intones, as if repeating a lesson from long ago. 'That's why I'm in the state I'm in.' She laughs. 'It's ironic,' she says.

The nun hears angry rattles, scratching across the strings of the pipa.

'Yes, it's ironic that despite all my efforts, it was me who got caught. In fact, you might say, it's tragic. Tragic enough for a lament . . .'

And then, as if responding to an unspoken request from Sister Mary Michael, the diva begins to sing in a voice both plaintive and proud, angry and mournful, and altogether enchanting. 'Who would have thought?' she sings. 'Who would have thought it would be me? Me who got caught . . . Despite having sold my heart . . . Sold my heart . . .'

* * *

Bing Fa had only meant to sell her hair that day in Guangzhou, nearly 100 years ago. It just so happened that for the number of coins she needed, she had to throw her heart in as well, she tells Sister Mary Michael. She hadn't had a choice. Her street performer father had picked up one of those illnesses itinerant entertainers caught out in the dirt and cold of the alleyways. They needed money for his medicine and had already pawned or sold everything else they owned. It had come down to her hair.

Bing Fa had good hair, a knee-length plait as black as a raven's back and as straight and strong as an acrobat's tightrope. But despite pushing open the doors of uncountable wig-makers' shops since dawn and holding it out to one old crone after another, none had offered the price she needed. She'd had to drag her feet deeper and deeper into that Chinese city's heart until she reached that place where the shopfronts were smaller and dimmer, but the offer prices strangely higher. Because they took more than hair, she had heard . . . And when she entered the dingiest smallest shop and the wizened proprietress pushed three heavy strings of coins towards her, she had realized this was indeed true.

'What else will you take beside my hair?' Bing Fa had asked.

To which the crone had answered, 'Why do you care?' She jangled the coins in front of the tired girl and said, 'This is what you want. You're not going to change your mind, no matter what I tell you.'

That was true, the young Bing Fa thought. Still . . .

'I think I'll manage the rest of my life better if I knew what I was missing,' she said.

'Well, you're a one,' the crone said, smiling not unkindly. 'But whatever it is, it won't matter a bit to you. All you'll regret is your hair.'

'Hair grows. There's no need to regret that.'

'Indeed,' the crone agreed. Then almost as an afterthought she added, 'As for the other thing . . . Since you asked, it's your heart.'

'People die without a heart!' Bing Fa exclaimed, clutching the buttons in front of that chest of hers, which hadn't yet grown breasts.

'Not the flesh one,' the crone replied. 'Compassion. The milk of human kindness. That's what I'll be buying.'

Bing Fa had tried to recall the instances when she'd seen compassion and kindness bring in a profit but hadn't been able to think of even one. That decided her.

'Well in that case,' she said slowly, trying to sound reluctant.

The crone's eyes glinted. 'You agree then?'

In answer, Bing Fa pulled at the crone's strings of coins and wound them around her wrist. Then she bent her head and lifted her plait towards the crone's long-bladed scissors.

She walked out of the shop straight-backed and proud. The crone had been wrong about her missing her hair, she decided as she rubbed the fingers of what would become her plucking hand against her bare neck. She didn't miss it, not at all. Without it, she felt light and unburdened. Free enough to forget her father's medicine and let him die. Yes, even that.

That was when the Madam had caught sight of Bing Fa, pulled at her arm, and asked if she'd like to sell herself too.

'In good hard cash, redeemable of course,' the woman assured. 'I'll give you the means.'

And the woman had been as good as her word. In Kota Cahaya, a two-week journey by sea from Guangzhou, the Madam had indeed taught Bing Fa the necessary skills to redeem herself.

First, she'd learnt to play the pipa. The strikes and plucks, the two-fingered down strum and up strums, the nine basic strokes for the right hand and six for the left. All learnt to the beat of Madam's fan falling on the emerging diva's knuckles in such a way her hands and fingers never swelled or flowered purple. The fan, beating and beating till Bing Fa had learnt to play 'major chords droning like pouring rain, minor chords whispering secrets, notes like the tinkling of pearls on a jade plate, like a nightingale among flowers, like a silver jar shattering and armoured horsemen clashing, and all four strings slashing, like silk tearing.' And after that, it was how to use the fan. How to take it out from under a bodice and splay the folds open then draw them close. How to hide behind it and smile with only the eyes. Then how to stand. How to pour a cup of wine and present it. How to pick up a piece of sweetmeat and offer it. To be blunt. How to offer herself for the best price possible.

But aside from one warning about attachment, Bing Fa had been given no lessons about the heart. She'd learnt nothing about how to protect it from a besotted lover. Nor how to deafen it to the call of bone from one's own bones and flesh from one's own flesh. Not that Bing Fa had asked. She hadn't given such matters a moment's thought, not even when she'd been wooed by the lovelorn and achingly handsome Tjoa Ek Kia.

Hadn't she already sold her heart at the wigmaker's? What was there to worry about?

Love, as it turned out. For it was love that had attached her to Tjoa Ek Kia's family and entangled her in his first wife's insecurities and his third wife's wants. It was love, or rather its other face—want—that got her involved with those hungry girls whom she'd tried to use. It was love that now kept her in the ash house, stuck.

'Stuck,' she cries at the nun. 'Unless you free me.'

* * *

The music in the room recedes. Sister Mary Michael returns to herself, thirsting, all Bing Fa's magic gone and only the sound of Arno Tjoa's reedy humming winding across the black top of the table towards her.

The fat boy is standing exactly where the nun remembers, at the far end of the table, next to his two dolls and the doll house.

'Magnificent, isn't she?' he says.

The nun nods. But she can't seem to speak yet. Reaching for the jar of water Cook has left her, she pours herself a drink.

'That's right, you're thirsty,' Arno observes. 'It's how it is. A bit of her is never enough. You're always left thirsting. You're hooked. And then, you'll have to do what she wants. No help for it.'

The nun nods again. That's what happens. What she expects. She's a Sister of Succour after all. Bait. She's supposed to be latched onto, to have her heart stolen. It's just that, despite all the shields she surrounds herself with, what attaches can sometimes be hard to dislodge. That has always been the danger. She suspects, this will be the case now.

But there is nothing she can do about it. She has already entered the story. Now, all she can do is follow its windings till she reaches its source.

'Is that what happened, with you and Girl?' she asks Arno. 'She gave both of you a bit, and you wanted more?'

8

Yes, Bing Fa had indeed seduced Arno and Girl with bits. But unlike the nun, it wasn't a matter of just two song lines in a chapel before dawn. In Arno's case, it had taken years. And even for Girl, it had taken quite a few months.

It isn't surprising of course. The boy and girl are not hollow as Sister Mary Michael is. They did not open themselves intentionally asking to be entered. And yet . . . and still . . . they had been entered. They had been manipulated. Bing Fa had connected them. She'd tied them up.

'And how!' Arno exclaims, when he recalls how it happened. Still not quite believing the good of it. Nor admitting the bad of it either.

* * *

Arno wasn't the kind of man who beat his brains over girls. Second maids arrived. And then, except in the rare instance when a cook left and the girl was promoted, they ran away or were sent home. When Girl arrived that November evening one year eight months and four days ago, he'd assumed she'd be simply another girl.

He was in his attic the night Cook came back with Girl. The French doors in the front were opened to the memory room, whose windows looked down to the road. The side windows in his working and sleeping areas were also ajar. He had heard everything. His aunt Irene greeting Cook and commenting on Cook's lateness. Her wondering if Girl was really twenty-three years old as her passport said. Her instructions about his Gran's bedtime and his father's supper and meal arrangements for the next day. Indeed, she was being so loud and bossy it was clear she meant for Arno to hear her and to go downstairs to help greet and settle the new girl.

No way was Arno going down though. He was at his worktable, curling his diva doll's hair. He couldn't afford to be distracted. Doing the diva's hair was a necessary, nightly task. Leastways Arno had thought then. He had to shampoo it, wind it around the mini bottle washer trimmed for the purpose, apply a stiffening agent onto the brush with a Q-tip then unwind everything without tangling. The task required 100 per cent concentration. And so, his only reaction to the new arrival was to tell the diva doll, 'Cook's back with a new girl.'

It wasn't a small thing, Cook returning. It meant Gran, who'd been taken to stay with his aunt Irene, was coming home too. As was his father B.K. Tjoa, who'd been camping out at his club. Arno and his dolls would no longer have the house to themselves.

Arno unrolled the last curl above the diva's right ear, patted her teeny nose and said, 'I'll have to put you back in the trunk during the day, dark as it is. After all we don't want Gran picking you up and messing with your clothes or dropping you, do we?'

The diva didn't reply, nor had Arno expected her to. Still, as he picked up an eye lash comb and began to fluff out her ponytail, he continued to speak to her, 'You're not to worry. It won't be for long. Gran's getting on. And my father's liver is so

scarred he'll be off too. It won't be more than a year or two. Not
so long in your scheme of things. Then I'll be in charge, and
you'll be queen of all this. A whole throne-room to yourself. A
concert hall even. If you like.'

Arno made the diva the same promise every night. Not
because he expected her to understand, but because making
the declaration made the small delicate tasks his hands were
doing feel bigger and more purposeful. As if it all meant
something and would lead to something beyond what he
could see or touch.

He started to dab the diva's body with a cotton ball soaked
in De-Solv-It, humming the tune that always came to him
during this part of the diva's toilette.

If Arno's father B.K. Tjoa had overheard his tone-deaf son,
he would have been surprised. For like Arno, B.K. Tjoa often
found himself humming that melancholy 1930's Shanghai tune
too. As it was, no living ears heard Arno's rendering of 'Qiu Shui
Yi Ren'. His father was at the casino he haunted every night and
everyone else in the house was busy. Only the diva doll in his
hands and her companions in their clear fronted boxes witnessed
his performance.

If anyone had asked Arno, he would have said he found the
melody curiously comforting. It seemed to envelope him in a
wrapping as soft and warm as the velvet underskirt he'd made
for the 'Raped Rose'. The melody made him feel somehow
safe and wholly loved. A ridiculous proposition, he knew. He
was glad no one was there to ask him anything about anything
and he could immerse himself in the practicalities of his diva's
toilette, paying no heed to the sounds of Cook and Girl settling
Gran in her room on the ground floor and later going down to
their basement quarters.

It was nearly midnight when Arno pulled one last time at the mandarin collar of the diva's scarlet qi-pao, slung her pipa over her shoulder and examined his handiwork.

'If you could talk,' he said to the doll.

He touched a fresh Q-tip against the glass stopper of a bottle of Chanel No.5 and dabbed it on the doll. Then he gave her a chaste peck on her faded white face and holding her in her stand like a candle, paraded her across the attic to his sleeping area.

Arno loved his attic. As a child, the space at the top of the house with its forgotten curiosities had been his make-believe treasure cave. He'd loved the way the light came in from the dormer windows and the air well that cut through the centre of the room, making shadowy monsters on the sloped ceiling. When he'd finished school and decided he was far too old to still be sharing the ground floor front room with Gran, he'd made the attic his private retreat. It hadn't mattered to him that the space adjoined the family's memory room in which Tjoa Ek Kia's and Big Mother's memorial plaques were placed. Later, when he began dealing seriously in Barbie dolls, he'd divided the attic into two at the lift and staircase landing, the front end for working on the dolls and their costumes, the back for sleeping. In the one section, he'd installed shelves for the dolls along its long side and put in a worktable, his fabrics, threads and accessories, and sewing machine. In the other section, which he'd separated with a heavy curtain, he'd left in place a high wooden bed which had been in the attic since before his birth. The very bed his father and aunts had been born in, according to his Gran. The bed in which he dreamt up stories of his diva's life.

By the side of the bed, Arno had positioned an upright 1920's steamer trunk made of crocodile leather and studded with bronze buttons. Ostensibly this was his nightstand. But it was also where his diva doll resided.

The trunk had originally contained four leather fronted drawers, three of which Arno had removed to make a display nook. In the centre of this nook, he'd placed the old doll house presumably made for his aunts. Three Ken dolls dressed in early twentieth-century style linen jackets and panama hats had been laid around it. The dolls, lounging on their sides, faced the front of the house, where Arno now set the diva doll and her stand. Only one last thing remained to be done before she would sing. She needed to be paid. And as Arno did every night, he plucked a hair from his eyebrow and dropped it into the slot of the letterbox on the front door of the house.

'There's your fee,' he told the doll with a loving pat. 'Now go and wow them.'

Then, duty done, he shut and locked the trunk and clambered onto his bed to sleep the sleep of the blameless.

* * *

Arno had slept through the first hours of Girl's first morning in the house. As had his father. And Gran. And Cook. Only what lingered in the walls of the house and the CCTVs his aunt Irene had installed, caught the girl wandering about.

It was quite extraordinary, Cook would say to the Labour Ministry investigators months later, when she was shown the footage after the accident. Extraordinary but entirely expected from someone like Girl, Arno had thought when the same footage was shown to him. Extraordinary because it had never happened before, and entirely expected because Girl was different.

No other new girl had ever gone exploring by herself on her first morning. They had all been intimidated by the modern glassed and mirrored insides of what should have been an old shophouse. Certainly, none of them had ever dared to go alone into Cook's domain, the kitchen. Not on a first day. But as Cook and Arno had seen on the CCTV footage, Girl had wandered all over the first floor; looking at herself in the glass, sitting in the armchairs in the entry foyer, and pretending to be a film star, a fashion model and heaven knows what else, before finally ending up in Cook's kitchen. Indeed, her itchy feet had taken her right to the red lacquered back door, which she'd opened. No other new girl had ever dared to open doors to look outside at the new country she'd arrived in on her first morning. And no other new girl had ever set off the security alarm on her first day and shocked the house awake the way she did.

The alarm set the mynahs to cawing and cackling in the back garden, then started Gran screaming to be let out of bed. B.K. Tjoa was forced up from his chaise longue and to his bedroom door, which he pulled open with a clatter before shutting with a bang. Did it matter who had orchestrated that? Whether it was a spirit named Bing Fa or simply Girl's propensity for trouble? Whatever or whoever, it was the whole jam bang clatter scream caw cackle of sound that had pulled Arno out of the delicious diva dream he was submerged in and roused him to the particularity Girl was.

Half-awake, Arno heard Cook thumping up the steel service staircase to attend to Gran. He heard her bumping into his father who was shambling down those same steps towards the security door controls on the landing wall. He heard Girl too, her light footsteps tip-tipping on the white marble as she scampered away from the kitchen back to the very same staircase.

Perhaps Girl had been running to get Cook to turn off the alarm. Perhaps she wanted to pretend she'd never been up on the first floor at all. Arno didn't know. What he does know and what he tells Sister Mary Michael is, 'That's when the dried out old twig met the fire. On that first morning. Halfway up and halfway down the servants' staircase.'

Because Cook had gotten up to his Gran and quietened her by then, Arno could hear his father's low slow voice saying quite clearly, 'Ah, so you're the culprit.'

And then Girl's light lilting voice protesting, 'No, I didn't. It was ghosts.'

Arno's father chuckled.

'Ghosts? It's not ghosts. The priests sent them packing years ago. It's the security system. Look.'

There was a pause when Arno's father must have jabbed the control panel to show Girl what he was talking about.

The screeching stopped.

'You new girls, you're always such sillies,' Arno heard his father say.

'I'm not a silly-' Girl started to protest.

And then, before she could get herself into further trouble, Arno had heard Cook calling down the staircase to his father, 'B.K. Big Sir! I'm so sorry she disturbed you.'

His father chuckled again. 'Yes, you should be. You better take her upstairs and show her everything fast. I don't need this happening again. Getting woken up like that when I've hardly closed my eyes,' he said to Cook. And after that, to Girl, 'Go on. Upstairs with you.'

Arno heard Girl mounting the steps. Obediently and steadily. Without pausing to look back at the employer she'd just had the temerity to answer back. If she had though, she might have seen what the CCTV on top of the stairs caught, the glint in B.K. Tjoa's eyes as he watched her walking up those steps, her hips swinging under the veil of her waist-long hair. Swinging the way he liked.

But Girl hadn't turned to see. And so, she hadn't learnt that first essential thing about B.K. Tjoa. How quickly his appetite was roused.

Cook had tried to tell her.

'B.K. Big Sir! And on your first day!' Arno heard her saying to Girl in the corridor.

'So, he'll be sending me home?' Girl had whimpered in reply.

'No!' Cook said. Then she must have drawn Girl to the mirror in Gran's room, for Arno had heard the hissing whisper that the air well channeled all the way up to his attic. 'Look in there at what he's seen. Such a thin shirt and wrap. And hardly anything else on. The problem is more likely than not, he'll want you to stay,' she'd told Girl.

In retrospect, Arno knew Cook could have got Girl sent away on that first day if she really was so concerned about his father. All she had to do was tell his aunt Irene that Girl was not twenty-three but sixteen and hence illegal. His aunt Irene never wanted any trouble with the law. But where would Cook have been if she'd done that? Cook's problem was that the turnover in the house was something awful. Girls didn't stay. With his Gran so old and so many rooms on so many floors, Cook couldn't manage on the second maids his aunts sent over 'as needed'. Without Girl, Cook would have to play a 'one-leg-kick-all', juggling Arno's Gran and his father and himself and the house all by herself. She'd gotten too old for that. So, she put it off. It was Cook's bad.

It was also Arno's bad that he didn't give his aunt the heads up about Girl's and his father's encounter. But he's not sorry about it. If he'd reported it, there wouldn't be a story to tell about himself and Girl. And how could he have borne that?

Cook and Girl must have stared at the mirror for a long time, for Arno was about to doze off again when he heard Cook say, 'Well Ma'am Irene will bring your uniform over later. Shirts and culottes like mine. That should cover you up some. And with your hair cut-'

'Cut my hair?' Girl asked in shock. And then, she exclaimed, 'No!'

Her 'no' had risen sharp and high through the air well to Arno's bed. That was when he'd woken fully to how unique she was. A girl protesting about a haircut before her first day had even properly begun, and with such certainty! It was as if she thought she had a say about the hairs on her head. As if she thought she was as good as a diva. Arno sat up in his bed and rubbed the balding spot on his eyebrow where he'd over-harvested his tributes to Bing Fa. Then he glanced at the old-fashioned wall clock opposite the bed. It was coming on seven. Not too early to wheedle breakfast from Cook if he was prepared to have her lay out every single little thing she'd done on home leave onto his plate as well. And he was prepared. Oh yes, he was! For suddenly, he was overwhelmed by hunger. And the need to have a look at the new girl.

9

It is the mention of Arno's eyebrow hair offerings that convince Sister Mary Michael he isn't merely a lonely boy obsessed with dolls and a second maid. He is indeed attached to the spirit that lingers in the house. And that Friday night, after Arno takes himself and his girl doll to bed, she begins to do the necessary. Leaving Cook to watch over the sleeping boy, she returns downstairs to cleanse his grandmother's room.

The nun employs all her tools: her crucifix, rosary, Holy Water and the St Michael prayers. She frees the hanging dolls, praying over each of them and blessing them with Holy Water before unhooking them from the door frame on which they dangle. She also blesses and sprinkles the diva doll, the doll house, the flower arch, every single garland and rosette on the carpet, and the carpet itself. And then she sprinkles the room and prays over it, from the floor and walls to the ceiling.

It isn't a proper exorcism. She'll have to wait for the Bishop to do that, and she can't call for him yet. It's early days. She hasn't enough information to make the pen and paper determination that will pass muster in an ecclesiastical court if it ever becomes necessary. The prayers and blessings and sprinkling are as much as she can do. And as much as her brittle bones will take. Hips and knees trembling, she puts the dolls, the doll house and the wedding decorations into the carton Arno brought them down in. And then she swallows her medication and steps into the lift to go up to Arno's attic, where she is to spend the night.

The air in Arno's attic is heavy, laden with so many emotions and stories the nun must stop and close her eyes for some minutes before she can comb though her senses to untangle them. There's anger, much more anger than she would suspect from her few hours with Arno. There's guilt. Over many things. Sex of course. Not unusual for a twenty-five-year-old Catholic man sent to a rich boys' Methodist school. But there's also guilt about his grandmother. And about Girl. A fair amount of loneliness. Not unusual again, given his appearance and manners. And then there are the stories, hanging from the sloping ceiling of the attic like snakes. All the stories Arno has made up with the diva's help. About the diva's origins. Her relationships with his grandfather Tjoa Ek Kia and his grandfather's old boss Towkay Ong. Her pain at being imprisoned. Her purported plans for freedom. Stories the house will certainly need to be cleansed of. But not until the nun can get to first cause and reasons. Not until the boy and his family are delivered.

Sister Mary Michael hopes she can do it quickly. She does not like the feel of it, the heaviness of the air up here. But tonight she has no energy left. The cleansing in the grandmother's room has drained her.

She pulls open the musty curtain leading to Arno's sleeping area at the back of the attic. Cook is snoring on the bare boards beside Arno's bed. There is no sign of the sleeping pallet the nun has requested.

Resigned to sleeping on the floor, she tip-toes through the room to Cook, and touches the sleeping woman's shoulder.

'Cook,' she whispers. 'It's Sister Mary Michael, I can take over now.'

Cook heaves herself up from the floor.

'Your pallet is in front,' she tells the nun.

She pulls aside the curtain, leads Sister Mary Michael to the work area and shows her the blow-up mattress made up with neatly tucked-in sheets, pillows and a light blanket. The pallet is laid on the floor in the middle of the room, equidistant from the wall against which the two sewing machines are placed, and the opposite wall of shelves filled with doll boxes from floor to ceiling.

'I hope this is OK,' Cook says.

Sister Mary Michael is sure her bones will welcome the mattress. But she is not sure about the dolls. She had not liked them when she saw them first, just after dinner, and she has not changed her mind after the hour spent cleansing the grandmother's room. Still, it has been a long day for both herself and Cook. She decides she doesn't need to broadcast her reservations.

'It's fine, thank you,' she says, then bids Cook goodnight.

However, the nun does not lie down on the carefully made-up pallet. Instead, after the sound of Cook's footsteps on the marble staircase have disappeared entirely, she returns to Arno's sleeping area.

As she reaches the great carved bed the boy is sleeping in, she runs her fingertips over the footboard to enquire of its history. It does not speak. Nor does Arno Tjoa's unnaturally still body. The nun goes up to him and puts a finger to his nostrils. No. The boy has not died. But it is as she suspects. It is not just his sedatives. Whatever had enlivened his recent crisis has withdrawn, leaving a shell emanating only the usual human emissions of breath and sweat, skin flakes and crotch-slime, nothing else. There will be no harm coming from his inert body this night, she assures herself. She can sleep next to him without fear.

But what of the rest of the room?

She looks quizzically at the upright steamer trunk by the side of his bed.

Covered in crocodile skin and dyed a rust red, the trunk seems to glow in the dim light of the shuttered and curtained room and beckon to her. And as always, she responds. She walks up to the trunk and lays her palms on its dry, flaked surface. The trunk emits age and experience, as if it has sailed the seven seas and carried its treasures safely back to this attic. She can trust it; it seems to be saying. She can sleep safely in the glow it casts. She can be as safe as the girl doll sitting on top of it.

Perhaps it's because Sister Mary Michael is so tired. Perhaps it's because her medication has kicked in and dulled her senses, all six of them. Whatever the reason, the nun forgets that in the language of beacons, red means danger. She forgets that all the beacons she knows are out at sea, set there as warnings to stop ships from running aground. She drags a small stick-back rocking chair from a corner of the room, sinks her bones into the chair and allows sleep to take her.

10

It is when Sister Mary Michael is rocking in the chair, dreaming of altar cloths and, candlesticks that Girl comes to her. She is floating halfway between Arno's back dormer and the wash yard she'd crash-landed in fifteen months ago, dressed in a white bridal gown. There's a scrubbing sponge in her hand, and she's looking disgruntled.

When she speaks, it is in a high insistent mosquito-like whine.

'It's my story more than Arno's or even Bing Fa's,' the girl declares. 'I'm the one they trapped. I'm the victim. The one you must free. So, it's my story more than theirs that you have to listen to.'

And then, without even an 'if you please' the story is dumped into the nun's dreams. Girl's story. In its entirety. From the beginning.

* * *

It had started at the standpipe in Girl's faraway village, the nun learns. Girl had been standing there waiting for her buckets to fill, her bare feet pressed against the sodden paving stones and her eyes streaming. She'd just been slapped for forgetting to top up her Ibu's water jars that morning. She was sixteen. Far too old to be giddy headed about such an essential chore. But she was still the spoilt youngest daughter who fell into scrapes then whinged and whined and burst into tears when she was found out and punished. So there she was, crying her eyes out. An overgrown child. Or so everyone at home had thought.

But the divisional administrative officer who was passing by had not seen a child. What caught his eye was a marriageable girl with eyelashes jewelled by tears and thick black hair flowing down her shoulders, a bedmate vastly superior to his dried-out wife of twenty years. Within the week he'd sent an offer to Girl's mother through a go-between, the Tjoa family cook who happened to be back in the village on home leave.

The administrative officer was a man of means, and the go-between was Cook, who was a cousin of Girl's Ibu and a well-travelled woman of good reputation. What reason was there for Girl's Ibu to decline the baskets of rice sent along with Cook as engagement gifts?

Girl could have listed a slew of them.

For one thing, the administrative officer was not Buffalo Boy, her childhood sweetheart. He was neither golden-skinned nor beautiful. Nor, as far as Girl was aware, could he sing buffalo herding songs. She had to get out of the engagement.

But she was already in pre-wedding confinement.

It was half a month before she could persuade her watchful sisters to let her out, and run to the bridge over the stream where Buffalo Boy was catching shrimp to tell him the whole story from the railings and rouse him to action.

'My fate's sealed if you don't do anything,' she shouted down to the stream, loud enough for all the passers-by to hear. 'I'm engaged. To be a second wife.'

Everyone had seen Girl and Buffalo Boy shrimping in the stream as five-year-olds, then bathing the buffaloes together as they got older. They'd ridden the beasts home on more than one evening, the boy's knees perched on the shoulders of one or other of the animals, the girl's legs wrapped around the boy's thighs, the hard buffalo hairs pricking into both their bottoms. When they'd grown so big even to glance at each other was unseemly, they'd devised other ways to continue pressing their bodies one against the other without being seen. And now, all of sixteen, she was staring down into the stream, her lips swollen and a trembling hand against her face, crying her eyes out. Buffalo Boy did not stop to think. He clambered up the embankment, wrapped his arms around her and, right there on the bridge where every passing trader and wood-gatherer could be a witness, kissed her and promised he would pay her bride price.

'Ten baskets of rice and him a herder, how's he going to pay?' Cook heard Girl's Ibu say to her daughter later, as she lifted the latch of the bamboo gate to Girl and her Ibu's house.

Details of Girl and Buffalo Boy's scandalous behaviour had already spread through the village like wildfire and now Cook had followed Girl home to announce the consequences. But bad news could wait, Cook decided. And so, instead of walking down the side of the house and turning the corner to the back garden right away, Cook stopped to hear what she could hear.

Girl's Ibu was sniffing.

Cook's cousin, Girl's Ibu, ran a cooked-food stall at the front of her house, and from the smell of burning firewood Cook knew she was preparing the day's offerings. However, the sniffs Cook heard were not those of a woman bending over a pot to check the seasoning in a sop buntut. Nor were they the sniffs of someone overcome by the spice of a hot sambal. Girl's Ibu had a vast vocabulary of sniffs. Sniffs of disdain—single haughty out-puffs accompanied by raised eyebrows. Guilt-inducing sniffs—repeated snivels suggesting her heart was breaking but no one cared. Investigatory sniffs—three in-breaths against the object of suspicion (a pot of two-day old rice or a jar of fermented shrimp or her daughters' underwear). These sniffs were entirely different. Was she crying?

'How's he going to pay?' Cook heard Girl's Ibu ask once more.

Girl's Ibu had set her youngest daughter's bride price high, as she had for her two older daughters. After all, she'd rationalized, there was the wedding feast to consider. Ten baskets of rice were nothing. And yet for a buffalo herder, Cook knew, it was way too much.

Still Cook heard Girl reply, 'He'll manage. He'll borrow.'

The sniffing stopped. Cook heard Girl's Ibu blow her nose, then exclaim, 'At one per cent a week! And him a herder. What will you eat then? Stones?'

Girl's Ibu hardly ever spoke about herself. But as everyone in the village admitted, she knew about money. There were rumours that as a young girl, she had gone away to make a living in the only way women could during her time. It was an acknowledged fact she'd come back at the age of twenty-five a rich woman with enough capital to buy land and start her own food stall. The subsequent years provided further proof that where this woman was concerned, a nothing could be turned into a little something and a little something could be turned into enough. Even with her first food stall destroyed by the volcano's outburst, she had fed and clothed herself and all three of her adopted daughters. The girls had gone to school up to the sixth year. They weren't rich, Cook knew. Moreover, as Girl's Ibu had grown older, she'd developed a softness for religious fundraisers. Still, through it all, she had managed to pay the Chinese rice trader and keep her second food stall running and a roof over her girls' heads. If she said her daughter and Buffalo Boy would be eating stones, it would certainly be so.

Cook heard Girl trying her luck anyway. 'There's love. With love, nothing's impossible,' she said.

'Love doesn't last with debt around,' Girl's Ibu replied. 'I grew up in a house full of debt. Believe me I know. With debt, everything else flies out the door.'

Cook heard a ladle tapping hard against a pot.

'You shouldn't believe those sob-stories playing on the Cini's televisions. Life's not like that,' Girl's Ibu said, before sniffing again. Once. Twice. And then, so many times and so quickly Cook couldn't have counted if she tried.

Girl's Ibu, who never cried, had broken down. And it was her wretched daughter who'd done it.

Unable to take any more, Cook bulldozed down the side of the house, rounded the corner and announced, 'Well, he's backed out.'

Girl's Ibu stopped sniffing.

'Sit yourself down on the back steps there,' she said to Cook without turning around. 'I've the fire going. We don't need any ashes falling on your expensive foreign veils.'

'No,' Cook replied, sitting down where she'd been in instructed, on the ramshackle backsteps which shuddered under her weight. 'Your girl has started a big enough fire. You don't need me burning up too.'

Girl's bride price would have paid for new backsteps, Cook thought, and even extra footings for the whole house. But now, there'd be no chance of fixing anything.

'I'm sorry,' she couldn't help saying.

Girl's Ibu had always been proud and now all she said in reply was, 'Well, we know what he's made of, that's something. He's so afraid of gossip he's lost his wits and forgotten what's good for him. It's no great loss.' She'd lifted her fingers and began to count for Cook. 'It's less than a moon cycle from the wedding so we can keep the engagement gifts. It's our right unless we choose to send them back. He won't make a fuss. He'd look petty. That's the last thing he wants people to think about him. No bride price, but still, it'll be five baskets of rice I won't have to buy from the Cini. And afterwards . . .' she smiled. 'Afterwards? You know how beautiful my girl is. They'll be waiting in line,' she said. As if the world hadn't changed.

But things had changed.

'Everyone's talking about how Buffalo Boy had one hand up your girl's baju and another undoing her kain,' Cook said. 'No one wants a cuckoo's egg in their nest. It's time you thought about something other than marriage for her.'

Cook had meant going abroad. But Girl's Ibu misunderstood.

'Don't you dare suggest that,' she growled. 'Not for my girl.'

It was even worse with Girl. She didn't simply misunderstand. She was agreeable!

'It's true though what Cook says,' she told her Ibu. 'I'm all I've got. Nothing's better if I don't marry Buffalo Boy.'

That was too much for Girl's Ibu.

'Am I hearing you right? How can you say having nothing is better than not marrying Buffalo Boy? And how can you even allow the thought of that other thing into your head? How can you be so stupid?' she shouted at her daughter.

'Please.' Cook pushed herself between the mother and daughter, then said to the girl, 'Now, answer me honestly.

Do you want to be married off to another man whom you don't know and don't care for, just because he's rich?'

Cook knew the answer Girl's Ibu expected, the one her two older daughters had given when presented with a widowed religious teacher and the idiot heir of the village's largest landlord. She also knew the answer this spoilt youngest daughter would give.

'All right. It's a no,' she said. And then she'd made her own offer. 'So, what about I give you the possibility of making so many zeroes you can pay your own bride price and marry whoever you want? What about you come to Kota Cahaya with me? To the City of Light? It's the foreign dollars from there that paid for my family's new house and my brothers' fields. It's what could pay your bride price.'

'What will I do?' Girl asked.

'You'll be a second maid. It'll be easier than working in a field or helping in a Cini shop here. One old Gran to look after. And the grandson, Arno Young Sir, who's no trouble at all,' Cook said.

She didn't mention B.K. Tjoa, Gran's son and Arno's father, who was trouble. But Girl had sensed something being withheld.

'They say you work in an ash house. There are ghosts in ash houses,' she protested.

'Not in this one,' Cook assured Girl. She hadn't made a search at the Land Office archives, but she knew the basic facts and was not interested in the rest of it, neither the rumours nor the rustlings at the top of the house. After all, unlike Sister Mary Michael, she was not the type of person who noticed such things.

'It was meant to be an ash house for another family. But they never moved in. There have never been any urns in it,' she said to Girl. 'As for the Tjoas, all their ashes are scattered at sea. It's just memorial plaques in the memory room up in the front of the attic. And only for the grandfather and his first wife, Big Mother. What's more, the whole house was blessed by a priest. So, there are no ghosts. I guarantee it,' she told Girl with the utmost conviction. 'As you can see, I'm alive, aren't I, with all my wits about me? And,' she added, 'I'm rich.'

This perked Girl's interest.

'How rich?' she asked.

'Not quite as rich as the Cini in the town or anyone in Kota Cahaya,' Cook granted. 'But rich enough for a villager.'

Still Girl shilly-shallied. 'Ibu's not young any more. I need to be here to help her,' she said. 'As for the bride price, Ibu can take the five baskets from the officer and credit it to Buffalo Boy and lend him the rest.'

Girl's Ibu was adamant though. 'Five baskets won't go very far. There'll be children. I collected you and your sisters from the midwife's back steps. I don't want to force you to leave your children there,' she'd said. 'It's not possible. You do understand, don't you? You don't have any other choice.'

'But Buffalo Boy . . .' Girl whined

Her Ibu's slap had come almost immediately.

'Well, you'll have to!' she said to her daughter.

Then, she'd turned to Cook and snapped, 'Take her.'

And Cook had. She'd seen to it that Girl's documents were altered so she was the right age, twenty-three and not sixteen. She'd bought Girl a ticket. She'd taken Girl by ferry and bus and two airplanes and a taxi all the way to the ash house and the lingering spirit she claimed did not exist.

* * *

'But she does exist. And now, she's caught me,' the girl says to the dreaming Sister Mary Michael. 'Which is why I'm here, talking to you,' she reveals, without guile like a child. 'I need you to tell me about spirits. Everything you know.'

As if it can all be taught in a dream, within a night.

'It's best not to know too much about such things,' the nun hears herself warning the girl, even as she sleeps.

'But you must,' the girl insists, spinning above Sister Mary Michael until her wedding dress turns into a billow of white lace and tulle, and her veil becomes a cloud through which the rust-red of the trunk glows.

'You must,' she cries. 'Bing Fa's wrapped herself all around me now, too tight for me or Arno to undo. You're the only one who can help. Otherwise, I'll have to marry Arno. And I won't. I won't!'

Her skirts flare, filling up the distance between her floating transparency and the nun. Sister Mary Michael feels Girl's wedding veil winding around her neck, pulling her towards Girl and drawing her hollow bones into the girl's shimmering no-body of a body. And then, it happens. Girl begins to pour herself into the nun's hollows and fill them.

Girl and Sister Mary Michael do not become one. But what Girl's young body had remembered, the nun too remembers. What she had felt resounds now in the nun's old heart and bones. The nun learns what Girl did not know. And with that knowing, the nun's own knowledge seeps from her bones and into Girl's ignorance.

* * *

Girl had known very little about spirits. Not enough to be careful of them. Nor to protect herself from them. Girl's Ibu hadn't encouraged questions. Girl had learnt what she could from her sisters. Bits and pieces they'd whispered to her on monsoon nights when the rain thundered onto their tin roof and her Ibu could not hear them. Bits and pieces. Precious little.

'There're demons and then there're ghosts,' Girl's sisters had said. 'Demons have bodies and rely on their own strength to get things done. Ghosts are smoke and air, but they can enter bodies and get those bodies to do their bidding. You can approach both demons and ghosts with offerings of food and flowers and you can buy their services with gifts like nail clippings or hair or blood,' they'd also told her.

'A sliver or a strand or a drop, that's all they want. And then they'll give you anything you want. The whitest skin and blackest hair. All the girls at school wanting to be your best friend. All the boys sending their go-betweens to your house. Everything,' her second sister had shared.

'But afterwards, they own you. And if you try to escape, it'll be like this,' her older sister had said, widening her eyes and wrapping her fingers around Girl's throat. She'd warned, 'Don't listen to her. Best not to owe anyone, men or ghosts.'

'Best not to owe anyone, men or ghosts,' Girl's Ibu would often repeat the next morning too, as if she'd heard everything they said. And if it was the rice Cini's delivery day, she'd say the same thing again after he left, with a few sniffs for emphasis. Not that Girl's Ibu followed her own advice. Like any other villager, she would sneak off to the graveyard with flowers when the rice in the bucket dipped too low. And if the rains were slow in coming, she could be seen putting out a few bananas under the fruit trees too.

* * *

Sister Mary Michael wants to tell Girl and her sisters and Ibu that those who linger have no power of their own, only what's lent to them; that they too are burdened by debts which grow exponentially, interest on interest like the loans due to rice-Cini. She wants to tell them that lingerers aren't free spirits but are obliged to do the bidding of their overlord. And she wants to disabuse them of the notion they can satisfy the spirits. Whatever the spirits say, neither blood, nor nails, nor promises can feed or free them. It's light and love they need. And all that's required to receive that is a turning back. Confession with contrition, then communion. That's what Sister Mary Michael wants to say.

It's too late for any of that though. Everything meant to happen to Girl has already happened. She has already fallen out of the tree. She has already been comatose for more than a year, first in the hospital and then in a nursing home. All the nun can do now is unbind her from whatever promises she made and allow her soul to go its way.

Girl had assumed dealing with spirits was a simple case of exchange. Flowers in a graveyard, bananas in an orchard, blood and nails, the hair she'd already allowed Irene Tjoa to cut. How much else could it cost? That's what Girl would have reckoned when she first began to deal with the spirit of Bing Fa.

The nun's sleeping body feels what Girl had felt when she asked that question, what she, Sister Mary Michael, has never experienced. There is the plaited hank of Girl's cut hair throbbing in its pouch underneath the pillow, screaming like an angry animal to be re-attached to Girl's body. And there are Girl's hands reaching under that pillow and pulling the plait out, and stroking it till her palms buzz with the static of its resentment. There are Girl's lips biting together. There is Girl's then-self, vowing to her future-self, 'Never again.'

Sister Mary Michael's hair had been waist length once too. But she had never mourned it. She had thought it more a trouble than anything and been more than glad to let it go at her Clothing Ceremony. Not a mere lock, like they did after Pope John XXIII's reforms, but all of it. First her braid taken at the nape of her neck like Girl's, then the rest snipped and snapped in handfuls unlike Girl's. Afterwards, the stubble, so closely shaven there seemed to be only bare skin under her young nun's fingers. And finally, to stop those fingers from one day regretting the loss, the veil.

They've done away with veils now. The dreaming nun has been allowed to run her fingers through her short grey hair whenever she feels inclined to for . . . Oh! She can't remember how many years it's been. But there it is, her dreaming self, doing it again.

In the liminal space between sleeping and waking, Sister Mary Michael shares the feeling of her own fingers running through her elderly nun's short soft hair with the girl.

'See, it's nothing special,' she says to Girl. 'Nothing to be excited about. Only hair that needs to be washed and combed and trimmed. A trouble you don't need to waste tears on.'

Those are the words the nun says. And yet, she herself must not be convinced. For even as she dreams in the stick-back rocker, pitching forward and backward gently, she can feel the sadness running through her bones. And the tears oozing from her eyes.

Why is she crying, the dreaming nun wonders? Is it for herself, because she's allowed all her wants to be squeezed out of her? Or is it for Girl, whose dreams have turned to dust?

11

During Girl's first few weeks in the ash house, she had thought she'd arrived in dreamland. She had found the ash house entirely wonderful. It was as if she'd walked into a TV serial and been given charge of all the machines she'd only ever seen on screen. There was the dust gobbler, which scooted around the marble floors by itself eating dirt. There was the rice cooker which didn't need watching but never burnt the rice. There was Gran's automatic bed that rose and fell and bent in the middle. There was the food cutter used for grinding Gran's food, and the rubbish eater which chewed up leftovers before disappearing it all down the sink hole. And then there were the dishwasher, the clothes washer, the clothes dryer, the fans and air-conditioners and the hot and cold running water. Never mind the strangeness of the house, its spaceship-like glass inside and its old lady outside. Girl had not believed her luck. To be working in such a house and with such machines. And to be paid for it!

But it wasn't two weeks before Girl realized she'd been given the wrong role in the show. She was playing the household drudge. However, miraculous the dust gobbling and rubbish eating and grinding and washing machines, they were nothing more than props to support her role as the person dealing with the sick and shit and slop.

'Dealing with sick' meant going out onto the five-foot way first thing in the morning to check for vomit and other traces of B.K. Tjoa's previous night's indulgences, then to disappear it all with a mop and Dettol before the neighbours could see. 'Dealing with sick' also meant going back inside and inspecting the rest of the first floor, the staircase and the lift and disappearing anything he left there too.

After that came the shit. Girl had to rinse off Gran's soiled sheets that she'd left soaking and put those into the washing machine. She had to take down the previous day's half-dried laundry and put them in the dryer. She had to hang out the newly-washed sheets. And when she was done with all that, it was up to the ground floor to Gran's room again, to sponge shit from her body.

Next was the slop. Gran had to eat. What went into her top end had to be blended into a mush which looked almost exactly like what came out the other end. Getting Gran to eat the slop was next. That took forever, with Gran screaming and spitting and trying to pinch and scratch the whole time.

'Dealing with slop' meant sterilizing Gran's spoon, bowl and blender too.

'You'll be sorry if Gran gets the runs,' Cook had warned.

It was a warning Girl took seriously. She had more than enough soggy heavy sheets to deal with. It wasn't worth it, stinting on the time spent sterilizing.

After Gran had eaten, Girl would wheel the old woman out for a sunbath in the back garden and massage her legs. It wasn't a total break. If Girl did not want to be kicked, she had to keep Gran occupied. Still, it was a change from the sick, shit and slop, squatting there at Gran's feet in the shade of the frangipani tree, breathing in the perfume of the flowers.

Supposedly Girl also had a proper break after she put Gran back to bed and cajoled her into having a morning nap. Supposedly that was when she could sit down for a cup of coffee and something to eat. But even though there was always something to eat in the house because Irene Tjoa didn't want to be featured in the newspapers for starving her help, Girl never had enough time to enjoy the food. Once Gran was put down for her morning nap, there would be the pin cushion animals and plastic blocks and whirligigs and photographs on Gran's big black table to tidy up, the koi pond to attend to, then Arno's attic and his doll boxes to clean, followed by more food preparation for Gran's and Arno's lunch, more dishwashing and sterilizing, another struggle with Gran over her afternoon nap, the kitchen's first wipe down, Gran to be woken up and amused, laundry to be folded and ironed, dinner, the kitchen's evening wipe-down, Gran's evening wipe-down, Gran's bedtime tantrum, Gran's toy table to be tidied again, and finally, the blasted koi fed.

As Cook had told Girl that first morning when Irene Tjoa cut off her hair, most days Girl didn't have time for anything but work. Certainly, no time for looking after waist-length hair. Despite all the machines in the house there were mornings when all Girl could do was drag herself up from her bed, wash her mouth and splash water on her face before running up to quiet Gran's screaming. There were nights when she fell onto her bed and her eyes closed before her head hit her pillow. Nights when she didn't remember that the hank of hair Irene Tjoa had cut was thrumming sullenly in the pouch under her head. And worse, there were nights when she did remember it but did not feel guilty for having forgotten on other nights. It was only hair after all. Indeed, when the hair on Girl's head grew out onto her shoulders again after two months, she didn't even wait for Irene Tjoa to cut it. She snipped it away herself and threw the locks into the rubbish bin without a second thought. As Cook had predicted, the hair was better gone. It was one less thing to worry about. That's how bad things were for Girl. Then.

Was it surprising she latched onto what Gran said that day, when Gran slapped her?

Arno's Gran didn't slap just anyone. She had to get familiar with them first. It took a month before Girl was slapped. In that month Girl had learnt to manage the vacuum cleaner she'd first thought of as the dust gobbler. She'd learnt to turn it on and off with a mere tap of a big toe and gotten it to roam only where it was supposed to and not go falling off the edge of the landing onto the fish-bone staircase or get itself stuck under the legs of Arno's worktable. She'd also been given charge of a smaller vacuum cleaner with a brush that she could run across the plastic surface of Arno's doll boxes.

On the morning Gran slapped Girl, she had finally managed to vacuum those box fronts properly, without dislodging any of them. She'd gone up to Arno's room to clean after strapping Gran into her chair in front of the big black table strewn with therapy toys and photographs and waiting for her to nod off. When she returned to the room though, she saw that Gran had woken, and was playing with three of Arno's precious dolls.

It was a mystery how Arno's darlings got down there from the attic. Initially, Arno had thought it was the girls. But all of them had denied it when questioned by Cook. The only possible explanation was that Gran was wheeling herself into the lift and sneaking into his quarters at odd times of the day and her wheelchair kept her so low the CCTV cameras couldn't catch her. Still, although that made sense, it did not stop Arno from screaming at the girls whenever he missed his dolls.

'If you don't want him screaming it's best you spirit the things back as soon as you find Gran playing with them,' Cook had said.

And that was exactly what Girl was trying to do the morning Gran slapped her for the first time.

Arno was in the dining room ploughing through a late breakfast. As he usually took an hour, Girl had thought there was plenty of time for her to get the dolls back up to the attic and into their boxes. But she hadn't accounted for Gran being contrary.

Girl had managed to gather up the woman doll in the kebaya and the man doll in a suit from the toy table before Gran could protest. But Gran was holding on to the teenage Barbie and not letting go.

'Mine,' she'd whined when Girl tried to twist it out of her hands.

When Girl pulled harder, Gran had raised her hand.

That thwack of palm against cheek echoed through the air well to the dining room as Arno set down his empty coffee cup.

This wasn't the first time Gran had laid hands on a girl. There was no reason for Arno to storm down the air well corridor and into Gran's room shouting, 'Gran, what's the maid done to you?' But he had.

'Where is she, the number two maid looking after you? What's she done?' Girl heard him asking Gran from the bathroom, where she'd gone to cry.

He was speaking slowly, so Gran would understand. And Gran had. More or less.

'It's not what the number two did,' Gran replied. 'It's what he did,' she said, pointing to the male doll Girl had left on the table. And then, she re-enacted the scene she'd already played for Girl at least once a week for the last month.

She sat the woman doll in the fold between her forearm and upper arm and knelt the teenage doll in front of it. Taking hold of the woman doll again, she wriggled its head and said in a voice that brought Arno back to his childhood, to when Big Mother was still alive. 'Remember, he went mad when she scattered his things. That's why I tied her to them and to us. And that's how it's got to stay. Tied. Remember. That's what's keeping his heart and mind together. And this family. So, don't forget.'

Girl had been told by Cook that Arno had no interest in stories about keeping the Tjoa family together. He'd stopped listening when he was nine. That was when Gran fired the old Cook for revealing family secrets she shouldn't have. First, that although Arno's aunts had told him he'd been named Arno after the river in Florence where his parents honeymooned, they had never had a honeymoon. Second, that his supposedly dead mother wasn't dead but had run away before he was six months old. But the current Cook had also told Girl, Arno was fond of his Gran, and he would humour her if he himself was in a good mood.

That day, he humoured her.

'Who're you talking about now? Whose heart and mind need to be kept together? Grandpa Tjoa's?' he asked her.

'Him and his second wife. I'm talking about the second wife,' Gran replied.

'The number two girl?'

'No, the number two wife,' Gran said.

Arno should have known who Gran meant. After all Girl, who'd been in the house for only a month, already knew the story: About Gran being brought before Big Mother. About the

second wife, Bing Fa the pipa diva, who'd bewitched Tjoa Ek
Kia from her grave. About how Big Mother wanted Gran to
become the third Mrs. Tjoa Ek Kia to replace that dead woman.
And about how Gran had agreed despite Grandpa Tjoa being
such an old husband.

'Such a very old husband!' Gran had said to Girl. 'But what
to do? We were so very poor.'

Gran never succeeded in winning Grandpa Tjoa's heart
although she and Big Mother had tried their hardest.

'Not important though,' she'd also told Girl.

It was the zeroes after the dollars that Gran and her family
needed. And to grow to a ripe old age, a Gran whom everyone
waited on hand and foot.

'A good ending,' she always said, every time she came to the
end of the story.

But somehow, Arno had not been able to connect what
Gran said that morning with the old family story. Instead, he
asked, rather stupidly, 'The number two maid. Are you saying
she hurt you?'

Girl heard Gran let out a very long disappointed breath
at that.

'How could Bing Fa hurt me? I had her under my thumb. I
tied her back up good and proper. We're all together aren't we,
we Tjoas? That's what matters. I'm not a fool like Big Mother.
What if Grandpa loved her more than Big Mother and me
together? As if love was any part of the bargain.' Gran replied.

As if love was any part of the bargain. Something made Girl's
ears prick at those words. Repeating them as she peeked out
from behind the bathroom door into Gran's room, she saw what
Gran had gained from her bargain. The table filled with all the
knick-knacks an old woman might wish for. The room that was

just for Gran. And outside the room, the rest of the three-story ash house she ruled over. It was everything Girl could have too. If only she gave up love.

It was much much more than she had ever thought possible.

Suddenly her eyes were opened to Arno's possibilities as well. He became someone more than the Arno Young Sir with the fat white face and palsied arm who dressed up Barbie dolls. He became the Tjoa heir.

That vision and realization prompted Girl to step out from behind the bathroom door.

Without considering the consequences, she called out, 'Arno Young Sir!'

Her voice was light and lilting, her tear-filled eyes shining, her small brown hand delicate against the hand-shaped welt across her left cheek. She was altogether inviting.

Arno registered her voice calling and turned, his flabby jowls spilling over his shoulder. Unlike the administrative officer though, Arno did not see Girl's lovely vulnerability. Rather, he looked past her limpid eyes and through her small breasts, her slim waist, the curve of her hips and her shell-pink toenails. All he saw was a second maid who'd been crying. All he realized was that he'd made a mistake about who had hit whom.

He frowned and muttered, 'Ah yes. Of course, you couldn't have hit Gran.'

Turning to Gran, he said, 'You've got to be nice to the helpers, all right? I don't want to call aunt Irene about another one running away.'

And as a parting shot to Girl, after he'd gathered up his dolls and was waddling away, he muttered, 'Don't take it too hard, you'll get used to it.'

12

It wasn't an entirely promising start for a grand romance, Girl had thought as she watched Arno making his exit. But Bing Fa, who'd been hovering above the door frames watching the scene play out had a different view. As she saw it, the underlying basics were there. Arno was lonely and the girl was full of want. Something could develop if she rubbed the two of them together. Enough heat, perhaps, to propel them towards the doll house. If that heat was properly channelled . . .

'I couldn't have done anything if there wasn't anything to begin with. You do know that, don't you?' she pushes Girl aside to tell the sleeping nun.

But all Sister Mary Michael says in reply is, 'Poor babes. You shouldn't have. Not even if . . . still . . . you shouldn't have . . .' And even though she's still asleep, the accusation in her voice cannot be disguised.

'Shouldn't have what?' Bing Fa retorts. 'Shouldn't have encouraged them?' She laughs scornfully. 'They didn't need encouragement. Take Arno, maybe he did have such a complex about his white face and withered arm he couldn't imagine Girl laying out herself as bait for him. But look at the size of him. He didn't become that way with one feed. There's a hunger in him. You see that, don't you?'

Still the sleeping nun continues to mumble, 'You didn't have to. It wasn't necessary.'

'Perhaps not,' Bing Fa agrees. 'But, you know, I don't latch myself onto just anybody, Sister. You must want something from me, before I make myself visible. Look at you and your hollows, how you needed my music to fill them. You started it,' she says to the nun. 'Same with those two. Girl started it. Perhaps she didn't completely understand what she was in for when she called out to Arno. But I assure you I had nothing to do with that first move of hers. And I can tell you, whatever regrets she might have had afterwards and however stubbornly she's been saying no so she can hold on to her dream of that Buffalo Boy . . . I can tell you . . . In the flash she sent that wish out, she'd cast the die. I felt the immensity of her desire. It was so strong, I couldn't resist. I had to help her become a Tjoa bride. I had no choice.'

The more truthful phrase, Bing Fa knows, is 'needs must', the girl's needs and hers. There was the key to Bing Fa's freedom, hidden away in the doll house, waiting to be revealed to its true owner. There were her failures, all those other hungry boys and girls who'd disappointed her in years past. There was time passing . . . Irene not getting any younger . . . Bing Fa could not afford to leave the fat boy and greedy girl to their own devices. She had to take possession of their bodies and bend their desire towards her purpose.

There are limitations, though, when one's puppets have wills of their own and when one's show is being played out in actual months and days. It has been more than a year since the girl fell from the tree. Her body has almost reached the end of its useful life. And without the girl, there is only so much she can make the boy do. Her play must take a new turn. Now, 'needs must' means engaging the nun.

'You of all people should know our limitations, we who don't have material bodies. There is nothing I could have made those two young people do, if they were unwilling,' she says to the nun.

At this the nun scoffs, 'As if!'

To which Bing Fa laughs.

'All right then, let me tell you the whole story and prove it to you,' she says, opening her hands in front of the sleeping nun as if parting the curtains of a theatre.

* * *

Arno had proved amazingly unresponsive to Girl. All her attempts to speak to him after their encounter in Gran's room had failed. He either ignored her or started stuttering and then scuttling away. Girl was fed up. She was being worked sixteen hours a day like a machine and she was tired of being tired. On the few days when she wasn't tired, she was sick of being bored. Bing Fa, whom she didn't know yet, was her ticket out.

Gran of course was the one who introduced Bing Fa to Girl. At first the diva had just been the second wife that the other dolls mentioned in passing. Someone a Big Mother doll would claim she'd gotten the better of and tied up. Or someone a younger Gran doll would be warned about by the Big Mother doll, because she, the second wife, was full of wiles and had her ways. Or the one a Tjoa Ek Kia Ken doll would describe to another Ken doll with just a single 'Ah . . .' filled with awe and want.

They were disjointed bits of information, but such delicious bits Girl couldn't help making a whole woman from them. In the fantasies she wove, the second wife Bing Fa was a beauty so lovely she couldn't be pushed out of Grandpa Tjoa's heart even after death. A lover so skilled a man needed only to describe her with an 'Ah . . .' to convey everything she was. A woman so dangerous, Gran had warned Girl directly, just the once, 'You've always got to keep your wits about when she comes around. Otherwise . . .'

Girl hadn't paid attention to Gran's warning. It was the one 'Ah . . .' that captured her imagination. Here was an enchantress with skills way beyond what Girl would ever learn from watching her Ibu, whose prowess the villagers still whispered about. Indeed, Girl suspected, she would not even learn as much from watching 100 TV serials of palace girls and empresses. She had to reach out to the spirit.

She decided to take her chance on a Friday, two months into her stay in the house.

Fridays were Girl's favourite days. On Fridays Irene arrived at the house with her driver sharp at nine, and after stopping with Gran for half an hour, left again with Cook for the market until at least lunch time. On Fridays, Arno went to the second-hand clothing depot and had lunch out. In between his leaving and the market party returning, Girl would be left alone with Gran and free to ask all kinds of questions including those about the mysterious Bing Fa.

On the Friday Girl chose to make her move, she was to have even more time alone with Gran. Arno needed to see about a new embroidery machine and had said he'd be out all day. Irene and Cook were going shopping for Chinese New Year goodies in Chinatown and didn't expect to be back before three.

'You'll have to see to Gran's lunch. Tofu and fish soup with fresh rice,' Cook instructed. 'You can do that yes?'

Girl nodded even though she wasn't planning to waste any time on cooking and had already decided to feed Gran the leftovers in the refrigerator. Gran wouldn't know any better. And there'd be no evidence if she gave the fresh slice of fish to the mynahs in the kitchen yard and sent the tofu down the waste grinder. Or so Girl hoped. Needs must, she justified to herself. To learn more about Bing Fa, she needed an entire drama by Gran with the enigmatic enchantress as the star. So no, she wasn't planning to waste any time on something as mundane as fish soup, tofu and fresh rice. Indeed, so eager was Girl to squeeze all the information she could about Bing Fa from Gran, she totally forgot about the CCTV cameras Cook so frequently warned her about. As Irene, Arno and Cook had been shown on the replays months later, she had wheeled Gran into the glass lift that neither cooks nor second maids were supposed to use, and two floors later wheeled her out without the slightest hesitation.

* * *

Once in the attic, Girl had set Gran in front of Arno's racks of dolls.

'Which ones do you want to make wayang with today Gran?' she asked.

Gran poked her head out from her shoulders like an old hen and scanned her black eyes over the foot-high dolls dressed in Arno's beautifully made costumes.

'This,' she said, pecking her thumb and index finger at a box by Girl's elbow.

The box contained an adult Barbie dressed in a flowered sarong and an elaborately embroidered purple lace kebaya.

'This is going to be Big Mother?' Girl asked, holding the doll out to Gran.

Cackling, the old woman grabbed it.

'Who else has such nice clothes?' she said before stuffing the doll into the pocket of her bib and closing her eyes.

She was done. But Girl wasn't. She needed at least two more dolls for the show she wanted to watch, a doll to play Gran and another to play Bing Fa. Squatting down, she examined the lower racks where Arno displayed his teenage Barbies and saw a slightly dislodged box. It contained a black-haired girl in a plain purple cloth and a cotton blouse that Girl had seen Gran playing with previously.

'You want this one also?' she asked, lifting the box up to Gran.

Gran peered into the box then raised her arm and shouted, 'You little fox! You want to be in my story!'

Girl ducked out of the way of the arm that looked so weak but had already hit and pinched her uncountable times since the first slap.

She wasn't Gran's target that day though. It was the girl doll Gran picked up and started smacking against the spokes of her wheelchair.

'I'll teach you,' she screamed.

'Gran. I'm sorry. I made a mistake. It's your wayang. Nobody else's. Only yours,' Girl soothed.

But Gran continued flailing the doll anyhow any which way, all the while screaming, 'I'll teach you! I'll teach you!'

She only calmed when Girl said in her most humble wheedling voice, 'Yes, teach me, please. I really want to learn.'

The tantrum disappeared then, like magic.

'Good girl,' Gran said in a voice almost like Irene Tjoa's, but not quite. 'All right, I'll teach you. Repeat after me thirty times—slave girls and bond maids are off limits. Start now!'

The order didn't make sense to Girl but she didn't want Gran turning red again or kicking her stupid so she'd be a burden to her Ibu. She did as she was told.

'Bond maids are off limits and slave girls too,' she chanted absentmindedly as she began to put the Barbie she'd rescued to rights.

Straightening the doll's arms and legs and pulling its clothes back in place was easy. Try as she might though, Girl could not bun the doll's stiff plastic hair back into the smooth chignon Arno had styled. She would have to catch him the minute he came home and make a confession before he started throwing wild accusations around, she realized. It would be an excuse to try talking to him again too, she supposed. Not that she needed an excuse of course, she argued to herself as she continued to chant. After all, she wasn't a slave girl nor a bond maid. She wasn't bound by Big Mother's spell.

Spell?

Girl stopped chanting and shot a quick look at Gran, who had nodded off. Gran looked feeble. Harmless even. But she'd almost managed to trick Girl into casting what seemed to be a spell on herself, the old witch!

She put the doll back into its box, brought her right thumb and ring finger together then flicked them apart to break whatever spirit tainted web she'd woven unknowingly. No, she wasn't going to be hexed. Not if she could help it!

Standing up, she reached down and tugged lightly on Gran's earlobes to wake her.

'I've finished praying, Gran,' she lied, 'But you Gran, you didn't finish your story yet.'

Gran blinked. Her baggy eyelids opened and her beady eyes swivelled here then there then everywhere like a hungry chicken.

'My story?' she mumbled.

Girl pointed to the Big Mother doll in Gran's bib-pocket.

'Yes, your story. You want to tell me your story but only Big Mother is here. We need to have you and Bing Fa too. Which doll is you Gran, and which is Bing Fa?' she asked, as she wheeled Gran slowly past the shelves of Arno's collection again.

Gran leaned forward and knocked her knuckles against a double-fronted box containing a woman doll dressed in Chinese clothes and a boy doll in a Western suit. When Girl took them out of the box, Gran snatched the boy doll to herself and cradled it against her stomach.

'My baby, my Big Boy,' she whispered to it.

Girl knew that Irene Tjoa, Eileen and the other sisters were Big Mother's daughters and that Arno's father, B.K., was Gran's only child. The boy doll had to be him and therefore, the woman doll was Gran. All she needed now was Bing Fa.

Tucking the woman doll into Gran's bib, she pushed Gran back along the rows of dolls they'd passed.

'Now, Bing Fa. Where is she?' she whispered, trying to keep her voice even.

Gran's head jerked right and left, then craned around.

'With Grandpa's button and pipe cleaner and shoelace and ear-pick, scattered everywhere, all over the garden,' she said.

'You mean she's gone?'

Gran cackled again. 'No. Big Mother got everything back and tied her to them.'

This confused Girl. 'Who scattered Grandpa's things? How did Big Mother tie her to them?'

Gran's answer didn't help. She said, 'With magic, what else?'

'I don't understand,' Girl said very softly, hoping against hope Gran wouldn't get annoyed and start screaming again.

Gran snorted. 'Didn't I tell you before? Pipa players don't like being tied. They want to choose. To go with the highest bidder. Grandpa Tjoa wasn't rich enough. When she first knew him, he was the handsome young Tjoa, not the rich old one I got. He had nothing in his pants pockets except his third leg standing at attention.'

She waved the boy doll she was holding at Girl. 'See this. It's a toy. They didn't have that word those days, but I learnt it from one of Irene's sons. Toy boy, that's what our Grandpa was for Bing Fa. A toy boy.'

Gran laughed at this, slapping her hands up and down on her thigh and swinging the helpless boy doll around like he was a dead rat.

'So why did she marry Grandpa Tjoa in the end?' Girl asked, both out of curiosity and to save the doll from further damage.

That set Gran laughing again. 'It wasn't her. It was him. After she died, he sneaked off to the Temple of Ghost Marriages and arranged the wedding.'

'A ghost wedding?' Girl hadn't known what that was then.

Gran explained. 'Yes. He got married to a paper doll with Bing Fa's name written on it. As good as bowing in front of the ancestral alter with the real woman, the monk said.' She laughed. 'Hah! He thought that was how he'd finally get her all to himself. In death if not in life. But she wasn't happy about that. Oh no! Tit-for-tat, butter for fat. Her spell against his spell. She went to her Madam in a dream and asked her to scatter his things. To break up his love.'

Gran opened her little eyes wide and flashed her teeth at Girl. 'You know what that did to him, don't you?'

Girl had seen enough of Gran's dramas to know the answer to that.

'Grandpa Tjoa went crazy,' she replied.

'Exactly. Scatter a man's love and you scatter his wits,' Gran said.

'Why did she do that? I would've been happy if someone loved me so much they wanted to marry me all the way through death,' Girl said.

'Maybe she thought all that love was a burden,' Gran said. She looked up at the doll cases then at her hands. 'Doesn't matter. We don't need to try to understand. We just need to keep Bing Fa under, like Big Mother did. Keep her under and keep Grandpa's head together.'

'And that was all Big Mother did, just keep Grandpa's head together?' Girl asked.

Gran had laughed and laughed at that. 'There wasn't a single bomoh who could guarantee anything else,' she said. 'What good is love if your husband's gone crazy and can't earn? That's what Big Mother thought at the time. Like I would have too. She took what she could get. And the rest . . .' Gran dropped her chin to the front of her chest. 'I'm tired,' she said. 'You tell me the rest. Show me you've learnt, like you said.'

Girl repeated what she'd heard so many times before. 'The rest is that the bomoh took Big Mother to the Madam's house and showed her where Grandpa's scattered belongings were buried. Then Big Mother dug them up and Grandpa got better.'

'But how did that happen?' Gran asked.

'You didn't say how,' Girl said. 'You skipped over that last time Gran.'

'And you want me to tell you now?'

'Yes please,' Girl said as meekly as she could.

'All right. Come here then.' Gran beckoned Girl towards her and lowered her voice. 'The bomoh told Big Mother to use her own hair to tie Grandpa's things together with some of Bing Fa's, then he made her sing one of Bing Fa's songs. And that was it. One string of things and one song and Bing Fa was bound and Grandpa back to himself. End of story.'

It wasn't the end of the story though, Girl thought. It was the beginning.

'Big Mother didn't burn the things?' she asked, to be sure.

'No. They were Grandpa's and Bing Fa's things. If she burnt them, she'd be letting Bing Fa go. Grandpa would go crazy again, maybe even die,' Gran, who was being unusually patient that afternoon, explained. 'She had to keep them together and whole.'

'And where did Big Mother put the things?'

Gran leaned in towards Girl and whispered, 'She hid them. But not so well I couldn't find them.'

She sat back in her wheelchair after this revelation, put the boy doll on her lap and crooned at it, 'I found everything and I untied her, didn't I? So she'd let me have you, my boy. You, your father's only boy. I had to do it for you, didn't I?'

Girl pulled at Gran's sleeve. 'You let Bing Fa go?'

Gran looked sideways at Girl and cackled. 'No. Why would I? I didn't want Grandpa to go crazy again either. I tricked Bing Fa, that's what I did. I made her agree to stay in the little house with Grandpa's things until my boy was born. But I never let her out again.'

Ah . . . At last, they were getting somewhere, Girl thought.

'And where's the little house Gran? Can you remember?' she prodded gently.

Gran's head jerked right and left then craned around the room. 'Here. Right here. In this house. Where else?' she said.

Gran's mind was wandering again. They were in a terrace house, sandwiched between two others. There was no annex or little house attached to it. How could the house Gran talked about be here? Despite having the whole morning free, it did not seem as if she would get Bing Fa's story after all. Despondently, she wheeled Gran into the lift and pressed the down button.

'Come. I'm going to cook now,' she said.

And since Gran was still clutching the boy doll, she added, 'You can tell me all about your boy when I'm making your rice and soup.'

* * *

Girl hadn't been interested in B.K. Tjoa, not as a boy nor as a man. She was afraid of drunks, and since Cook had ordered her to keep out of his way, she saw very little of him. To Girl, he was a whiff of cigarette smoke and a chuckle overhead when she was out in the back garden with Gran and he happened to be smoking on his balcony one floor up. Sometimes she heard him singing softly in Chinese as he walked from the lift to the front door. And sometimes very late at night, if she was still working in the wash yard, she would recognize his stumble in the kitchen above and then hear his slurred voice chiding the kitchen cupboards for moving about and not keeping to their places. He seemed good natured, an elderly uncle who unfortunately left distressing traces of his drinking habits all over the house. Perhaps unpredictable. Even mischievous. But certainly not dangerous.

She wasn't thinking when she asked Gran, 'Was B.K. Big Sir naughty?'

Gran frowned unexpectedly. 'Mothers shouldn't bad-mouth their sons you know. You'll need to ask somebody else,' she said.

They were in the middle of Gran's lunch. Girl was spooning slop into Gran's mouth and within pinching distance. Since she didn't want to be pinched, she asked more indirectly, 'Was B.K. Big Sir like Grandpa then?'

Gran swallowed and giggled. 'He's exactly like his father, the very image.' She stroked the shoulders of the boy doll she was cradling. 'No arguing at all that Grandpa Tjoa was my boy's father. Everybody could see from the moment I pushed him out. And when he grew up . . .' She stroked the doll's legs. 'See these strong legs, this straight back.'

Like Buffalo Boy's back and legs, Girl had thought. But she would have to set Buffalo Boy aside until she finished her contract. She pushed the image of him away and went back to feeding Gran and pretending to be an absorbed audience.

She asked what she'd asked before, but in yet another way.

'So, B.K. Big Sir was very handsome like Grandpa Tjoa?'

Gran swallowed and giggled again, her head wagging back and forth. 'Maybe Grandpa was handsome in his photographs. But me, I only knew the dried-up old man.'

Girl giggled along. She had seen the photographs of Grandpa Tjoa and B.K. Tjoa as young men on Gran's toy table. They did indeed look alike. But it was also true that the yellow hang-skinned B.K. Tjoa whom she paid so little attention to looked nothing like those photographs.

'Yes, come the years, everything wrinkles up,' she said tactfully.

'Not down there. Down there he was always ready,' Gran said with a wink, clutching the boy doll's crotch.

'Grandpa Tjoa or B.K. Big Sir?' Girl wanted to be clear.

'My boy? I told you not to ask about my boy. I mean my husband, you stupid girl.'

Girl let the insult go. With Gran, stupid was simply another name for second maids. This talk with Gran was getting her somewhere though. That's what mattered.

'But Grandpa Tjoa was old already. And you told me, Grandpa Tjoa never forgot Bing Fa. So how?'

Gran shrugged. 'Those herbs Big Mother put in Grandpa's soup made his third leg stronger than a goat's. Bing Fa got his heart. But down there any hole would do. If not me, then Big Mother.'

She hugged the boy doll closer and said to it, 'You know, don't you, my boy, what happens down there has nothing to do with love?'

Girl had heard her Ibu saying the same thing to her sisters before sending them off to their lives of comfort with the widowed religious teacher and the landowner's idiot son. Still and all, Girl had continued to hope. There were those TV serials, those worlds where love overcame. Perhaps in this comfortable house where the refrigerator was never empty and water and lights came on with a flick of the fingers, this might also be the case.

She stroked Gran's cheek. 'They say your baby can only look like its father if you love him. Maybe you loved Grandpa Tjoa even if he didn't love you?'

Gran's right eyelid dropped then lifted in a definite wink. 'Close your eyes and go blank, that's how to get a son looking like his father. Disappear from the scene. Let his papa take over.'

This was not what Girl wanted to hear. But what did Gran care about what a second maid wanted? She was already rattling on. 'Me? I'm not a dreamer. Big Mother was the one who kept hoping. Even if she told me making his mind whole was more important, she was always thinking the more she could keep

Grandpa with her, the more he would love her. She was so full
of what she wanted there was no space for him. That's why she
dropped those six girls, all looking like her except for Irene.
Clever with the herbs and the spells, stupid with her heart, that
was Big Mother.'

She tapped the lapels of the boy doll's suit. 'She got a
shock didn't she when your father died and your sister Irene
told us about his will,' she said to it. Then, turning to Girl, her
eyes bright with glee, she told her, 'It turned out, after all Big
Mother's efforts and all the time gone by, he still wanted to be
buried next to Bing Fa. Hah!'

'Buried,' Girl said. 'And where would that be, where
Grandpa and Bing Fa are buried?' she asked.

Gran squeezed her wrinkled hands together around
the boy doll, like a spiteful child squeezing a small animal.
'They're not together. Big Mother burnt him, scattered his
ashes in the sea, and stuck a memorial plaque for him upstairs
in the memory room. Later I did the same for Big Mother.
Told her ashes to go travelling with him so I could have the
house to myself at last. As for Bing Fa, Grandpa buried her
in the Cantonese cemetery at Bright Hill. But that's been
dug up by the government. Same with the Temple of Ghost
Marriages where he kept their marriage tablet. All gone. Lost,'
she said to Girl.

Gran was not in the least distressed. But Girl was.

'Lost?' she repeated. 'All lost?'

Gran shook her head so hard Girl thought it would fly right
off her scraggy chicken neck.

'No. No. No,' she said. 'I told you, she's in the little house.
They're both there, their spirits tied up together. I should have
burnt the house when Grandpa died but Big Mother said, if we

kept them tied up, the family would be together. So, it's still here. Somewhere.'

This was Gran's second mention of the house. It had to be a real place then, a place Girl could go to.

'Can you tell me Gran,' she began as calmly as her thumping heart allowed, 'Where is Bing Fa's house?'

Gran blinked and squinted at Girl. 'Who are you?' she asked.

'The number two maid who looks after you Gran,' Girl replied promptly, humbly.

Gran nodded, brought the boy doll up to her lips and said to it, 'Not our flesh and blood then, is she? Not a Tjoa son, right? Only a servant, yes? So, it's not for her to know, is it?'

Girl almost throttled Gran.

'Stupid old hag, I wipe your nose and clean your arse, I'm closer to you than any of Grandpa's flesh and blood,' she almost shouted aloud. But she didn't.

A Tjoa son would know, Gran had said. There were two Tjoa sons in the house, B.K. Tjoa and Arno. Girl knew who she'd have to go to.

13

As fate, or perhaps Bing Fa, would have it, on that Friday when everyone was supposed to be out of the house till teatime, Arno was mere steps away from Girl.

Arno had walked into the house minutes before, carefully balancing his new embroidery machine against his belly and holding it in place with his one good hand. But the box had begun to slip. To prevent it from crashing onto the floor, Arno had leaned backward against the nearest wall, slowly squatted down onto the floor and set the box aside on the marble floor. Then, he'd stretched out his legs and called for Girl to help him.

The wall was next to one of the door panels separating Gran's room from the corridor. And just as Arno opened his mouth, Girl had slid it open, stepped out and tripped over his outstretched legs. And as Girl fell, Arno had heard a voice suggestive of the warmest intimacies, the most boundless and unconditional love, and the promise of everything, say, 'Look. As you wished, I've brought help.'

Girl had been carrying the three dolls she and Gran took from the attic earlier and they'd flown out of her hands when she fell. The one dressed in the purple Nyonya costume had landed between Girl's back and Arno's belly, with its lace kebaya flung open and the tiny crystal shirt fastenings scattered on the floor. The doll in Chinese clothes had landed across Girl's right shoulder with its face buried in a fold of Arno's T-shirt. And the teenage Ken doll that was supposed to be the Chinese doll's son had somehow lodged its head inside Girl's collar with its upside-down legs stuck against the nape of her neck and its feet pushing at the short ends of her hair. As for Girl, she was in Arno's lap, her back snug against his chest.

Arno placed his weak hand on Girl's back and told her, 'Don't move. Let me get my dolls first.' Then using his good right hand, he pried the Chinese doll from the fold in his T-shirt and set it on the floor. Next, he pushed Girl slightly forward and freed the doll dressed in Nyonya clothes from between them. And last, he reached for the upturned teenage Ken doll inside Girl's collar.

Arno was careful not to touch Girl's skin. He didn't want Girl making any molest complaints against him. His aunt Irene had enough trouble putting out the fires his father B.K. started. But when he circled his fingers around his doll's feet, he couldn't help touching Girl's hair. The ends of her unevenly cut hair had thick blunt tips that felt almost artificial. The filaments were an unusual black with blue and purple tints. Doll hair, he thought, as a shiver of pleasure ran through him.

Unable to stop himself, he leaned into the shining black strands to steal a sniff.

Girl didn't smell of doll. She smelt wholly human—salty with a trace of sour and a bit of sweet. And what else? He took another breath. Was that a tinge of coconut oil? Sweat? Smoked fish? Tears off a pillow? He leaned in closer and took a third breath.

Girl sat as still as she could and allowed Arno's face to inch nearer. Only her eyes moved, sliding sideways and up to the painting of the three musicians on the wall.

'Isn't this what you wanted? Haven't you prayed for the opportunity to get close to him, the Tjoa heir?' their mocking faces seemed to be saying.

And in truth, how much closer could Girl be to Arno? There she was on his lap. And there he was with his fingers on her hair about to bury his nose into the back of one of her sea-shell ears. If she had wanted him close, then the force called Bing Fa was granting her wish. He was very close indeed.

She shifted her weight backwards and into him.

Bing Fa does not know why Arno rolled Girl off his lap, she tells Sister Mary Michael. But he had.

'I need to get this upstairs,' he said, struggling to his feet. He pointed to the box containing the new embroidery machine. 'Can you run up and get my trolley?'

Perhaps Girl was disappointed about the turn of events. But if she was, she didn't show it. She'd simply stretched out her slim smooth arms and said, 'We got these. No need for a trolley.' Then she'd squatted and lifted the box onto her right shoulder.

It was not so heavy for Girl. Much less than the bags of rice she'd taken off the back of the Chinaman's truck for her Ibu. Much less than the bales of dried grass she'd helped Buffalo Boy carry. Indeed, the package was so light she had to wonder what kind of man Arno was and how he could be the heir of everything around her yet be unable to manage even a cardboard container.

Obviously, Girl had not shared these thoughts with Arno. All Arno had seen on Girl's face that Friday was a desire to be of assistance as she stood up and said, 'I'm ready.'

'Right.' He nodded, gathered up his three dolls and led the way past Gran's sliding door panels into the air well corridor. At

the lift, he pressed the door open and walked in, beckoning for
her to follow.

'I'm not allowed,' she said.

'You are if I say so,' he told her.

She stepped in then, almost triumphantly, it seemed to
Arno. As if she'd won a bet. 'Not a slave nor a bondmaid,' he
thought he heard her mumbling. A village chant, to protect her
while going up an elevator, he supposed. Whatever, it was none
of his business.

Up in the attic, he pointed to his worktop.

'I want it there,' he said.

His worktop was nothing like Gran's huge toy table. It
was the size of a school desk, with an extra flap protruding
from one side. His existing sewing machine was already on
the main desk. It would be tight if he put the new embroidery
machine on the adjoining flap, but he couldn't think of an
alternative.

Girl, however, had.

'No. There's something better,' she told him.

She set the box down on his work chair, crossed the landing
to his sleeping area and stopped at the crocodile skin trunk
crammed between his bed and the wall.

'This has wheels. We can roll it to your sewing place and
put your new machine on it,' she said. 'It's just right.'

It wasn't just right.

'Leave that trunk alone,' Arno shouted as he waddled
towards her.

'But, see . . .' Girl swung her hip gently against the front of
the trunk. 'It's not too high and not too low.' She turned and
bent her knees, assuming a sitting position, then put her hands
out over the top of the suitcase and mimed someone sewing. 'It's

exactly right,' she repeated, tilting her head at Arno as if she was a model in a sewing machine advertisement.

'I said no.'

This time, Arno spoke slowly and very quietly.

Girl looked up, recognizing the change in his voice and the warning it implied. But she'd become a five-year-old again, as bewitched by the rust-red crocodile skin trunk as she'd been entranced by the blue-green wet hide of the monitor lizard she'd tempted into her Ibu's garden with a newly-slaughtered chicken. Held by the red lights inside the lizard's coppery eyes, five-year-old Girl had ignored her Ibu's coaxing to come away and instead had continued to inch toward the lizard. Her Ibu had crept up to Girl, scooped her in her arms and walked her away backwards, all the while hissing at the lizard. Now it was the steamer trunk's flaking leather and the tarnished greens of its bronze buttons that snared sixteen-year-old Girl. And it was Arno, who wormed his hand into the crook of her arm to gently drag her away.

Girl drooped against Arno's belly. 'I don't understand,' she said.

She felt as if she'd just been pulled away from the jaws of some gnashing, chomping creature. But she wasn't in a back garden at the edge of a jungle, escaping a dog-sized lizard. She was between four walls in an attic room on Green Hill in the centre of the richest city in the region. There was nothing wild and hungry for her to be saved from.

'That's where the house is, the doll house. Inside the trunk,' Arno said. 'We can't move the trunk. She wants it there. In that corner.'

Girl's eyes widened. She had sent a wish out and it had been answered. She had been led to what she wanted—the little house and Bing Fa.

She struggled out of Arno's arms and turned to face him, her eyes fierce.

'Can I see her? And the little house?' she demanded.

Arno hesitated, then nodded and took her hand in his. Together they tiptoed towards the trunk like small animals, drawn to the dark inside of some terrible beast, the beating hope in their breasts making them deaf to their fear. But Girl could not be deaf to her Ibu's voice, which had been whispering the wisdom of ages to her all her life. It came to her now, urgent and admonitory. 'What if the thing you want, the thing that's so near, turns around and bites you?'

Girl stopped right where she was. Pulling Arno's face towards hers, she asked him, 'What's the doll house?'

'I'm not sure,' Arno said.

He truly was not sure. When he'd first discovered it, he'd thought it was merely a replica of the ash house made for his aunts to play with. Later, when he'd invented his bedtime ritual for the doll (or at least thought he had), he'd seen it as a convenient vessel for his offerings. Frankly though, it had not actually occurred to him to ask the question.

Hoping for an answer, he cocked his head towards the trunk. Girl followed. Breath bated, they waited.

They were expecting a revelation. What they heard was the front door opening two floors below and Irene Tjoa telling Cook to be careful with the duck eggs and the bird's nest.

'We're so lucky to have found that red bird's nest. It'll do B.K.'s liver a world of good,' her voice pierced into the attic.

The spell that had taken hold of Girl and Arno shattered.

'You better go down. They'll need your help bringing in the groceries,' Arno said.

His voice as it echoed off the attic ceiling rumbled in its usual way, slow and low. The afternoon sunlight shining in from the west dormer window made its usual square on its usual place against the opposite wall. And the crocodile skin trunk stood exactly where it always stood, squat and solid, its skin a dull rust, its screws a faded copper. Not threatening at all.

It was as if everything Girl and Arno had experienced had never happened.

14

Irene had blamed herself when the Ministry of Labour showed her the CCTV footage of the girl going up and down the lift that Friday, easy as she pleased. She should have known trouble was brewing, she who could smell deceit in a Cook or a second maid from fifty paces. Why she herself had caught the girl slipping down the steps that day, when she and Cook came in from the market. But as her sister Eileen had taunted after it all blew up, what had she, Irene, done about it?

'What were you doing up there?' she'd asked the girl.

To which the girl had replied, 'Cleaning the staircase.'

Irene had looked the girl up and down, from the top of her small head and down the front of her pink-buttoned work shirt to her small feet, bare against the white marble floor. Such a slow careful examination usually elicited some confession or other from a girl, but it hadn't from this girl. She'd simply stared back at Irene, her eyes wide and innocent.

'Why weren't you in Gran's room watching her?' Irene asked.

The girl had her answer all ready. 'It's nap time. At nap time, I clean the stairs.'

'Not B.K.'s quarters though, correct?'

'Also, but only when he's not at home,' the girl replied. 'Like today. Especially today, because it's market day and Cook doesn't have time.'

She'd answered everything perfectly correctly. And yet if Irene were to think about that day, something had been off. That po-faced expression on the girl's face was too good to be true. As was everything else about her, if Irene were to believe Cook. How well she managed Gran. How quick she was at her tasks. How Arno hadn't complained even once about his dolls going missing since she came.

No. It couldn't all be true, Irene had thought. But she was already giving so much time and money to the ash house and its occupants, it wasn't funny. She'd just spent half the day pushing and shoving her way through the Chinatown crowds to get everything needed for the Chinese New Year Reunion, notwithstanding that being a daughter she wasn't even allowed to attend it. And there was still the rest of her day to go. Tea with the church ladies, a meeting with the family trust accountants, shopping for her grandson's birthday, and dinner with her husband.

Life was short and she was tired, that's what she'd thought. So what if she was the oldest Tjoa daughter and had to take the responsibility along with the privilege, as Big Mother was always saying? She wasn't a son, was she? And she didn't have the time nor the energy either. All the manoeuvring to retain her position. All the horse-trading with Eileen just so things would go smoothly. Noblesse oblige be damned, that's what she'd thought. That's why she'd simply let the girl off and gone to Gran's room to make her goodbyes.

Things would have been different Irene knew, if she hadn't let her guard down that Friday. But things were what they were. She couldn't afford to waste time on regret.

* * *

Irene wasn't the only one who'd let Girl off easy. Cook had too.

No doubt when Girl stepped into the kitchen, she'd said, 'You might have hoodwinked Ma'am Irene, but not me.'

But she hadn't pushed matters when Girl gave her a befuddled look and said in that light, lilting, innocent voice she always used, 'Why whatever do you mean Cook?'

Cook had come back from market laden and didn't have time to dig into Girl's lies.

'There's lots to clear and put away,' she said to Girl from the floor, where she was squatted, unpacking a basket of vegetables.

Girl looked at the kitchen's counters and the white-tiled floor covered with produce.

'What's all the food for?' she asked, squatting down next to Cook.

Cook pushed the basket of vegetables towards Girl. 'Prayers to the ancestors at the Reunion Dinner on New Year's Eve,' she answered. 'This is an ash house after all. Did you forget?'

Girl sniffed quick and sharp, like her Ibu. 'I'm not a fool,' she said. 'I've taken a good look at this house. No altar in the front room. No table for offerings. No jars or ashes. Only those marble tiles up in the attic in that room in front of Arno's, and that perfume of dead roses and jasmine. It's not me that forgot. It's the owners.'

That was too pert for Cook. The girl needed a put down, no question.

'Looks like you didn't read the characters over the front door then,' she said. 'You know what they say? According to the old Cook who was from China, they say 'Dedicated to the Tjoa Ancestors.' She dipped into the basket she'd pushed at Girl and pulled out the first thing at hand, a string bag of onions.

'Yes, Tjoa ancestors. Ancestors who need you to put away their onions and such,' she said, plunking the bag at Girl's feet.

Girl wrinkled her nose and set the onions behind her.

'Ancestors whose ashes were scattered in the sea,' she retorted.

'True,' Cook had to grant that. 'But Catholic or not, all Cini have a reunion dinner. And it's only polite to invite the ancestors, especially if you've scattered their ashes and are living it up in their ash house. That's what I'd do too.'

'But why? Why are we inviting ghosts to dinner when everyone says there're no ghosts in the house?'

Cook tapped her fingers on the styrofoam box of preserved New Year meats she'd just opened. The girl was beginning to irritate her no end.

'It's the custom. And we're not feeding real ghosts. We're doing it in memory of people who died,' she said.

That answer didn't satisfy Girl. 'So, you don't think there are ghosts in this house?' she asked again.

Cook repeated what she'd been told and what she'd already told Girl. 'Big Mother had the priest who baptized her come and throw water everywhere. The house should be clean.'

'Should be. But is it?'

As if she hadn't heard Girl, Cook continued with her count of sausages, waxed duck thighs and waxed meat. And then, after a good few minutes of quiet, she said to Girl, 'So, what were you doing leaving Gran alone in her room and tripping up and down the stairs?'

If Girl hadn't been so anxious to show off her new-found knowledge of the ghost in the crocodile-skin trunk, she might have held her tongue. As it was, she scooted closer in to Cook, lowered her voice and said, 'I was upstairs with Arno Young Sir and you know what he told me? He says there's a spirit inside that suitcase next to his bed. What do you think of that?'

Cook showed Girl what she thought by slapping her big fleshy palm down on the Girl's knee. 'I knew it! You were up there meddling about with God knows what!'

Girl wriggled her haunches. 'I was bringing his new sewing machine up for him,' she said.

'Well, you're done with that now,' Cook said.

She leaned into the basket of vegetables, brought out some heads of winter mustard and tossed them in front of Girl. 'You know what they say about the devil and idle hands. You're better off peeling this and checking for cabbage worms than worrying about all that ghost nonsense.'

'Well, I don't think it's nonsense and I am going to worry about it,' Girl had muttered as she snapped the mustard leaves off their stalks. 'That Bing Fa knows a lot. If she's up there, I'm going to get in touch with her.'

'Didn't your Ibu tell you there are reasons why people run when they see a ghost. If there's a dead woman up there, I'd leave her be if I were you,' Cook warned.

'But you're not me,' Girl replied.

She splayed her fingers out to show Cook her fingernails stained green with mustard leaf sap and said, 'I'll turn into a vegetable if I'm stuck here in this kitchen much longer!'

'No, you'll learn some cooking skills. And I don't see anything wrong with that,' Cook retorted. She pushed another bundle of vegetables at Girl, watercress this time. 'What's more, from what I heard, that second wife was a famous singer. I've only ever heard you whine and wail. It's a bit of a stretch isn't it, you wanting to sing on stage? Much better that you learn what I have to teach. A good cook can always find a position. Your

Buffalo Boy will appreciate that more than a singing girl out all night with all sorts.'

'If I wanted to be a cook, I could have stayed at home with my Ibu,' Girl said. 'I'm going to do something different, instead.' And then she'd shocked Cook with her plans. 'I do love Buffalo Boy desperately. But now, like in the TV serials, I'm going to have Buffalo Boy appear at the end. I'm going to get a rich man to marry me first. Then, after using his money to set up a nice business or two, I'll leave him for Buffalo Boy. It's not easy. But I know I can do it with Bing Fa's help. So there!'

It was such an unbelievably foolish idea Cook hadn't given it any credence at all. She didn't even bother to tell Girl to stop being so silly. It never occurred to her that Girl would hurry back to the attic the moment she was done cleaning the kitchen and try to persuade Arno to open up the doll house again.

15

Arno was still awake when Girl came back to the attic just before midnight. He'd been on his bed, surrounded by the accessories for his new embroidery machine and trying to understand what each could be used for, when he heard her padding across the room toward him. She had the robot floor cleaner clutched to her chest and a dust cloth slung over her shoulder as if she was preparing to clean. At this time of night, it was preposterous. And considering the strange waking dream he'd been visited with before dinner, she was altogether quite unwelcome. He scowled, then dug his head deeper into his shoulders, turned back to the bits and pieces he was fiddling with and tried to wish her away.

Her heard her sniff a slow investigatory in-breath. Later, much later, she would tell him that he'd smelt of defiance and fear that night. She'd recognized it because it was oftentimes her own reaction to a raging Ibu. But what was he defiant about? And who did he fear? Surely it could not be her? Unable to stop herself she'd followed her nose to find out, walking almost right up to him.

'I'm busy. Are you too stupid to see?' he snapped.

Arno didn't usually speak this way to girls, any of them. Dismissively yes. But never so disrespectfully. Never like that.

Girl didn't even blink though. Instead, she'd shown him the vacuum cleaner she was holding and said, 'But Arno Young Sir, the vacuuming. I've to do this every day and I missed it today. Why don't you go shower and I'll get it going? And then I can quickly give your doll cases a wipe too,' she suggested, smiling tentatively.

'And leave you alone? With her?'

He knew that Girl understood who he meant by 'her' and he had expected her to back off and go away. And yes, Girl's Ibu had taught her that sometimes the best way to go forward was to retreat. So, she had taken three steps back.

'Okay. I'll go to your work area and clean the doll boxes first. Then when you shower, I'll come back here.'

That pull back hadn't been enough for Arno. 'I don't need you doing anything up here tonight,' he said.

'But what do I say to Cook and Ma'am Irene if they see that your room's dirty tomorrow morning?'

'I've to finish a Peranakan wedding set by New Year or I'll lose a lot of money. Tell them I said no cleaning till I'm done.'

'Ma'am Irene wants the house cleaned top to bottom before Chinese New Year. It's one week away. Cook will surely scold me if she comes tomorrow to check and your room's still dusty.'

Arno harrumphed, bouncing himself up and down on the bed and jiggling the mattress and embroidery machine pieces.

'So, will you shower soon Arno Young Sir?' Girl asked again, ignoring his mini tantrum.

It was too much. He picked up a presser foot, aimed it at her and threw. It hit her hard and sharp on her right shin.

'If you don't understand English, you understand this, don't you?' he said. 'Scat! Shoo! Go!'

Girl hadn't run off though. She hadn't even stooped to rub the sore spot. Sometimes, as she'd learnt from her Ibu, the only way to get what one wanted was to stand one's ground and push back.

She told him, 'I'm not a cat, Arno Young Sir.' And then, stepping forward, she asked, 'What are you scared of? Show me. Let me help you.'

Arno pulled his knees up to his chin and stared at Girl. There was nothing scary about her. But he had nothing he wanted to share with her. And there was nothing he needed her help with. Sure, his diva had come to him in a waking dream just before dinner and told him quite clearly why she'd delivered Girl to him and what he was to do with her. He hadn't liked the plan. At the time, he hadn't been a believer in marriage. The only thing issuing from the short-lived and rarely-spoken-of union between his runaway mother and wretched father had been himself. Notwithstanding his diva's arguments in the waking dream, Arno didn't consider himself, waddling maimed Arno Tjoa Jia Hao, an outcome worth repeating. As for the companionship of a good wife who might provide solace, the only good wives he knew were his aunts. Punctilious in their duties towards their husbands. Careful in the supervision of their children. Attentive about every detail of their tables. And always ready to tell him what to do and how to think. They were not the best advertisement for wives. And anyway, he'd told the diva, he didn't need a wife. Even if she, the diva, was just a doll whose story he spun from imagination, she provided all the companionship he needed.

He looked warily at the girl standing at the foot of his bed. She was not a doll. Not a cat either. She wasn't even just a newly-arrived second maid. She was much more troublesome.

She was a human being who behaved unexpectedly and aroused complicated feelings he didn't need or want. He had to keep well clear of her. His diva's suggestions were nothing but manifestation of something in his deep dark unconscious, or more simply, his hormones acting up. He didn't have to satisfy those hormones, he told himself. Not by marrying anybody anyway. Moreover, he reminded himself, he wasn't his father. He was committed to treating women with respect.

'Sorry. Didn't mean to be short,' he said. 'But I do need to get my machine set up. I've got a deadline worth a few thousand dollars.'

That hadn't deterred her. Instead, she picked up the presser foot he'd flung at her, inched nearer and held it out to him. 'I can help,' she said. 'My middle sister, she makes kebaya for a Cini man in our town. He lent her a machine like this. Sometimes, I worked with her.'

Arno had found out later that Girl was lying. While it was true her middle sister embroidered on a contraption that looked vaguely like Arno's machine, it was nowhere near as sophisticated. And Girl, who was known to be clumsy despite her delicate appearance, had certainly never been allowed near the borrowed machine.

Arno had not held that against Girl. It had been worth her while to lie, he supposed. After all, he had told her he'd be earning a few thousands on just that one commission. She had probably figured that if she was not to be given a chance to get at the spirit in the crocodile-skin trunk, then she might as well try to learn a marketable skill.

Whatever Girl's reasons, she looked straight at Arno, keeping her eyes as wide and steadfast as she could and willed him to believe her, just as she'd done earlier in the day with

Irene. And Arno had not been able to resist that wide-eyed look of seeming sincerity.

Happily, Girl turned out to be a natural. She needed only one glance at the instruction booklet to pick out the open-toe embroidery foot he had wanted to use. Another quick consultation and she was off to his work area and sitting at the machine, showing him how to attach the embroidery frame to the machine's base.

Of course, she didn't get everything about the machine on first acquaintance.

'This, I don't understand,' she said, pressing her palm against the LCD screen to the right of the machine arm.

But what a quick study!

When he called up the patterns from the machine's memory, her index finger had gone to the images of the flowers immediately.

'I like this one,' she said and then, without his telling her what to do next, she picked up the touch pen and tapped on the icon of a rose.

She smiled as red petals bloomed and filled the screen. 'How can I make more?' she asked.

'More? Like a bouquet for a medallion? Or like a row for a border?' he asked back.

She wrinkled her nose, thinking. She hadn't known what a medallion was of course. 'Both,' she ended up saying. And handing him the stylus she'd said, 'Show me.'

As Arno had tapped, copied and pasted to compose a borderless medallion of three roses framed with leaves and buds, he'd realized that Girl had given him an idea he could use for his stalled Peranakan bridal commission. Roses were a departure from the traditional motifs he normally gave the clients. But he felt the design would still be authentically Peranakan. After all the Peranakans had loved all things Western. They would have known about red roses representing love and would quite credibly have used them as wedding symbols.

How amazing, he had thought, that a girl from a village would intuit this? As his diva had told him in his waking dream, Girl was indeed a woman after his own heart. Not to be a wife. His diva, or rather his own unconscious, had got it wrong there. But a helper. Quite possibly . . .

For the next hour and a half, Arno and Girl played with the screen as Cook slept, making variations on the rose theme for the bride's clothes, and sturdy trellises twined with leaves and visited by clouds of bees for the groom's jacket. Arno had no idea it was nearly two when finally, he transferred the patterns onto the red and blue satin which would be tailored into the dolls' actual robes. It was Girl who brought him back to time.

'I've to go Arno Young Sir. Big Sir will be home soon. It won't be good if he sees me up here,' she said.

No, Arno thought. That would be bad. Girl had no idea how bad. But he didn't want to let her leave.

'One more pattern?' he pleaded.

She shook her head.

'It's Saturday tomorrow. A long day,' she said.

Back then before Gran died, Saturday was indeed a long day for Cook and Girl. It was when Arno's aunts and their families all came for dinner.

'Yes, it's Saturday tomorrow,' Arno agreed. Girl had to go. But he wasn't going to let her leave without a thank you. Or an invitation. 'Well come again, if you can. This time is good. After you've cleaned the kitchen. I'd like that. We make a good team,' he mumbled.

'All right then Arno Young Sir,' she answered with a quick flash of bright teeth.

He smiled back, a huge watermelon slice of a grin that cut right across his face, and then offered her his good hand. 'We'll be partners. So, no more of that Young Sir rubbish. I'll be Arno to you from now on,' he said. 'Let's shake on it.'

Obviously, Arno knew the saying about bamboo doors pairing only with bamboo doors and wooden doors with wooden doors. He was giving Girl ideas beyond her station. A Tjoa heir asking a number two maid to call him by name! Arno could imagine how his aunts would squawk. But this number two maid was going to be on his team. It seemed right.

He walked with her to the landing and watched Girl as she went down the fish-bone staircase, walking the way his dolls would if they could, with her upper body erect and her tummy tucked in tight, the swing in her walk coming from her hip sockets so she swayed as her feet stepped one in front of the other, heel to ball. He continued to stare as she hurried down the last two steps to the ground floor and noticed that as her little feet glided past the koi pond, they did not make the tap-tap-tap that feet trapped in high heels made. This would have been how his diva doll would have walked if her feet were free to unbend, he had thought then. If his diva doll were human. If she could come to life and become a breathing vital body. If . . .

It was only an 'if'. Arno had known it wasn't possible. His diva was just a doll. The real girl was the one in the air well two stories below, step-stepping out of his line of sight and through the door to the service staircase.

16

Bing Fa closes her retelling with the bittersweet ending of the Butterfly Lovers opera, playing it so gently the plaintive notes fall like tears onto the half-dreaming nun.

'Now do you see?' she says. 'Do you see how they would have done it themselves anyway? All I did was provide the opportunities.'

The nun's eyes open, but she does not answer. Instead, she stares fixedly up at Arno's dormer window as if she hasn't heard Bing Fa.

'Sister, I'm talking to you,' Bing Fa needles the nun. 'You must have heard me!'

'You said they got there all by themselves,' the nun murmurs, still barely awake.

'That's right. What do you have to say to that?'

'Well, that's your story,' the nun answers, more fully awake now. 'But . . .' She turns away from the window to look up to the ceiling and at Bing Fa, as if she can really and truly see her. 'What happened afterwards, that was you,' she says, her lips puckering with each accusing syllable.

'Yes.'

Bing Fa can't deny it. That had been all her doing.

* * *

It was Saturday—the day after Arno and Girl's first work session. Girl was tripping up the steel service staircase, congratulating herself. She had passed all the tests. She had successfully lied to Irene about cleaning the marble staircase. She had told Cook she would be reaching out to Bing Fa and Cook hadn't forbidden her. She had gone back up the steps and stood up to Arno. She had sat at his embroidery machine and traced out roses for him. And now it was morning and she was running to Gran's room and would go to Arno's attic again if she could find a moment between the old lady, her sheets, the koi and preparations for dinner. Arno had asked her to be his partner and work with him on the doll costumes. She was not to address him as 'Arno Young Sir' but by name. A future was opening for her. Not a rich husband who would buy her an ash house of her own but the start of a business. She was making progress. One stone at a time.

One stone then another, feet searching and hands grasping . . . That was how Girl and Buffalo Boy climbed down to the village stream when they'd been children not even as high as the shoulders of the buffalo. The stones they'd climbed were good stones, as large and flat as the slabs on the fish-bone steps in the ash house. Less safe perhaps because they were covered with thick moss. But more fun because on that moss, Buffalo Boy could trace flowers for Girl.

Buffalo Boy used twigs and his fingers to draw his flowers, producing petals that had seemed as soft as velvet, with pistils and stamens that throbbed and writhed as if they were dancing. They were flowers far superior to the ones Arno had made with his machine the night before. And for a very good reason Girl realized. For was not Buffalo Boy himself filled with life in a way Arno wasn't?

A picture of Arno and Buffalo Boy standing side by side came to Girl just then, and she giggled. The fact was Arno was no match at all for Buffalo Boy. Why he wasn't even particularly clever. Despite his twelve years of school, Girl had understood the diagrams in the machine's instruction book with far less trouble than he had. No, Girl thought. Even if Arno could earn thousands of dollars in less than a month and qualified as a husband with means, he was an exceptionally sad specimen of a man. Not much of a body and not much else either. No, she decided as she stepped out into the air well corridor from the steel staircase. No matter what she'd thought before, Arno wouldn't do. Not at all.

That was when Girl heard the voice for the first time.

'But he'd be so much easier for you to control,' the voice said to her. 'Clever ones are a headache. You wouldn't want that.' The voice sighed. Then it added, 'Believe me, I know.'

'Believe me, I know . . .' Those were words Girl's Ibu said all the time. But Girl's Ibu would never have said them in such a warm intimate way, as if she was sharing a secret with someone dear. Girl felt immediately singled out and special, safe and loved. She was overwhelmed. Suffocated. So suffocated she had to wonder how something as light as a voice had such power?

She stopped in front of Gran's door panels and sniffed. Danger—that was what was in the air. And a sweet sad yearning that brought the smell of dead roses and jasmine to mind, the same smell that hung in the memory room. Still on that Saturday morning, Girl had not been troubled by those hints of danger or the smell of tears and death. Full of her small victory over Arno the previous night, she slid open the door panel to

Gran's room and as carefree and easy as a child, walked straight to the side of the old lady's bed.

Gran was cooing at the sunbeams reflected onto the ceiling from the koi pond. She had not screamed to have her roll belt removed right there and then when she saw Girl. Nor had she pinched and scratched when Girl began to unfasten the tabs on her soiled diaper. Her luck was turning, Girl thought. It had been a good evening with Arno and now it might even be a good day with Gran.

'That's right isn't it?' she said. 'We're going to have a good day, aren't we?'

Gran stopped cooing.

'If you're trapped half here half there, every day's the same,' she replied.

Girl knew this wasn't true. The old lady was certainly more alert that morning than the morning before. Still, she wasn't going to get anything except a blue-black bruise by disagreeing. She pulled out a double sheet of wet wipes and went on with what she was doing.

Showing the wet wipes to Gran, she said, 'We'll give you a quick wipe first, yes?'

This was the routine every day. The same question, exactly how Cook had taught her. 'Because old people like to know they're in control,' Cook had said. Cook had also told Girl, 'Don't expect the same answer though. Old people's minds are weak and they wander.'

'Or perhaps,' Girl had said to Cook a month into her stay, 'Some old people simply like fooling other people around. Maybe that's why Gran sometimes screams at me, and sometimes pinches, and sometimes lies flat and pretends she's died. Maybe Gran's just a mean old lady.'

'Be that as it may,' Cook had answered, 'You do the same thing every day and you take whatever she gives you, whatever day it is.'

That Saturday morning Gran grunted.

Taking that to be permission, Girl flattened out Gran's soiled diaper, lifted her hips and slid the diaper away, leaving the disposable bed pad under her.

'It'll be a bit cold, yes,' she warned before applying the alcohol-soaked wipe onto the wrinkled skin in circular strokes that were not too hard and not too soft.

Gran grunted again. And then she asked, 'What were you talking to Arno about so late last night?'

Girl's hand stopped circling. How could the old lady have heard what happened in the attic? Voices rose, they didn't fall. She herself had never heard Arno's or B.K. Big Sir's voices when she was down here in this room. And besides, the old lady was deaf. How could she know?

'Don't dither. Didn't you hear me? I asked you a question,' Gran said more loudly.

Girl rolled up the used wet wipes, tucked them into the folded diaper and pulled out another double sheet. It was proving to be a good day for the old lady's mind, if not her mood. There was no escape. She confessed.

'I was helping him with a new sewing machine. It's to make flowers. Roses maybe,' she said.

'That's all?' Gran asked.

More than enough for a start, Girl thought. But all she said was, 'Yes. That's all Gran.'

The old lady spat. 'Tchahh! You're not one to take advantage of your opportunities!'

It was best to play dumb Girl decided. Saying nothing, she tucked the second round of wet wipes into the folded diaper and pulled out more. 'Almost done now,' she said, wiping the old lady's buttocks. To distract her, she added, 'You know, we don't have wet wipes in my village. We use cloth. It's a lot of washing.'

The old lady nodded at that. 'Because in this world, there's a lot of shit,' she replied, before closing her eyes.

Dozed off again, how inconvenient, Girl thought. She'd been about to sit the old lady up and wheel her into the bathroom for her shower. Now she'd have to wake her. And who knew how the old lady's mood might have changed after a ten second nap?

But Gran began to speak again.

'I had to clean my father. It was unbelievable, how much of it there was. How it got on my hands and under my fingernails. It was impossible to wash away,' she confided. 'That smell. On my hands. I know. Believe me I know . . .' she whimpered, shaking her head from side to side.

'Oh, Gran,' Girl said.

Gran might have become a rich old lady but she had been a poor young girl once. Girl and Gran, they were the same. She tucked the wet wipes she'd been working with into the diaper and bent over to give the old lady a hug. Then she noticed the shit stains on her hands. 'I'm going to wash my hands. I'll be right back,' she said, gathering up the diaper and soiled wipes.

'No, you won't,' Gran replied.

But the voice Girl heard coming from Gran's mouth was not Gran's. Nor was it Gran's strength that wrapped the arm attached to her body around Girl's shoulder and pulled Girl down towards her chest.

'You'll stay right here and listen, understand,' the voice said into Girl's right ear.

And locked against the old lady's chest, Girl couldn't even nod.

The voice had known Girl would agree anyway.

'Good girl,' the voice purred. Then in a murmur that seemed to draw Girl close once more, the voice shared, 'I had to sell my hair too, like you had to cut yours. You had to work here. I had to buy medicine. It's so sad. So very sad.'

And once again Girl felt singled out. Allowed in. Loved.

'The thing is . . .' The voice paused here to emphasize that Girl was being given a piece of the wisdom of ages. 'People like us, we start at the bottom. We've got to take our chances when we get them. Otherwise . . .' The arm against Girl's head nudged her to look left. 'Otherwise, you see.'

What Girl was being made to see from the corner of her eye was the old lady's free hand snaking towards the folded diaper Girl was clutching. The hand pulled the diaper from Girl then dragged it towards her face.

'This is all you'll get. Shit. We've got to take our chances. Otherwise, we'll always be stuck at the bottom, wiping bottoms,' the voice said. 'You do understand, don't you?' it asked, not unkindly.

Girl tried to nod again.

'Yes,' the voice agreed. 'That's right. So close your eyes and throw yourself at that fat boy, no holds barred.'

The pressure against Girl's neck eased. The hand holding the stinking diaper fell away onto the bed pad. Gran began to gargle and gasp. Her chest heaved as if to expel something. Then she coughed, opened her eyes and squinted at her own shit-stained hand.

'You, what have you done?' Gran said, her beady eyes staring accusingly at Girl.

* * *

Five-year-old Girl's Ibu had asked the same question after she tore the chicken from Girl's hands and threw it at the lizard to save Girl. It was an unnecessary question. Girl could see what she'd done. The lizard had trampled down Ibu's tomatoes and kacang plants. Ibu's chicken had gone into the lizard's maw. A total waste. It was unforgiveable. She'd crept under the house, rolled into the tiniest ball possible and tucked herself between the footings.

Ibu had left Girl there till dusk. And then after she'd set out dinner, Girl had heard Ibu saying into the floorboards directly over her hiding place, 'Are you going to stay down there all night, waiting for the lizard to come back for you? Or are you waiting for the tigers instead?'

Girl never let on how glad she was to be allowed back into the glowing house, help herself to a handful of warm rice from the food tray and later lay herself down bolstered between her two sisters; to be safe in a house on stilts with front and back steps drawn up, protected from anything and everything prowling below.

But a voice which sneaked into her head and spoke from someone else's mouth wasn't quite the same as a flesh and blood animal, Girl understood. She would need more than walls to escape the spirit she'd invoked. All she had was want. That was like pouring oil on fire.

* * *

Girl had felt the spirit following her as she wheeled Gran into the kitchen for breakfast. The spirit had stopped speaking but Girl knew she hadn't gone away. The spirit wasn't Ibu. She would not be turning and walking away in a huff to attend to an endless list of chores. This spirit had all the time in the world to hold her breath and wait.

The spirit's silence was everywhere. It was hiding under the squeak of Gran's wheelchair and lurking inside the gulps, gasps and gargles of her breakfast. As Girl sank the spoon into Gran's bowl of mushy oat slop. As Gran winched her chicken-beak mouth open. And as her toothless mouth gummed and gummed. It escaped from each of Gran's swallows in impatient little explosions, filling the kitchen and smothering the spits and sizzles from Cook's pans as she busied herself with the preliminaries for the big Saturday meal.

There was something familiar about the feelings lurking behind the spirit's silence. It was the shivering insistent hunger Girl remembered from the times when her Ibu owed the rice-Cini and the rice in the basket had fallen to a hand's depth, which had to be saved for customers. It was the kind of hunger that announced itself in bubbles and squeaks from the emptiness of her guts when she walked past the Cini shophouses and caught the smell of the stewing Cini pork she wasn't even supposed to call food. It was a hunger that came with shame and anger . . . A dark and shrinking shame at being so hungry, and a red flaming anger at an Ibu so proud she'd rather Girl starve than allow her to beg. Herself, Gran, the spirit. They had all, at one time or another, been hungry angry girls, Girl realized.

'It's okay. I understand,' Girl had whispered. And closing her eyes, she had said into the centre of the silence, 'Let me help.'

Immediately, Girl felt the air around her cool and the spirit seemingly tossing her head as she withdrew. And try as Girl might, reaching her arms out as far as she was able, she could not hold on to those disappearing folds of silence. Instead, it was Cook's hands that reached for hers, gripped at them, and pulled.

Girl opened her eyes and found herself in the glass tube kitchen staring at her reflection. She was sitting on a metal stool next to the eating counter. It was breakfast time. Gran was sitting in her wheelchair in front of the reflection with her mouth open and her tongue thrust out at the actual Girl. Next to them, Cook was saying, 'She wants more, can't you see? Give her more.'

So that was what Girl did. She dipped the spoon into the bowl of oats and lifted it up to Gran's mouth. The kitchen filled once more with the gulps, gasps and gargles of Gran eating breakfast. The spirit was gone. There wasn't even the echo of her hungry expectant silence behind the clanging of Cook's pots or underneath the drone of the traffic rising from the freeway behind the house.

Girl felt empty, how she'd felt when her favourite serial *My Lover from the Stars* ended. She was back where she was most mornings since she'd come to the ash house—in the kitchen, pushing slop into Gran's flailing failing body while Cook chopped and sliced and boiled and fried. This was her life, a number two maid's dead-end servant's life, the life her Ibu and Cook wanted her to live with no end to it, ever. And there was nothing she could do about it except kick loose the brake on Gran's wheelchair and push her roughly through the shining red door to the back garden.

'Time for your sunbath,' she said, using the exact same words Cook had told her to use, her foot pushing the brake down, her hands mindlessly strapping Gran in and then pushing her big straw hat onto her head in the same old same old way. Afterwards, unwinding the garden hose, bringing its nozzle to the bottom of the frangipani tree where the mynahs lived, and turning the water on. As she usually did.

Back in Girl's village, the villagers planted frangipani in graveyards not in gardens. Back there, mynahs didn't nest in frangipani but in fruit trees. Yet the mynahs had established an unlikely home here overlooking the freeway. They'd found ways to feed themselves. At Girl's feet, for example, was a mynah picking at a chik-chak it had killed. There were another two on the parapet surrounding B.K. Tjoa's balcony, quarrelling over a piece of meat they'd scavenged from the garbage. And up there on the rooftop was the fourth bird, the commander, keeping watch. All of them thriving. As she could too, Girl supposed. But how?

She considered what the spirit had said about marrying Arno. But, no, she decided. She would not let a ghost push her toward marrying him, certainly not the ghost of a woman who wasn't even the marrying kind. She could do better she knew. If she let go of love as Gran had said. And . . . She stared up at the pair of birds fighting over the piece of meat . . . If she was prepared to fight, as all the best heroines in the TV serials fought.

But even the best heroines, like the most persistent mynahs, could be stymied by forces beyond their control. Just when it seemed to Girl that one of the fighting mynahs was getting the better of the other, the bird on the rooftop squawked a warning, and the pair flew off in fright.

B.K. Tjoa had stepped onto his balcony and scared them off.

'Morning!' he shouted to his mother. And then, as if he'd just noticed Girl, he stopped, stared, and gave her a cheery wave. Knowing her place, Girl did not return the wave. But B.K. Tjoa smiled at her anyway, flicking down the piece of meat the birds had abandoned as he did so.

The meat arched towards Girl as surely B.K. Tjoa meant it to. It did not reach her though. Before it could hit the ground, the two birds who were fighting over it swooped out from their hiding place, snatched it mid-air and carried it away. Their fight resumed, as if it had never been interrupted.

Girl looked up at the balcony. It was empty. B.K. Tjoa had retreated to his room. But beyond the balcony and above the rooftop, the sky glowed blue. And behind her, the growl of the freeway coursed up her bare soles to the top of her head, announcing the presence of uncountable truck drivers going about their business. There was a whole world out there filled with men whom she hadn't yet met because she was on her three-month probation and not allowed out of the house, Girl realized. But once this was over, Irene Tjoa had promised that she could go to the remittance centre with Cook to send her pay home. And after six months, if she behaved and her debt to Cook was settled, she would very likely get half a Sunday off every week too, to do as she pleased. Meanwhile . . .

Girl clenched her fists. She would not take Bing Fa's advice. Arno was an opportunity, her best opportunity if she wanted to start a business sewing dolls' clothes. For a husband though, she wanted better. As Bing Fa had wanted better. Hadn't Gran told her Bing Fa had wanted the freedom to choose, even in death? Why wasn't Bing Fa allowing her the same freedom?

It was something she'd have to ask Gran about, Girl decided.

17

Girl never got the opportunity to pick Gran's brain. Chinese New Year arrived and she was caught in the whirlwind of ritual meals at the ash house—the New Year's Eve Reunion dinner, the first day New Year open house when the family came to pay their respects to Gran, and then the second day tomb visitation brunch set up in the memory room. Afterwards, she and Cook had been sent to help at the various aunts' New Year parties. What with the excitement of the cash-filled ang pows being handed around like tissue paper packs, the raw fish tossings and the suppers to be prepared for the late-night mahjong and poker parties, Girl hadn't managed to steal even a moment with Gran aside from those scheduled for feeding and washing her. It was a month later before things settled enough for Girl to remember her decision to consult Gran. And by then, contrary old biddy that the old woman was, she'd sickened and become completely unresponsive.

On the morning Girl remembered she needed Gran's advice, she was pulling out Arno's and Big Sir's sheets from the laundry chute and feeling out of sorts about her lot in life. Irene Tjoa liked Cook to run a tight house. However, since Cook could not control B.K. Tjoa and could only prod Arno gently, there was just Girl to keep in line. Thus, Cook's nagging about Girl keeping clear of the Big Sir and being too close to Arno. Her instructions about dusting the surfaces of Arno's doll boxes. And also her ridiculous rules about how to examine Arno's and B.K. Tjoa's disgusting men's sheets soaked with sweat and stained with you know what.

'Close up, with your eyes and nose,' Cook had said to Girl.

But of course Girl didn't look that closely at those sheets. And for sure she didn't sniff. There was no reason she could think of for using her Ibu's just enough to find out but not enough to choke on in-breaths. Unlike her Ibu, who was checking for important information like the monthly flow from Girl's and her sisters' virgin bodies, or signs that their virginity might have been stolen, or even worse that they'd been infected with some disease or seeded with a child, there was nothing of that nature Girl needed to ferret out. She had no powers to punish either Arno or B.K. Tjoa. She couldn't lock B.K. Tjoa up when he spilled drink or vomited on his shirts and sheets. Nor could she beat either father or son when they stained their inner clothes. She brought the laundry up to her face only because she had to demonstrate she was following instructions for the benefit of Irene Tjoa's CCTV cameras.

Men did what men did. Girl had been with Buffalo Boy and knew what it was all about. She couldn't control what the two Tjoa men got up to. Her job was to fluff out their good shirts and pants, mark any stains with tape and then to put them into a laundry bag for Irene's driver to take to the cleaners. She had to pre-spray the stains on the towels, sheets, jeans, sleeping and exercise clothes and underclothes and put them in the washer. She had to rub the collars of the T-shirts with Lux liquid, soak them overnight in the big copper washbasin, then handwash them with lots of bubbly Lux soap flakes. All that, yes. But only that.

What did Girl care about Cook's instructions? Cook wasn't going to report her to Irene Tjoa. A girl like her who could tolerate Gran and manage to keep bedsores off the old woman's skin wasn't easy to find. Neither was one who would fetch and carry for Cook without complaint. Indeed, Girl realized, she was doing all the laundry now, almost all the house cleaning, and most of the peeling and chopping and seasoning. All Cook did was clean B.K. Tjoa's quarters, plan the menu, go marketing and order Girl around. She was almost a boss lady! If she'd climb into B.K. Tjoa's bed, she'd be mistress of the house. And God knew, Girl thought resentfully, with herself at Cook's beck and call, Cook had surely enough spare time to do that.

But a voice in Girl's head had corrected her immediately.

'She's not the kind to think that way. Anyway, she's run to fat and reeks of the kitchen. You don't expect your B.K. Big Sir to allow her in his bed . . . Really, really, really . . .' the voice had sneered.

Girl's heart jumped. Bing Fa was back!

The voice continued, 'You, you're the only one who can be mistress of this house. It's just who you pick to get there, the father or the son.'

Girl remembered the administrative officer's fifty-year-old pen-pusher's fingers slipping his name card into her camisole when she went to collect her new passport. That had been barely tolerable. She shuddered. No, not B.K. Tjoa's alcohol-pickled hands. Never.

'Well, it's the son then,' the voice said.

Arno . . . Girl went to the washer, pulled out his now clean undersheet, lifted it over the clothesline and spread it out to examine. The stains he'd left from whatever morning fantasy he'd woven were gone. She brought her nose up to the sheets. The fish stink too, she noted. All she could smell was the lemongrass scent of the fabric softener, the same smell that came off Arno's hand soaps and body washes. A good clean smell for what was a reasonably good reasonably clean man. An innocent. Not at all like his father.

Girl's mind began to wander. The feel of Arno's hands on her body would be quite different from that of the administrative officer's, she imagined. Or of his father's. Arno had small hands with pointed fingers, roughened by sewing, but always clean. As for the rest of his body, it was probably washed and lemongrass scented too, like his soaps. And not wrinkled. Doughy perhaps. But tolerable . . . Except, why should she have to tolerate anything when the dead woman speaking to her had held out for so much more?

Ignoring her Ibu's advice never to engage a spirit, she looked up into the quiet warm air around her and said, 'My mother didn't need a man and neither did you. Why are you pushing me towards him?'

The damp sheet on the line billowed up to caress her face and she felt a cool draft snaking around her neck.

'You're slow little one,' Bing Fa said. 'It's not a question of you needing anyone. It's about making them need you so you can use them. I did that and your mother too. We sold our hearts. But you . . . Sure you left your cowherd to come here. Sure you sacrificed your hair to stay. But I know you, you're not the kind to sell your heart. So, what else can you trade if not your body?'

There was nothing else she could trade, Girl realized.

But that wasn't the right question, was it? The right question was what she'd be trading her body for?

She pondered that as she went to get Arno's top sheet from the washer. Would she trade her body for the sheets?

Arno's bedding was made of very closely woven cotton. 'A wonder to lie on but a chore to iron,' Cook had said. Girl didn't know about the first part of Cook's comment and hadn't asked Cook how she'd come by that piece of information, but she was sorely aware of the truth of the second part. The sheets had to be dried on the line, so their wrinkles could be pulled straight by their own sodden weight. And even then, it took almost an hour with a hot iron to smooth the remaining puckers out of the whole set of over and under sheets, pillowslips and bolster cases. A pain indeed to take care of.

No, Girl decided. She didn't care how good the sheets were to sleep on. She'd certainly not trade her body for them.

'But a number two,' the voice teased. 'What about a number two maid of your own to take care of these sheets?'

It's the smallest things that cause us humans to stumble, the innocuous little things that trap us. Like the bread and lentils that cost Esau his birthright, Sister Mary Michael might have told Girl. Or a girl child who hadn't even learnt to say 'Mama' Bing Fa might have added. What was it in Girl's case?

No, Girl had thought, she didn't want a number two maid. But a new telephone would be nice. And maybe genuine name-brand ripped jeans. Better yet a pair of sneakers. Plus, perhaps a denim jacket, a tube of Korean lipstick, some eye shadow . . . In fact, why not a whole range of Korean seven-step face care products? A push-up bra? Some dangling earrings? A thousand and one small luxuries from the television began to pile up in her imagination inside a house built for comfort and security. Everything Gran had and more, provided she left love out of the bargain.

'But only temporarily,' the voice reminded. 'I'll guarantee that.'

Girl believed her. She would have it all, she decided. Lipsticks and comfort. Security and freedom. Money and love. Businesses and a home life. Her own bride price and Buffalo Boy. And beyond that, sewing shops and rice fields that would feed the two of them and their children. Everything in her own name so she could be her own woman and Buffalo Boy would be beholden to her and never beat her or put her out for someone else even when she grew old and ugly. And so, there and then in the wash yard, she lifted her face to the shafts of sunlight piercing through the frangipani tree and said, 'Yes.'

Yes, she would trade her body to get from where she was standing to where she wanted to be. But she wouldn't regret it, she told herself, not even temporarily. She knew exactly what she'd be giving it up for. That future, that seeming impossible future, was worth it.

She had time, she thought. She didn't have to squander her body on anyone anyhow. She had a two-year contract with just three months gone. She was here in Kota Cahaya, the City of Light overflowing with opportunities. She would learn what she could from Bing Fa but she wouldn't let Bing Fa push her towards Arno, or worse, B.K. Tjoa. Now she'd set her sight on the correct future, it was very clear what she needed to do. She needed to continue working with Arno to learn from him and to earn enough tips to get herself a mobile phone. She needed to keep well in with Cook so she'd be allowed to go out with Arno on weekdays and by herself on Sunday. And she absolutely had to go back to drawing out Gran.

It was Gran who could teach her how to keep Bing Fa in hand. After all, it was Gran who'd declared over and over,

'I tricked her. I got her back in the house. I locked her in. And still, she gave me what I wanted.' How could she have forgotten that?

She pegged the last of Arno's pillowcases onto the line then rushed upstairs to Gran's room.

* * *

The smell in Gran's room was foul as usual. Unusually though, Gran was quiet. Not snoring in great gulping gasps. Not gargling. Not choking. Her eyes were opened but she did not acknowledge Girl's morning greeting, not even with a blink.

'You're going to give me a good day, yes?' Girl said to her, varying the usual question to get Gran's attention.

But Gran had continued to stare at the ceiling where the reflected sunbeams played and allowed Girl to clean her without fussing at all.

Girl had felt a surge of sympathy for Gran then. What a sad fate for an old woman, to be left alone and tied down all night with four security belts. And Girl herself doing the dirty deed. This would never be allowed at home, she thought. Never. Ever.

Feeling suddenly very angry, Girl pulled at the belts and released Gran.

Then she brought her up to a sit.

'In the chair and to the shower now,' she said.

Usually, Gran struggled at this point. That day though, she sagged.

Girl looked at the deadweight in her arms. How contrary of Gran to play dead right now when it was her talk Girl needed.

But Gran wasn't playing. She was really and truly not having a good day.

* * *

Gran was not to have any more good days, not as Girl would reckon anyway. She'd been silenced. No matter how hard Girl had shaken her, nothing had come from her mouth but drool. And no matter that Girl had screamed for Cook and B.K. Tjoa, neither had been able to do anything either except stare. It was only when B.K. Tjoa came to his senses and called his sister Irene that things began to happen.

Not that any of it helped Gran.

It was just noise and confusion as Cook leaned into Girl and wiped her face with the corner of her apron and B.K. Tjoa sat on the edge of his koi pond and shouted into his phone, 'She's my mother. Don't you tell me what to do. I'll call an ambulance if I want to!'

And the phone crackling and dying, followed by Cook's phone ringing and Cook mouthing to B.K. Tjoa, 'Ma'am Irene.'

And B.K. Tjoa telling Cook, 'Turn the speaker on.'

Which Cook had not done.

Which had so infuriated B.K. Tjoa he'd grabbed the phone from Cook and screamed, 'Don't you go telling my servants what to do when I'm standing right here!'

And the speaker being turned on.

And then Irene Tjoa's voice floating clear and cool into the air well and restoring order.

'There's no need for this high drama,' she'd said. 'There's all kinds of germs in hospitals. It's the worse place to send her. It's her time. We'll just keep her at home. The GP will know how to manage it. Call him now.'

A 'GP', Girl discovered, was the ordinary family doctor who came regularly to attend to Gran's aches and pains.

Girl had watched enough TV to know rich people with seizures went to intensive care immediately. They were never left in the care of 'one-leg-kick-all' doctors who came to visit in short-sleeved shirts, khaki pants and sandals. Nor were they assisted by shifts of second maids, sent as and when from the aunts' houses. They had emergency nurses in uniforms.

'It's not right,' she told Cook after a week of this seemingly inadequate care.

Cook shrugged. 'Right. Wrong. It's not up to me,' she said.

She slid a plate of fried eggs, rice and sambal across the counter to Girl. 'Eat. It could be a long wait. You want to keep your strength up.'

'What do you mean, a long wait?' Girl asked.

'It's her time,' Cook repeated what Irene Tjoa had said.

'You mean, they're all waiting for her to die and that's why they're not doing anything.'

Cook set her own plate of rice and eggs onto the counter before replying, 'At home we don't do anything but sit and wait when the time comes for seventy- and eighty-year-olds. Gran's ninety-two. What's the fuss?'

The fuss, Girl thought sadly, was that she had lost her chance to get the information she needed out of Gran. She would never find out how Gran kept Bing Fa under control now. But she could not tell Cook that.

She stabbed the yolks of her eggs till they ran into the rice and mixed everything up every which way. 'I'm upset because I thought she'd be treated better,' she said. 'After all, she isn't an old woman from a village like ours. She's different.'

Cook thought about that as she chewed. 'Everybody dies,' she said after a while. 'We're cleaning her. There's no pain. One of you girls is always with her. She won't be alone when it's time. What more do you want the family to do?'

'I don't know. For her family to be more sympathetic, I suppose. Not be like Arno.'

'It's Arno Young Sir to you,' Cook reprimanded, without going into what there was to emulate and not to emulate about Arno. 'Eat,' she said again, tapping on the edge of Girl's plate. 'Then take yourself off to the shower and to bed. You've got the cleaning and ironing to do when you get up. Those two men aren't going to stop wearing and changing clothes simply because Gran's laid up. Life goes on you know.'

And life did go on. As the days passed and Gran lay in her bed almost dead to the world, B.K. Tjoa continued his daily excursions to the casino. Indeed, as if it was possible, he was coming home even more drunk than usual. As for Arno . . . Although he was perfectly sober, he did not bother to visit the sick room, not even once. It was like Girl's Ibu had told Girl. Men's hearts couldn't be relied on. Not even when the mother and grandmother who doted on them was dying.

Poor Gran . . .

18

Bing Fa smiles. The girl had been entirely mistaken about Gran's state, she tells Sister Mary Michael. Gran's last seven weeks had been one of the best times of her life. It's just that no one had realized it, except for Gran and Bing Fa.

Gran had not expected the gift of those last seven weeks. As she'd gotten older, she had come to the conclusion no end of trouble came with wishing. Heaven knew where it had already gotten the lot of them, her and B.K., Arno and his runaway mother. She was suspicious about what happened after she was stricken. It had to be another of Bing Fa's tricks. It was too good to be true how alive she'd become. Whatever Irene, Eileen and their gaggle of sisters were saying, 'stricken' and 'dying' weren't the correct words for the state Gran found herself in.

However, the phrase 'Don't look a gift horse in the mouth' had come to Gran after a few days. It was the first full sentence she'd learnt at the English lessons Big Mother sent her to. Then, Gran had taken the phrase to mean that she, the young bride, should not look too closely at her aging husband Tjoa Ek Kia. Not at his yellowing teeth nor his big flaking wrinkling body nor the old dying smells that came from it. After all, hadn't he agreed to support her mother and feckless brothers in a style way beyond what they were accustomed to? And for life? Her marriage to Tjoa Ek Kia was a gift. As was the strange fact that after her stroke she was more alive than she'd been for a long time. All she had to do was accept it.

Gran's spirit body was so alive it could go everywhere and see and hear and feel what everyone was feeling, her B.K. Big Boy and Arno, Irene, Eileen and the other sisters, Cook, and even the girl. Indeed, Girl was so full of want Gran couldn't have shielded herself even if she wanted to.

I want . . . I want . . . I want . . . Those feelings emanated off the girl's body and pulsed against Gran's newly-animated spirit body non-stop, insisting Gran rouse herself, and open her eyes and ears and mouth and tell her everything Gran knew about Bing Fa. Because she, Girl, absolutely had to know. Absolutely. The problem was that Gran couldn't do what Girl wanted. She hadn't then acquired that faculty Bing Fa had developed over 100 years—a voice. She hadn't yet managed to command anyone's attention, let alone enter anyone's mind and speak clearly to them.

Still those spirit ears of Gran did hear. And on Girl's first Sunday out, two weeks delayed on account of Gran's seizure, what Gran heard was greedy gasping animal grunts. The girl was rushing past Gran's room to meet some of the other second maids and she was counting bills, extra money she'd gotten from Arno's last commission and the overtime Irene was paying for cleaning Gran's stricken body.

Gran remembered feeling the stiffness of those fifty-dollar bills under Girl's fingers, and hearing Girl's thoughts as they jumped all the way home to her village and to her Ibu . . .

The girl's Ibu used to roll bank bills into bamboo tubes and hide them in the rafters, all the while telling her daughters, 'One can never have too many zeroes.' And then when needs must, splitting the bamboo tubes, smoothing the money out and justifying, 'But it's no good sitting around not getting used.' At which point the daughters would turn into jabbering monkeys, chittering and chattering about buying this and that at the market. And the girl's Ibu would begin to pant, like a fox in heat.

That's what Girl had been like on her way out of the house that Sunday, a fox in heat with dollar bills to spend in her paws. And she was still panting when she came back in later the same day.

Gran had heard Girl sneaking past the front room to the kitchen and had followed with her spirit-body. Slip-sliding like a snake, Gran's spirit went through the wires and out the CCTV camera to the ledge above the red lacquer door, where she had a clear view of Girl pulling clothes out of a plastic bag. They were sparkly pieces. A pink top. A pair of jeans. A small vest. Everything ripped to show the skin Girl seemed intent on displaying. She was parading herself like a whore and Gran could see not just her but her reflection in the red lacquer door too. Both were twisting and turning. And being recorded for the girl's Buffalo Boy in the new phone she'd just bought.

The phone. All the next week, Gran's newly acute spirit ears heard Girl whispering into it non-stop. The calls had been to her sisters, to give messages to her Ibu who did not have a phone. And, of course, to the Buffalo Boy. There they were, all hours, exchanging their sweet nothings and making their plans. Him looking for work on a construction site. Her going to find a rich boyfriend to wind around, marry and winkle capital from to build a business before divorcing him with a settlement. Them getting back together after that and marrying.

It had amazed Gran that Girl had shared her plans with Buffalo Boy and that all he'd said about those plans was 'very good' and 'thank you very much'. The fool!

Not that the prospect of Buffalo Boy had cooled Girl down. She reeked of her unquenched desire. Gran didn't need a spirit nose to smell it. Her stricken one was enough. The smell burnt off Girl's baby breasts and hard little buttocks and went everywhere, including up the air well. To Arno, who didn't know what to do with it. And to Gran's B.K. Big Boy, who knew all too well.

Gran had prayed then that it wouldn't happen again as it had with Arno's mother: Her B.K.'s nostrils flaring, his eyes opening for a look-see, and finally the pounce. It was true Gran had told Girl to give up love and marry a rich man. But she hadn't been thinking about her own B.K. Nor Arno either.

* * *

It had surprised Gran, how things developed between Arno and Girl. And yet was it that unexpected?

It was the hot season, coming to the end of March, tomb cleaning time when no new bride and groom orders came in. Arno had finished his last commission, a wedding set for a Guangzhou client. All he was doing was waiting for an air ticket there to deliver the ensemble. There was plenty of time for him to sit with her, his apparently stricken Gran who doted on him. Yet Arno hadn't visited. Not even once all those seven weeks. Instead, he'd spent the time in the attic, soaking in the pleasure of Girl. A live girl hot with want not more than three feet away, her fire so close it licked at him.

Girl and Arno hadn't gotten up to hanky-panky. It was just them sorting Big Mother's old batik and Arno talking his head off, 'The world this . . . Human beings that . . .' Nothing going on at all, but just the right kind of nothing to allow one fat lonely boy to fall in love.

As for Girl, there was no reason for her to be up there to help with anything. But there she was every free minute she got. Gran supposed it was worth the girl's while. It was no effort keeping quiet and letting Arno talk. Less boring than watching an old lady lying like a log in her sick bed. Or lying down in the pokey servants' room when it came around to her rest time. Or hanging about Cook.

Unlike Cook who always shut the little thing up, Arno allowed Girl to ask questions when he ran out of breath. Girl could ask Arno anything. All the 'Ws'. 'When' he found the diva. 'What' her life was like. 'Why' he put her in the trunk. 'Where' he got his stories about her from.

That 'where' led to the unbelievable.

Gran's spirit eyes saw Arno blush when Girl asked him that question. And no wonder. It wasn't nice the rubbish he got up to by himself under his sheets, even if he couldn't help it. But how was poor Arno to know he wasn't the one responsible for those sex-drenched stories interrupting his sleep? How was he to know it was really Bing Fa, gone into his head, who was making him dream those things? He couldn't. That's why his cheeks had turned as pink as the hibiscus on the swatch of Pekalongan in his hands when Girl asked where his stories came from. Still, he didn't need to do what came next—ask the girl if she wanted a wedding doll made from the Pekalongan.

Gran could hardly believe what she was seeing—her grandson, Arno Tjoa Jia Hao, the Tjoa heir, hiding behind a scrap of Pekalongan batik, making a veiled proposal to a second maid.

Girl didn't want Arno though. Even then.

She giggled. 'No one in my village needs doll wedding sets,' she said. 'If you want to give me something, give me ang pow. It's a waste using up the Pekalongan if good money isn't being paid for it.'

After Arno insisted though, she'd backed down. 'Maybe a simple top and a cloth then. In good cotton. No patterns.'

Arno had taken it as a yes. Even if it wasn't.

The little fox! Sitting there, doing nothing, and all the while her claws were sinking into Arno!

But spirit body that she was, Gran couldn't confront Girl. And even if she could have, Gran knew what Girl would say. She'd say she was simply making good use of her time. She'd say she was taking the opportunity to learn from Arno. Arno was her friend, she'd say, even if he paid her. She found him entertaining in his own way, with his strange ideas, Girl would argue. She'd tell Gran not to blame Arno either. Arno wasn't forcing her to do anything. It was her choice. She was choosing to be kind. That's what she'd say to Gran. And when Gran thought about it, it wasn't just herself who couldn't argue against that. Neither could her poor Arno.

Poor Arno knew nothing, Gran realized. Not about life. Not about death. Not about how a girl could love a fool cowherd and still sell herself for a better future, just as she had given up her fantasies to marry an old man. Arno could never do what Gran had done and what Girl was planning to do. After all, Arno wasn't a poor girl from a nobody family. Not like Gran. Not like the girl. How could he know about the very few choices poor girls had?

* * *

If Girl had a choice, Gran would have lived. Indeed, Girl had done everything to make it happen. She'd called the ambulance for Gran even though Irene had already told everyone there was nothing anyone should do. 'Come the time, you're to let Gran go,' Irene had said. 'Sit and watch and call me when Gran's breathing stops.'

But that night, when Gran had turned white and the breath between her lips was lighter than feathers, Girl hadn't just sat. She had upped and done something.

She did it together with Cook, the two of them like one, Cook whom Gran thought loved her, and Girl who didn't know if she loved Gran. One of them had gone to phone for the ambulance while the other slapped Gran, rubbed mentholated oil into her nose and called to her spirit. When the ambulance arrived, one had walked beside Gran when they wheeled her out while the other locked the front door. Then, they'd both climbed into the metal coffin on wheels and swerved down the hill and onto the freeway with her.

They'd squatted on either side of Gran, the two of them hanging onto the hand straps and Gran buckled and tied like a nanny goat on the way to slaughter. And all the while the sirens had cried, like wailers already come for their share of the funeral feast.

'Will she be okay?' Gran heard Girl ask.

'Yes. For now,' the ambulance attendant answered. 'But with old people, it's always hard to know.'

And after that, Gran had heard Cook say, 'It doesn't matter. Either way, she'll be mightily pissed.'

'She' meaning Irene, not herself, Gran understood quite clearly.

Who would have thought that it would be Cook who would change sides, Gran mused? And before Gran was even gone.

Gran had taught Cook everything: Everything Big Mother had taught Gran, and more . . . Not only those assam and masak lemak dishes and Nyonya kueh. Also how to fold napkins into roses, how to lay out a tea tray, how to make scones, how to cut persimmons.

'Always cut persimmons in six but lay out only five on the plate,' Gran remembered telling Cook. 'Because odd numbers looked nicer in circles,' she'd explained, before handing Cook the extra piece and saying, 'To taste.'

Poor Cook. She'd been such a scared little thing when she first came, such a country bumpkin she hadn't even known what a persimmon was. The sweetness of them, that's what Gran gave her. And the soft and sour and salt and heat and crunch of everything else. And yet it wasn't Cook who couldn't bear for her to die, it was the girl. What did you know?

Gran understood. Cook had herself to worry about. If Gran died, Cook might be blamed. She might be sent home. Or the police might be called in. Why, Cook and Girl might even be sent to jail. But these were only potentialities. What was certain was if Gran lived, Irene would chew them out well and good and spit them out too.

Irene, the Tjoa queen bee . . .

Gran had mused about her too. Who would have thought Irene would be as full of want as the girl? She'd been so polite. But it was an act. Her mask had fallen once she thought Gran couldn't see or hear anything. 'Stricken', that's what Irene and Eileen and their gaggle of goose sisters had thought about Gran. That's why there'd been all that discussion right in front of her. About how the words on the trust didn't say what Big Mother and Tjoa Ek Kia had told everyone. How 'descendants' included females. And how they'd finally be able to get their hands on the trust to manage it right. Because the words were clear. As clear as Gran's spirit ears, which unknown to the sisters, had heard everything. Everything as clear as a bell.

Gran heard everything in the ambulance too.

Girl, angry and muttering at Cook, 'Why did you bother to help if you wanted Gran to die?'

And Cook telling Girl, 'Gran's lived a good long life, already. It's her time. There's nothing for Gran to regret, if we let her go now. Not from what I see.'

Cook had no imagination, that was her problem, Gran had thought. She couldn't possibly have imagined how Gran's spirit body had been going everywhere, learning everything about everyone including what was happening in their bodies and inside their heads. It was almost, Gran had realized at that moment, almost as if she had become Bing Fa. Almost. Except for getting her voice into heads. No. All Cook had seen was Gran lying in her fancy sick bed, seeming half dead. It would be a mercy Gran dying, that's what Cook would have thought.

But it wouldn't be a mercy dying, it came to Gran. It would be progress. She would be going beyond, beyond lying there and listening to Irene and Eileen and the other sisters hatching their plans. She'd become like Bing Fa, able to go inside their heads, to muddle them and the plans they were making. And more importantly, she'd be able to get inside Arno's head to tell him how to use Bing Fa to stop them. And to tell him how to keep Bing Fa down afterward . . .

Arno. It was for his sake that Gran decided to leave her body and die. It was because she had to get in his head and speak to him. To warn him.

Girl had different ideas. She needed Gran alive and back at her toy table, enacting those plays where she was big with her

B.K. Big Boy . . . Where she was laughing . . . Because she'd learnt the secret of how to keep Bing Fa under.

'Wake up,' Girl had said to Gran, every day of those seven weeks. 'Don't you see life is good?' she'd kept asking. And when none of that worked, when they'd all ended up in that steel coffin on wheels, what did she do? She pinched Gran down there, in that place nobody had touched since Tjoa Ek Kia died.

The cheek of her!

That pinch decided Gran. There and then. The girl might call and pinch all she wanted. Blood was stronger. No. Gran wasn't going to wake up. She was going to Arno. To get her voice inside his head.

She opened her eyes and gave Girl a last look. And then, she was gone.

19

Arno was in Guangzhou, in a budget hotel, fast asleep after receiving a godly wad of US dollars for delivering his wedding set. He'd brought his diva doll along, as she'd told him this was her hometown, and propped her up against the window to look down at the streets she'd left nearly a century ago. Then he'd turned the music system to the old Shanghai music channel, stepped into the shower and lost himself in the water and the wailing singers.

The music system, seemingly playing only different versions of his favourite song, had woven a barrier around Arno and blocked out everything as he washed and then slept. He had not heard the phone calls coming in from Irene, Cook and his father. It was only when the music stopped near dawn and everyone alive had given up on him, that Gran could approach and do what she'd flown all the way there to do.

Gran had waited all night, gathering herself and shedding years and layering flesh back on bone. She'd become so thick that when she landed on Arno's chest her weight nearly suffocated him. He tried to push her away but she'd anchored her gigantic thighs across his rib cage and her bottom onto his belly. Material and present, she was all there, impossible for him to ignore.

She put a hand over his face and then, just like Bing Fa, she sent herself into his head, the whole enormity she'd become, the swell of the batik-wrapped stomach that stretched above him like a balloon, the upright lace-covered breasts like hillocks, and above the hillocks, her face, like a moon.

She smiled down at him.

Arno recognized the smile, that almost not there smile she reserved just for him and his father. It was a smile that told Arno, especially Arno, that no matter his arm, or his limp, no matter his exam results, no matter what, he was special to her.

He hadn't seen that smile for years. But there it was on Gran's face in Guangzhou. She was dead, although he hadn't realized it yet, but she was thicker and bigger than she'd ever been. And she was giving him her smile again and with it, her love. More of it than he'd ever seen.

Arno wasn't ready for so much love. He tried to close his eyes and look away. And when he couldn't, because she was in his head, he tried to tell her how sorry he was for not visiting her. And how bad he felt, for counting the days until she would die, because . . .

'It's all right. No need to be sorry. I'm your old Gran. I understand,' she said to him. Then she picked up his diva doll from the window behind her, tapped his eyelids open with it and ordered, 'Listen now.'

She pointed at the doll she'd set on her stomach.

'This doll's going to tell you to open the doll house and tell you to burn everything inside. She'll promise you anything if you do it. But you're not to listen to her. If you do, you and your father and the rest of the Tjoas and everything you all have will turn to dust. You're not to believe her. Not ever,' she said.

'She's rubbish,' she concluded, tossing the doll over her shoulder right back to where Arno had placed her, propped against the window looking down at modern Guangzhou and out of Arno's line of sight.

'Listen,' she said again into Arno's ear. And then she began to tell him what he had to do. 'One, you're to pretend to obey Bing Fa. Two, you're to unlock the doll house and take the things in it out. But you're not to untie the string. You must ask Bing Fa for a favour first. And then, still not untying the strings, you're to lock everything up again. You've to pretend that yes, you'll free her and burn everything. But you tell her, you'll only do it after she grants you your wish.'

Arno hadn't liked that. White was white for him. Black was black.

'What if she gets angry? What if she keeps coming back to remind me? What if she haunts me?' he asked Gran.

'She's already haunting you,' Gran told him. 'Besides, you don't have a choice. Bing Fa's a liar. You've to fight fire with fire. Tell her to wait till you have children. Promise to let her teach your children her song. Give her a deposit to convince her. Hair. Some of yours. Or the children's. Just remember, don't take her things out again. Never, so long as you're alive.'

'She won't like that, being kept in the dark forever,' he'd said.

'Not the doll,' Gran told him. 'I mean the string. It's the string and the things and spirit tied to it I'm talking about.'

She explained it all over again. 'First, the promise to Bing Fa. Second, the favour from her. Third, the feint, to get her locked up again. To keep her under.' She repeated, 'Under. You must remember that. You must keep Bing Fa under.' And then, she'd pushed down on Arno with all the weight she'd built through the night.

Arno's ribs creaked. He pointed at the doll and said, 'She's overheard everything and she'll tell Bing Fa.'

'No,' Gran said. 'She's looking out the window trying to find the spot where she left her father. She's not paying attention. And she doesn't need to. It's you, Arno, who's got to pay attention. Pay attention to me, your Gran. You've to do exactly what I've told you. Pretend to say yes to Bing Fa, then give her a few hairs. Pretend. You have to pretend.'

And then, she rubbed her nose against his, how he'd liked when he was little, and told him. 'I've to go now. Don't forget. I won't be able to come back to tell you again.'

'Why can't you come back?' Arno asked.

Gran hadn't answered. Instead, she kissed his cheeks and breathed him in to remember him by. She breathed and breathed and breathed, taking in all his smells, powdered baby, sweaty boy, fish stinky teenager, sour fat adult. She breathed until her swelling spirit body began to stretch the patterns of her sarong and the lace across it, until the skin holding her together turned to gauze, then tissue paper, then shreds of light.

'Gran!' Arno called out as he tried to put his arms around her. But there was nothing for him to hold on to.

* * *

That was the only time anyone saw Gran after death, Bing Fa tells Sister Mary Michael. She'd thinned and thinned after that and then dissipated into nothing. It wasn't what she expected. She had expected to be like Bing Fa, who might have been spirit or ghost or demon, but certainly wasn't nothing. But after warning Arno, Gran had lost her purpose for existing. What could she expect? The only thing left of Gran was the photographs of the magnificent funeral which Irene had commissioned, and her plaque in the memory room, installed there seven days after her death.

20

Gran's funeral was a typical Irene Tjoa production, which is to say it was grand, well organized, well publicized and well attended. Everyone was there. The great and the small. Those with reputations. Those without.

Gran was, after all, the third Mrs Tjoa Ek Kia. It didn't matter that the said numbered Mrs Tjoa hadn't known most of the visitors and most of them hadn't known her. They all came anyway. Children from the orphanage Tjoa Ek Kia built and from the university he endowed. Friends of Irene and her sisters and their children and grandchildren. Old men who used to be boys at the rubber trading company. Rival traders. A judge Tjoa Ek Kia had given a scholarship to. A cabaret dancer and her daughter, one of them an old mistress.

The cabaret dancer and her daughter were both so ancient none of the sisters had any idea which of them had been the mistress. Irene didn't really care. Her father had been called many things—an old goat who lusted after young flesh, a leading businessman, the soul of generosity . . . And indeed, he had been all of these. The man who had married his third wife because she was young and had sweet meat on her. A leading businessman who'd made enough money to provide for that young woman's family and herself well past his demise, and even for her son and her son's son. And yes, the soul of generosity even discarded mistresses mourned. It was only right that all those people came to see her father's last wife off.

It was also right, Irene thought, that the others had come, the ones who'd neither known her father or his wife. Those friends of her husband and her brothers-in-law. It was only right that they too sat there through the hours of prayers. It was respect due her and her sisters, and in that way an indirect tribute to her father too. He would've been proud, she told herself. Proud . . .

* * *

As far as Arno was concerned though, it was a farce. Those grandchildren of his aunts who never even greeted him and whose names he could never remember. There they were, the crowd of them, playing at being buzzy bees, arranging and re-arranging flower wreaths, printing out prayers, quarrelling over who was to do what at the funeral service. They weren't Tjoas, not one of them! And certainly, they were not of Gran's blood. What did they have to do with her, especially when their grandmothers, his aunts, were already plotting to get at his father's and his inheritance?

They were all vultures, that's what. Those who were organizing the funeral, and those who came. The priests especially. They were the biggest vultures of all because they were going to get the biggest share. His aunt Irene has promised half of the proceeds from the sale of the house to them. Those frocked faggots!

It was a whole fake ah-kua wayang and Arno hadn't been able to take it. He'd thrown the prayer sheets handed to him down on the floor and stormed off home.

His aunt Irene had called on the phone and hissed and hissed. But he'd refused to go back. And then on day three, his father B.K. Tjoa had got himself so disgracefully drunk he'd spread his long body out underneath Gran's casket for all to see. There was nothing anyone could do to get him standing. His aunt had to arrange for him to be carried to her car, sent home to the ash house and wheeled up to his bedroom in dead Gran's wheelchair. And after that of course, she wrote the two of them out of the act.

Arno hadn't cared. He'd hunkered down and busied himself with plans for a new project. Since Gran was not to get a genuinely felt send-off from his aunts, he'd decided he'd do it himself. He would create a funeral tableau as magnificent as his grandfather's and send it up in flames in the backyard on the day of the funeral.

He'd barely gotten started though, when Girl persuaded him otherwise.

Irene had sent Girl and Cook after Arno and his father with instructions to keep their eyes on the two men. She'd ordered Cook to sober up B.K. Tjoa and then give him just enough of the devil drink to keep his shakes away, but not so much as to conk him out. Girl had been told to keep Arno calm, with his pills if necessary. And both Cook and Girl were to get the two men dressed and ready for the driver to pick up on day five, the day of the funeral. Seeing as it was Irene paying their salaries, both Cook and Girl took her instructions seriously. And so it was that Girl had gone up to the attic to speak to Arno after a day and a night of leaving him to fume.

'Gran would rather you be at the real funeral, you know,' she said to him, without preamble.

'And what makes you think you know Gran better than me, when you've been here less than half a year and I've known her all the twenty-four years of my life?' he retorted.

'Because, if you don't go, your aunts will take over your family money, and Gran wouldn't want that,' she'd said.

He laughed. 'It can't happen. Everyone knows which descendants Big Mother and Grandpa Tjoa meant the trust for. There's no doubt.'

Girl had gotten angry then.

'The only thing there's no doubt about in dead people's heads is worms,' she said. 'If I were an administrative officer, especially in this country where you can go to jail for giving envelopes to officials and the law's the law, no arguing, I'd certainly not rely on what people said. Only the written down words matter, that's what I heard your aunts saying. Also, even if you're right, where are you going to find the money to argue with your aunts? As it is, we're all living off Ma'am Irene and if she stopped the money . . .'

The argument about Irene Tjoa's money and Arno's lack of it had half convinced Arno.

Then Girl had added, 'You should go anyway, because it would make Gran sad if you didn't. I know it.' After which, she'd told him about her grandmother. 'My M'buk was so poor she collapsed in the fields with mud still on her feet. But when she breathed her last, she had everyone with her, her sons and daughters and grandchildren. She was poor but she didn't die alone. Not like Gran, who only had Cook and me and the ambulance attendant. Nobody from her blood, just servants. And foreigners at that,' she'd said. And then, she'd asked, 'And now, you won't even send her off?'

It was the scorn on Girl's face. That's what un-manned Arno and sent him to Gran's funeral.

* * *

Arno had gone to the funeral in his very best whites, a raw silk shirt and linen trousers. And he'd tried to look and act the part of the descendant. But it hadn't helped. Like rotten meat calling to flies or young girl flesh to old men, the money had called to his aunts anyway.

On the seventh night after Gran's death, after they'd collected her ashes from the crematorium and sprinkled them in the sea and installed her memorial plaque with her photograph in the memory room, his aunts had swooped in. They'd been like the mynah birds in the garden, falling over themselves for the scraps Cook threw out. Red on white on black, red nails and white teeth, all sharpened bright against their black mourning gear, all ready to pick and tear at his inheritance.

He should have known of course, the way his aunt Irene was going about the preparations. It had been nothing like those seventh night stories Gran had told him. No one had sprinkled flour on the floors or hidden in the bedrooms waiting for midnight to come so they could sneak out to check for the dear departed's last footprints in the flour. No, they hadn't done anything like that. They'd eaten dinner, and then, the lawyers had crowded in and there'd been the meeting.

It had all been so unexpected.

* * *

Irene would have preferred less drama and certainly less mess. But life was too short for regrets. The important thing was she'd tied up everything by the end of the evening.

Irene had wanted everything decided quietly, out of earshot of the servants. That's why she had Gran's room cleaned and set up for the meeting. She hadn't managed to get everything moved to the attic, out of sight and out of mind. To pacify her brother B.K., she'd allowed the girl to leave Gran's toys and photographs in the room, on a display shelf. But that little concession and a bottle of thirty-year-old Macallan had calmed B.K. enough to allow the girl to polish the table, set out chairs and lay out pencils, papers and folders.

Still, the meeting had been rocky.

Perhaps, Irene had comforted herself after it was over, she'd simply been unrealistic. Perhaps it was just impossible to crowd those multi-millions in assets, six plus two disputants and three lawyers in a four-by-four metre room and not expect a blow-up. Although she'd buttered up Eileen and prepared all the other sisters, it was a fair amount of money and she and her sisters were the indomitable Big Mother's daughters. Besides, whatever might be said about B.K. and Arno, they had Tjoa Ek Kia's red migrant blood flowing through them. Things could not be expected to go smoothly.

B.K. had lighted the fuse by grabbing one of Gran's whirligigs and throwing it at the lawyers, then walking out. Encouraged by this, Arno had swept all the rest of Gran's things off the shelf with an impossible to mute whoosh and clatter, while spewing out a stream of scatological obscenities, and then slamming open all the sliding doors in the room and running up the air well staircase screaming he was never ever going to give in. Ever.

Irene had to thank heaven the neighbours were well-bred enough to pretend they hadn't heard anything and did not call the police.

Noise aside though, Irene hadn't found Arno's and B.K.'s walkout unexpected. That was what they always did. They wiped their hands off things. They refused to take responsibility. They walked away and let other people deal with the mess, scatological obscenities notwithstanding. That's why she and her sisters had mounted the coup. It wasn't because they were greedy even if some people would come to that conclusion. It was because they were the people most suited to be trustees, not drunken B.K. nor crazy Arno. It was a good thing those two had walked out; had in effect surrendered. That, Irene had thought, was exactly how it should be.

21

Bing Fa had waited eagerly to see what would transpire next. She'd arranged the sets and groomed the players. It was time for the last scene and for Girl to play her all so important part.

Everyone in the house had retired except for Girl. She was in the back garden, sitting under the frangipani tree picking at her fingernails and waiting. She had not known what she was waiting for, but she was Bing Fa's latest and most promising prospect, and what she was waiting for was Bing Fa to call her onto the stage.

Bing Fa obliged, with a rousing whoop.

Girl recognized the diva's voice immediately. Who else could it be calling to her, now that the old woman was dead and the Tjoa sisters had declared war on the Tjoa men and her position in the house was so uncertain?

She wrapped her arms around herself, hugging tight, and whispered, 'Yes?'

Bing Fa had no time for her jitters.

'Go! Go! Go get it!' she said, bubbling into Girl's body so that her sandaled feet glided through the kitchen, into the dining room and through the air well corridor towards the front room, as if on air.

The room was almost exactly how Girl had last seen it. Irene and the others had recovered enough of their senses to tidy away all signs of the commotion. All the folders had been removed from the toy table. It was empty and polished, with not even a thumb print disturbing its shining black surface. The things that Arno had swept off the display shelf, were back in place. Not as Girl arranged them but in neat rows, the pin-cushion animals in the front, the blocks behind them, the whirligigs at the back. The photographs, which had been in untidy stacks to the right of the toys, were now re-stacked from largest to smallest. The smallest photograph was the size of a passport photo. And weighting it down was a rusty key no bigger than a thumb nail.

Girl's fingers picked up the key. But Bing Fa blew gently and she set it down again. Then, as Bing Fa intended, Girl picked up the photograph. It was a very old picture, tinted in pink and pale blue, the colours almost all washed out. It had been stuck to the back of a larger photograph so no one had known it was there all those years Gran had shuffled and re-shuffled her collection of images. Bing Fa had ensured it was hidden, biding her time until that hour and that night when Arno would dislodge it when he swept everything off the shelves. Until Irene would re-arrange the pictures systematically, so it would lie on top. Until someone like Girl would discover it. Along with the key.

Girl pulled the flex-armed lamp she used to check Gran for bed sores towards the photograph and turned the light on. And there the diva was on the century old paper.

'Bing Fa,' Girl whispered.

'Yes, that's me, Bing Fa. The enchanting inimitable pipa-playing slut. Me!' Bing Fa announced with mock solemnity, allowing only the faintest hint of amusement to show through. 'Not what you expected?'

Bing Fa didn't need Girl to answer aloud. If one were Girl, with the kind of expectations nurtured by years of watching TV serials, one would think she, Bing Fa, was the ugliest woman ever. Bing Fa had no eyebrows in the picture. And the photographer's light had caught her high thin nose at the wrong angle, so the bridge looked as sharp as a knife's edge. What's more, her eyes and lips looked so cleanly cut in the image it was as if they were three slits slashed through the paper by a letter opener.

Girl traced a finger on the blue the photographer had tinted on Bing Fa's eyelids and the pink smudged around the closed line of her mouth, and then across the hair-line and around the side of her cheek to the tip of her too-sharp chin, making a question mark. 'Those painted lids . . . That barely pink mouth . . .' Bing Fa heard her murmur, 'Surely, they're not enough to make a man love her beyond death?'

Bing Fa had known Girl wasn't going to understand anything about messages with the pipa and fans and teacups and how by those means, she'd managed to persuade everyone she was as classic a beauty as the ones who drowned fishes and caused wild geese to fall from the sky. It was a different time. A different world. Instead, what Bing Fa said to Girl was, 'You don't want to look like all those actresses on TV who've gone under the knife. They're so alike no one can tell them apart. That's not the way to stand out. You want to be like me. Never cut. Nothing changed from the day I was born. Everything original. Always. In more ways than one.'

'What do you mean?' Girl asked.

She was interested. Which meant, Bing Fa had to pull back.

'You wouldn't understand. You haven't had the training,' she said with a sigh, as if that was the end of the matter.

'I could learn,' Girl volunteered.

Bing Fa backed up some more. 'You'll have to pay,' she said.

It wasn't about Bing Fa wanting payment. It was just the way people were. They didn't appreciate anything they got for free. It always seemed more valuable when they were made to pay. Whatever it was, their need for it suddenly became greater. More urgent.

'All right then,' Girl said. 'I don't have much but-'

Bing Fa swished the air about, as if it was a hand waving away Girl's nothings.

'I don't want anything of yours, except perhaps a small favour,' she said to Girl. She had sensed she sounded suspiciously disinterested. But Girl hadn't noticed.

'Well then?' Girl asked.

'That little key, the one lying on top of my photograph. Go get it,' Bing Fa said.

'This one?' Girl asked, pointing to the tiny rusted thing.

'Yes. That one. Pick it up,' Bing Fa said, as slowly as she could.

Some of her eagerness must have shown, for Girl did not pick the key up. Instead, she reached out and tapped it lightly with the tip of her index finger.

'What's it for?' she asked.

Bing Fa swished the air about again, hard this time, like the whip of a slap. Girl raised her hand to ward it off. But of course, there was nothing there and her hand flailed as it pushed against emptiness. She lost her balance and tilted into the display cabinet, grazing her forehead against the edge of a shelf.

'Don't toy with me, girl,' Bing Fa cautioned her.

Obedient now, Girl wrapped her fingers around the rusted key, took it back to the table and placed it beside the photograph.

'Good girl,' Bing Fa said.

'And what do you want me to do with it next?' Girl asked, meekly.

'Oh, nothing for the moment,' Bing Fa answered, her voice airy with unconcern. 'When you have time, you might polish it to get rid of the rust. Then put it away in that bag of yours where you keep your hair.'

But now, Girl was wary of making mistakes. She needed to get the details right. 'And afterwards?' she asked.

'Afterwards, you can have the father, or the son, or both. And me too. At your command,' Bing Fa told her.

Girl wasn't going to allow herself to be bought though, not with what Bing Fa was offering. She drew herself up readying herself for an argument, and said, 'If you don't mind, I don't want Arno. Nor B.K. Big Sir either.'

'Well, if you learn your lessons well, you can have anybody,' Bing Fa teased. And then, from habit, she plucked three plink-plink-plinks on her pipa.

Bing Fa had lied of course. Her plans did not include anybody else, only the Tjoas. Still Girl fell for it.

'Really?' she asked.

'I got everyone I wanted, didn't I?'

Never answer a question directly if you can do so with another question. That was something else Bing Fa had learnt from Madam. But Girl was not to be side-tracked so easily.

'You did that before Big Mother trapped you,' she said. 'How do I know you can do what you say now you've been trapped? After all, if you're so powerful, why are you still here?'

That was the question, wasn't it? But Bing Fa couldn't tell her the real reason. That would've given the game away. She swished the air again to give the impression she was tossing a whole head of hair, and said, 'I'm married into this family, aren't I? All those Tjoas, Irene, the others, the Big Boy. They're my children. Why should I go anywhere else?'

She paused then before offering, 'I'll let you have a free lesson. How about it?'

Bing Fa was behaving like a market vendor, someone Girl could understand. Somebody like her Ibu who would often offer a free taste in the hope she might sell a whole plate. Pathetic, she could hear Girl thinking. But what did Bing Fa care? Girl would learn soon enough how many ways she had, and how many wiles. Not one of them pathetic.

'What do you want me to do for you?' Girl asked.

Bing Fa filled the room with a soft caressing breath. And then she lay it out in front of Girl. Her lie. The same lie she'd told Arno's runaway mother and his grandmother.

'Unlock the doll house and let me out,' she said.

And there was the expected question coming from Girl, as it had come from the other two. 'What will you give me in return?' Girl asked.

'Like I said, a lesson,' Bing Fa replied.

Girl pounced on the offer. 'What? What will you teach me?'

'Mmm . . . Let me think about it,' Bing Fa replied.

It was all for show of course. She'd known exactly what she'd give the moment Girl reached out to her. Still, one needed to go through the motions. 'Do you think your mother's beautiful?' she asked.

Girl wrinkled her nose. She had never thought to ask that about her tall angular mother. 'If you're talking about old women, Arno's aunt Irene is beautiful,' she replied.

'Her!' Bing Fa exclaimed before blowing a dismissive swish of air through the room. 'You'd change your mind if you saw her without her war-paint.' Irene had inherited good instincts though. Bing Fa could vouch for that. 'Like mother like daughter,' she told Girl. 'There's no need for lessons for her.'

'Oh?' Girl said.

Bing Fa caught herself. It wasn't necessary for Girl to follow that question to its end. Irene wasn't the subject of Girl's and her tete-a-tete. 'Your mother,' she said, putting the conversation back on course. 'Don't you think she walks like a queen?'

Girl thought about it a while, then nodded. 'Yes. Especially when she's walking back from market with the basin of vegetables on her head.'

'Exactly. And when she's behind her food stall, doesn't she look like she's holding court? It's almost as if she's doing the customers a favour when she takes their money for her soup and rice, don't you think? Maybe her food isn't so special. But she makes people want it. Because it comes from her hands and she's made herself special. Do you see?

'But I'm not like Ibu,' Girl demurred, sweeping her hands over the very slight swells of her breasts and hips. 'And anyway, you said, you'd be telling me your secrets. I can go home and look at Ibu all day if I want to know hers.'

This time Bing Fa made the air in the room pulse so hard Girl's head flicked to the left, as if she'd been struck on her right temple. Which she had. It was a move Madam would have praised if she'd been alive to see, Bing Fa thought. And she hadn't even needed a fan to execute it.

'You won't learn anything if you don't learn how to use what's yours,' she continued after Girl had recovered. 'Your Ibu and I, we did the same thing . . . at the most elementary level anyway. We both turned what was most undesirable about ourselves into beautiful illusions. Your mother—her height. She became the queen anyone could conquer for half an hour.

Myself—my eyes, my mouth. Don't they challenge? If you were a man, wouldn't you want to penetrate them? Penetrate me?'

Girl picked up the photograph again and stared at it.

A flicker of understanding ran through Girl as she recognized the fire that seemed to hide behind the slits of Bing Fa's eyes, a fire that might bring an old man to life or light a young man's path.

Girl put a finger on the pink smudged lips, stroked them in wonder and drew her breath in. 'That's why,' she whispered. And then she set the photograph down, and asked, 'But I . . . What do I have?'

Bing Fa swirled another drift of warm soft air around the room. 'You cry too much, don't they say?' she asked.

'My sisters do. Yes. Ibu also. They do say that.'

'But the administrative officer saw something else?' Bing Fa prompted.

Girl twisted her mouth. 'That dirty old man. I don't care what he saw. It's what Buffalo Boy sees that I want to know about.'

'Buffalo Boy . . . the end who has no means,' Bing Fa teased.

'I don't need reminding how poor Buffalo Boy is,' Girl retorted.

'Precisely,' Bing Fa agreed. 'And you too. As poor as a flower, that's what we used to say in China. But flowers have their charm. And flowers stained with tears . . . Well, you've got more than enough tears.'

She let that idea sink into Girl's head.

'Tears. You want me to use my tears?' Girl asked.

'You can't be a cry baby all your life,' Bing Fa told her in a reasonable teacherly tone. 'But that water inside, you can use that. Men have a thirst. Take a look.' She blew on the top of

Girl's head gently so it began to tilt downwards and she was again looking into Bing Fa's eyes in the photograph. And then she asked. 'Do you see water?'

Madam had taught Bing Fa everything about the tremendous power of suggestion. Girl began to see the flames in Bing Fa's eyes swirl and turn to water; the water of the stream she and Buffalo Boy had played in, and the water at the bottom of the well she had drawn from, and the water in the waves that smashed against the sea of her dead grandmother's village. The waters of home. In no time at all, she was sniffing and tears were gathering under her eyelashes.

Bing Fa had her!

'Oh, be done with that! Swallow those tears down,' she told Girl.

'I can't. If I'm sad, that's what . . .' she sobbed.

'Of course, you can. Become your tears. Become water,' Bing Fa said.

Now, that was a new thought for Girl. 'Become water? How?'

Bing Fa didn't have time to do what Madam had done, have Girl practice watery scales and dance to water music and memorize songs about rippling streams and silent lakes and surging seas. There was no time. And anyway, Girl didn't have that single-minded focus Bing Fa had possessed. She kept it short. 'Try this for a start,' she told Girl. 'Walk like water.'

'How?' Girl asked.

Bing Fa had the fleeting thought that perhaps she had chosen badly yet again. That perhaps, despite all her want, this girl too would fail her like Gran and Arno's mother had. But there was no doing without trying and she'd already come this far. There was no loss going a bit farther.

'Walk from the hips. Heels first then balls of your feet then tips of your toes, like you always walk,' she said to Girl. 'But at the same time, remember the stream and remember Buffalo Boy with one hand under your blouse and the other untying the knot of your cloth. Remember it all.'

'That's it?' Girl asked.

'Yes,' Bing Fa said. 'That's it. Give it a try. You'll see.'

Girl stared down at Bing Fa's photograph and brought the key to her cheek. Then she smiled, a soft satisfied smile and walked out of the room swinging her legs from the hips, stepping each foot down heel first before rolling onto the balls and lifting off the tips of her toes. Placing one foot in front of the other. Trying to walk like water, as Bing Fa had instructed.

22

Girl flowed all the way down the service stairs to her room, chanting, 'Walk like water. Walk like water.' The next morning, she started again the instant she swung her feet out of her bed and onto the floor. And she was still at it in the afternoon, as she walked one bare-footed step at a time up the fish-bone staircase to B.K. Tjoa's quarters with his afternoon snack. Still whispering, 'Walk like water and not spill it . . . Not spill it . . . Not spill it . . .'

B.K. Tjoa was still at home sleeping off his drunk. In normal circumstance, Girl wouldn't be anywhere near him. But Irene Tjoa had spearheaded a coup and Bing Fa had been swishing and stirring. Circumstances couldn't be normal.

B.K. Tjoa had most illogically blamed Cook for everything that happened the night before. Irene's meeting would not have taken place if Cook hadn't agreed to prepare the seventh day dinner in the house. There'd be no seventh day at all if Cook had called the doctor and Gran had not died. Indeed, Cook should have barred the doors against Irene as soon as she got hint of the plot.

'And who would have paid us then?' Cook had dared to ask.

At that, he'd called Cook a parasite and a two-faced traitor and banned her from ever setting foot in his quarters again.

This is how the scene had played after that, before Girl found herself trying to flow up the fish-bone stairs.

'Twenty years of service and he calls me a traitor. He doesn't deserve any of the things I do for him, the ungrateful sot,' a swollen-eyed Cook had told Girl even as her stubby fingered hands were carefully laying out pads of bird's nest into one of Big Mother's heirloom soup plates.

'Then why are you still making his evening soup?' Girl asked.

'I'm the cook, aren't I? They pay me to keep enough flesh on his bones so he doesn't look like a skeleton, don't they? So that's what I'm doing,' Cook answered. Still, she was wounded enough to declare again, 'But I'm not putting up with him any longer. End of my contract, I'm gone.'

'You, me, we've hardly reached six months in our current contracts. It'll be ages before we can go home,' Girl reminded her.

'Yes, that's why I'm doing what I need to,' Cook replied. 'Besides . . .' she prodded the bird's nest with her index and middle fingers, 'This bird's nest is good for him, Gran used to say. He's lucky Ma'am Irene still forks out the money for it every month. Although now, Ma'am Irene and B.K. Big Sir are at odds . . .' Cook left the thought dangling.

'Won't matter anyway. It's only coughed up gunk from a bird with a scratchy throat,' Girl said.

'It cleans the liver. You see how he comes home every night, barely able to stand up straight. And the yellow in his eyes. That's what it's for,' Cook explained.

'He could stay home and stop drinking. Stop gambling too. That would save money.'

Cook snorted. 'A single man! I'd rather he hunted outside, thank you very much.'

Girl considered that carefully before saying, 'I guess you're right. B.K. Big Sir's hardly beautiful. I wouldn't want him touching me up. Although some girls might, if he paid enough.'

Cook hadn't thought that last remark worthy of a reply, and Girl, having settled it in her own mind, returned to the task before them.

'I wouldn't eat this,' she said, wrinkling up her nose at the bird's nest which she'd heard cost its weight in gold. 'Give me a nice fish stew or meat my teeth can sink into. Only Cini are stupid enough to pay a year's wages for a snack made from bird spit.'

Cook laughed a sour laugh. Then, she set some goji berries at the centre of the bird's nest pads and said, 'Well you couldn't eat it even if you wanted to. Cini pay high for everything coming out of the jungle except us. It'll cost you a year of your wages if you want a plate of that.'

'We're good with those bear-gall leaves you planted in the wash yard,' Girl replied. 'Actually, they'd be good for B.K. Big Sir too.'

Cook shook her head. 'They won't eat bitter. What's more our leaves are free. You know how they think. It can't be good if you can pluck it from a pot in the wash yard, right?' She showed Girl the murky yellow chunks she'd retrieved from the pantry's top shelf. 'This is what they like. Rock sugar flown in from up-country with a price equal to your airplane fare. One way.'

'Plain old raw sugar! And you don't think Cini are stupid?'

Cook looked pointedly sideways towards the CCTV cameras in the corner of the kitchen, where the ceiling met the walls. 'Well, if I did, I wouldn't let them hear me saying it,' she said in a low whisper.

'Nobody's here to hear except Arno and Big Sir. And they've both taken their pills and are sleeping like the dead,' Girl replied.

Cook shrugged, looked once more at the camera in the corner and muttered, 'Houses have ears.'

Cook had been pounding the sugar chunks in a mortar with a pestle as she and Girl were talking, and now she sprinkled the pounded crystal over the bird's nest pads and goji berries. 'See, instead of bothering yourself about this, that and the other, you should be learning how to do this,' she told Girl. 'How to make a gold flower with fire in the middle and star powder all over.'

'With sugar I can't afford,' Girl added truculently.

Cook shrugged again. 'Well, if you want to see it that way.' Then having decided she had nothing more to say about Girl's foolish thinking, she continued with her lesson. 'Now, after that's all done, you put the soup plate on a stand in the electric steamer and let it steam for four hours. And when that's done, all this stardust will have turned into liquid sunshine.'

* * *

Gold flowers . . . stardust . . . liquid sunshine . . . Bing Fa had smiled as she heard those words coming from Cook's mouth. She hadn't expected such whimsy from the stolid, garlic-scented and oil-spattered woman. But Bing Fa had given her performers plenty of leeway. As Madam often quoted from the Classics, 'There are not more than five musical notes, yet the combinations of these five give rise to more melodies than can ever be heard. There are not more than five primary colours, yet in combination they produce more hues than can ever be seen.' So why not such surprising whimsy from Cook?

Cook wasn't wrong about the bird's nest either. After four hours in the steamer, the ingredients had indeed turned into noon-bright, the pads of bird's nest clear like glass and the rock-sugar melted into a thick golden syrup underneath which the orange of the goji berries shone like tiny sunbirds.

Just the thing to whet B.K. Tjoa's appetite, Bing Fa had thought. Just the right thing to put in front of him before the main course.

'I can see how Big Sir might want to eat this,' Girl said.

'Might. Might not. We won't know until you take it upstairs,' Cook said.

'But I'm not allowed.'

'He's banished me. Someone's got to do it.'

'Both Ma'am Irene and you told me that I'm especially not to go near him when he's in a bad mood and drunk. I can't go up,' Girl protested. But to no avail.

Even when a director gives his or her performers free play, the players have certain tendencies the director can count on. Bing Fa had counted on B.K. Tjoa shifting blame. She'd counted on Cook's loyalty and how hurt she'd be. And she'd counted on Cook insisting the bird's nest be delivered and bullying Girl into doing it. It was all developing splendidly.

Cook cocked her head towards the ceiling. No sounds came from the floor of the room above.

'He's dead to the world. You'll be fine,' she said. 'The amount he drinks, he'll need this. And he doesn't want me going up. We don't have a choice.'

Girl looked at the plate. It was full, almost to the point of over-flowing. 'It's too much. If you want me to take it up, we need to scoop some out,' she said.

'We'd be wasting the goodness in the syrup,' Cook replied.

'It won't be a waste if you drank it,' Girl suggested.

Cook's jaw dropped. 'What? Drink it? How can you even suggest that?'

And now it was Girl's turn to be shocked. 'You mean you've been cooking it all these years and never ever tasted it? Not once?'

Cook pursed her lips. Her eyes slid up to the CCTV camera once more. 'I think we shouldn't waste it,' she said, exaggerating her lip movements so they could be clearly read by whoever would be looking at the camera footage. She lay a tea-towel onto a tray, set the soup plate on top of it, and said loudly enough for the microphones to pick up her voice, 'Here take it up. Big Sir's asleep and it's fine for you to go.' Then, turning her head away so the camera wouldn't catch her, she added, 'Use the towel to catch any spills.'

Girl laughed and replied, 'I've gone up and down those stairs for quite a few months already and never had an accident. There won't be a spill, you'll see.'

'Marble's treacherous in its own way,' Cook said. 'You should always take care.'

But Girl laughed again. 'That staircase? Why, back home, before they connected the water, I used to go up and down the bank to our stream twice a day and never lost my footing. Not once. I can walk up to B.K. Big Sir's blindfolded if you want me to,' she boasted.

Bing Fa had counted on that too, how Girl might over-estimate her abilities. How she wasn't going to pay any attention to Cook telling her to take care.

* * *

Girl was a creature of instinct. She had always moved as she felt. If she had to plan, she would stop, puzzle over the problem, make her decision and only afterwards act. What Bing Fa had asked her to do—to think while doing—was new for her. There was the bird's nest worth its weight in gold that she was balancing on the tray. And then there were her feet, stepping heel to toe from one white marble slab to the next. And finally, there was her having to whisper her thoughts aloud, 'Water's soft. Water bends. It's graceful, like a dancer. Thirst quenching. Fire cooling. And what else? Water's smooth. Water is? Cold? Is . . .'

It wasn't the marble steps that undid her. It was the floor rug. Even when a girl's nature is water and she's practicing walking like it, there's still the possibility that her very solid little toe might get caught in the fringe of the old rug next to an old drunk's chaise longue. There's still the possibility she might stumble.

In the TV serials Girl sneaked, such a stumble would have been followed by the tray tilting in slow motion and the soup plate (always a very valuable old one that had been in the boss's family for centuries) sliding off, bouncing on the rug, then breaking into picturesque quarters and waking the old man. In actual life Girl managed to straighten up and pull the tray towards her chest. The indeed very valuable soup plate that had been part of Big Mother's dowry was saved. There was no crash or clang to wake B.K. Tjoa from his stupor. Only half the bird's nest and syrup splashed out from the soup plate. Of this, none fell on the marble floor. A part slopped onto the tea-towel. The rest of the spill ended up on the rug, which being old and dry as dust, sucked up the syrup with the thirst of 100 years. The bird's nest pads which had fallen out were left stranded in clumps, all around Girl's feet.

She stared at the mess. B.K. Tjoa was still snoring in his rattan chaise longue, his back to her. Above her head, his ceiling fan continued to whirr. It was as if nothing had happened.

Quick as a thief, she lowered herself onto the rug, set the tray down at her feet, then cupped her left hand and began scooping up the clumps of spilled bird's nest. She had retrieved almost a handful when the chaise longue creaked. Its occupant had rolled over. But, sneaking a look, she saw his eyes were still closed. She could continue with her rescue. She moved the soup plate from the tray onto a dry bit of rug and poured her gleanings back into the plate, stirring a finger around the jumble of bird's nest pads and red putty goji till she'd recreated a storm-ripped semblance of Cook's original masterpiece. Then she rolled the soaked tea-towel up carefully to one side of the tray, lifted it, and drained the liquid on the tray into the plate. It was hardly enough to cover the top of the bird's nest pads. She would need more.

'I'd rather not,' she whispered to no one in particular. But she did it anyway. She took the soaked tea-towel firmly in both hands and wrung it out onto the bird's nest pads.

It was an insult to Cook's handiwork and still the plate was only three-quarters full. She needed to get it all the way up to the rim. She unfolded the towel, flattened it on the wet rug around her feet and pushed down hard to sop up as much of the syrup as she could. She was sopping up hundred-year-old dust too. But she could not afford to think about that. The chaise longue was creaking more insistently. Very soon she'd be caught sticky-handed if she didn't do what needed doing. She pressed down even harder. When the tea-towel was nicely soaked she rolled it up again, brought it over the soup plate and, shutting her eyes tight, twisted the towel. She squeezed till no more syrup seeped through her fingers. And then and only then did she open her eyes.

What she saw was pond-water clouded with pond-scum. Cook's liquid sunshine was gone. And she'd be going herself too, she supposed. Without her bride price. In debt for the cost of her airfare home. All because of a stupid bowl of bird saliva. Which she might as well taste, she thought, now she had nothing to lose.

'Perhaps it's better than it looks,' she mumbled, before dipping a finger into the muck and bringing it to her mouth.

The dust-laden syrup was disappointing. Sickeningly sweet with a mouldy aftertaste. Not worth a year of her wages, Girl thought. She turned and stole a last look at B.K. Tjoa, seemingly still asleep on his chaise longue and blind to the terrible things she'd done. And then she stood up. What was done was done. And if she had to be sent home, well, so be it. She set the soup plate filled with pond-water onto the side table beside B.K. Tjoa, picked the tray up from the floor and tiptoed away.

So intent was she on escape, she did not turn around to check if she'd left any traces of the spill behind. And so, as on her very first morning in the house, she did not see B.K. Tjoa and the look in his eyes. Nor did she see the sugary trail of girl-sized heel- and toe-prints on the marble floor, going all the way from the side of the chaise longue to the landing.

23

It was Arno who discovered the trail of sugar. He had spent most of the day trying to sleep off the tumult of the family meeting and had become entangled in yet another sex-laden dream featuring Tjoa Ek Kia and Bing Fa. He woke feeling as if he'd been led through a bordello and been tumbled on every one of its mattresses. To clear his head, he stumbled out to the landing. It was as he was standing there that he'd seen Girl slipping down the fish-bone staircase like a stream of water.

He called down to her, but she did not turn and smile up at him like she did most days. She kept going, leaving a trail of glittery footsteps after her.

The fact that the footsteps started from his father's landing had set Arno's alarms off. Girl was only ever supposed to go to that floor when B.K. Tjoa was out, and he was still in, as Arno could surmise from the drone of his father's air conditioner. Arno had heard his father ranting at Cook earlier, too. It was exactly the wrong day for Girl to be near his father. When she did not answer him as she usually did, even after he called out a second time, he rushed down the stairs to find out what the matter was.

What Arno was greeted by when he walked onto his father's landing was magic. Footstep after footstep of shining sugar crystals drying against the marble like flecks of precious metal washed from a stream. The tracks got darker nearer the staircase as the sugar dust mixed with dirt, but to Arno they still seemed like glitter out of a dream. He knelt and placed his palm against one of the prints, a powdery heel mark, and tried to imagine it was Girl's flesh-and-blood heel glittering in his hot sweaty hand. And then, as with all good fantasies, his came true. There they were, her two feet, in front of his face. They were damp, having just been washed, but he saw with joy that a sprinkling of sugar dust remained, stuck to the side of her ankle.

He bent his head down to that ankle and almost placed his lips against the glittering dust, but he held himself back at the last moment. Instead, he looked up and asked, 'What happened?'

'I spilled some of your father's soup and I'm back to clean it now,' she said, showing him the bucket and mop she was holding.

'His super expensive red bird's nest soup?'

'Only a bit,' she said.

But when she pushed his father's door open, Arno had seen the trail of sugar all the way to the chaise longue. It was way more than a bit.

Girl managed to get rid of it fast though. It took her only a few swipes of her mop to disappear the footprints. And then she was out of the room again, the door closed and B.K. Tjoa apparently dead asleep through it all.

'You won't tell, will you?' she pleaded.

Arno would not have told. But she'd given him an advantage, for once. Unable to resist, he took it. 'What will you give me to make it worthwhile?' he bargained.

'I'll share a secret with you,' she said. 'Please just keep quiet until after dinner and then I'll show it to you. It'll be worth your while. Really.'

She'd looked at Arno as if she would die if he didn't say yes, as if a river of sorrow was going to spill out of her eyes. It was almost enough to make him tell her he was only teasing. But he did not. By the time he managed to open his mouth, she was already halfway down the staircase, and it was too late to say anything.

'It was my bad,' he confesses to Sister Mary Michael on the Saturday morning after the nun's arrival in the house. 'My bad.'

* * *

It hadn't been Arno's bad Bing Fa thinks irritably when she hears him telling the nun about it. Without her prompting he would have been incapable of taking that opportunity when Girl offered him the trade. Girl had returned to the kitchen on tenterhooks only because she, Bing Fa, had whispered, 'Why not?' into Arno's big stupid head.

She doesn't bother to enlighten the nun about it when Arno tells her though. And of course, she hadn't bothered to enlighten Arno about it when it happened. A man laden with shame was so much easier to bring to a boil than one with a cool clear conscience. She'd left Arno there on B.K. Tjoa's landing, simmering with anticipation nicely seasoned with guilt, and turned her attention to his father instead.

* * *

B.K. Tjoa had taken his time getting off his chaise longue and dressing for his evening out. He had ignored the bird's nest, which lay where Girl had left it, on his side table. But on his way out, he'd stopped, stared at the soup plate and the mess in it for a moment, then picked it up and walked down the stairs with it.

Bing Fa had been given a jolt as she watched him taking the fish-bone steps, his feet falling swift and sure like a far younger man, and all the while not a spill from the dish in his hand. It was almost as if she was watching the young Tjoa Ek-Kia going down the narrow staircase from her room in the sing-song house to the street below. There were the same wide shoulders and straight back being carried away on the same strong legs, the big muscles of the same calves flexing under white linen trousers. Indeed, she'd thought, B.K. Tjoa was as grand a man as his father. But only on the outside. On the inside even B.K. Tjoa's own mother would have to admit he was nothing but an empty heartless thing, without a conscience and without shame. Nothing like his father Tjoa Ek-Kia, who despite everything Bing Fa faulted him for, always asked before taking and always paid for what he took.

B.K. Tjoa had proven immune to Bing Fa over the years. He'd grown up with everything and never had to hunt to satisfy anything, not even the itch in his crotch. He would feed, if she threw a bit of meat his way, but that was all she could make him do. He was that lazy. Bing Fa had never meant for B.K. Tjoa to do anything in the production she was staging. But then she'd heard him ranting at Cook and banishing her from his rooms. And Bing Fa had realized how much more interesting her production would be if she included him, with his nose for girl-flesh. When Girl was running from the chaise lounge, Bing Fa had brushed herself around Girl, picked up her scent and wafted it across the room to the half-sleeping man. His nostrils had flared. He raised himself onto his elbow. And from below hooded lids, his connoisseur's eyes had followed that small stream of girl-flesh as she rippled away.

It was because of Bing Fa that B.K. Tjoa had strode down the stairs with the soup plate in his hands. It was because of her that he had followed Girl's girl-fresh smell all the way to the kitchen. It was her bad, Bing Fa knew. But she brushes away the small prickle of shame she feels. Needs must, she tells herself. She was running out of time. She had to do it.

* * *.

Girl was ironing Arno's sheets at the far end of the kitchen when B.K. Tjoa stepped in. It wasn't usual, and she suspected it had to be about the bird's nest. But she kept her composure, and merely gave him a small respectful nod to acknowledge his presence.

'It's Big Sir,' she whispered to Cook, who was standing in front of the microwave heating up leftovers for their dinner, her back to B.K. Tjoa.

Cook was surprised by B.K. Tjoa's presence in the kitchen. But he had hurt her feelings, and she supposed this was his way of making amends. Turning around very slowly, to show she wasn't going to simply forgive at the drop of a hat, she greeted him with a short, 'Big Sir.' The rest would be up to him.

'The bird's nest,' he said to her, setting the plate on the counter. 'You didn't cover it. It got cold. And dust got in.'

Cook shrugged. Pointing to Girl with the back of her elbow, she said, 'You didn't want me up there, so I sent her.'

'She's new. You're in charge here. You know I rely on you. I always have. That's why sometimes I get upset and say, well, you know . . .' He left the apology implied.

It was enough to soften Cook. 'I thought as you were home, you wouldn't need a cover,' she tried to explain.

He raised a palm to stop her, then tapped the side of the soup plate and said, 'I suspect my sister Irene will go on and on about my liver if you tell her I wasted this. You share it and we won't mention it got cold.'

'The bird's nest? For us Big Sir?' Cook was flabbergasted.

He smiled. 'It's our secret,' he said to Cook. Then he called to Girl over Cook's head, 'Our secret, right number two?'

'Me?' Girl peeped up at him through her lowered lashes.

He chuckled before saying, 'Yes, you.'

Cook would have known that chuckle. It did not mean he was wishing Girl well. But she'd been distracted by the prospect of finally getting a taste of the much-vaunted red bird's nest.

'Yes, Big Sir. We'll do that,' she said. And before his back was turned, she'd already taken two soup spoons from the cutlery drawer. 'You heard that,' she said to Girl as soon as he was out of the room. 'You wanted a taste and now you've got it.'

'Mmm, no,' Girl replied. 'You have it all.'

24

There are two kinds of sins, Girl had overheard Irene Tjoa saying once. A person might do something. Or a person might intentionally not do something. Girl had committed both kinds, and one kind twice over. First, she'd spilled the bird's nest. Second, she wasn't telling Cook the truth about it. And third, she was encouraging Cook to eat it all. She had to make amends.

Although Cook was not there to see, Girl was especially careful cleaning the kitchen that night. She mopped the floor again despite it being already whiter than white and re-wiped the dustless black counters till they shone like night. She also gave the rings around the bottoms of the faucets a mid-week brush with Cook's special white paste, and carefully painted vinegar around the transparent rubber edgings of the sink. The black glass cooker surface got an extra polishing. And then, she re-arranged all the leftovers in the fridge. When she was done, the kitchen was so commendably clean even Irene Tjoa couldn't have faulted it. Girl, however, still felt dirty with sin.

She left the kitchen and went down to the servants' quarters, resolved to confess everything to Cook. But Cook was sleeping, a happy smile on her face. She was feeling good about the soup. There was no reason to feel so guilty, Girl decided. Everything was fine. Almost. Except for Arno.

She went to her bed, pulled her pouch out from under the pillow and felt inside it for the little key and the photograph she'd nestled in the coils of her hank of hair. They were all she had to trade for Arno's silence. She gulped. Giving up the key and photograph were all right, but her hair . . . She gave the plaited hank a goodbye pat. Then stuffed everything back into her pouch and headed for the attic.

* * *

Arno was sitting at his worktable playing around with ideas for the plain blouse and cloth he'd promised Girl when she appeared. She was in a faded T-shirt and an ankle-length sleeping cloth of an indeterminate shade of pale. But the blue of Arno's neon work lights had given everything an aqua tint so that she looked like she was under water. A Mermaid Barbie, Arno had thought, his mind turning away immediately from the project at hand to the makeover he'd give Girl, to turn her into a perfect mermaid.

There was nothing he could do about the hair she'd cut short at her neck, except perhaps weave some seaweed green tulle into the crown of her head and let them fall about her neck. But there was that totally unsuitable patchwork pouch that could be replaced with a crotchet string bag trimmed with scalloped edges, decorated maybe with a scattering of mother-of-pearl beads. And for her top, a tight aqua-coloured tube, paired with a clinging skirt flared at the bottom and embroidered with jewel-coloured scales.

It was such an exciting concept he would've started work on it immediately if Girl had let him. But she had other business on her mind.

'I've brought it, the secret,' she said, pulling him out of his marine fantasy.

'Oh!' Arno had exclaimed stupidly before he remembered why Girl had come up to the attic. But then instead of telling Girl he didn't need to trade any stuff with her as he'd previously intended, he asked instead, 'Well, what do you have?'

Girl folded down on the floor all in one move, like water it seemed to Arno. Then she pulled at the string of the pouch and spilled out its contents.

'This,' she said.

Arno saw a faded photo, a key-shaped charm and an arm-length plait of hair, glowing as if it was alive.

The plait, that was what he wanted, Arno knew immediately. But it was not what Girl offered him. She handed him the key instead.

'We can open that doll house inside your crocodile-skin trunk with this,' she said.

'But my diva's in the trunk,' Arno protested. 'We don't want to disturb her.'

Girl was not to be denied. She rolled up onto her feet, squatted on her heels and proceeded to stare Arno down. 'The diva spoke to me,' she said. 'She wants me to let her out.'

Who was Girl to speak for his diva, Arno thought crossly? But then he realized she wasn't speaking about his diva doll. She was speaking about the diva who was the love of his grandfather's life.

'Which diva?' he asked just to be sure.

'This one,' Girl said, pointing at the photograph.

Unlike Girl, Arno thought the photograph showed the most beautiful face ever.

'Look at it,' he said to Girl. 'That wonderful white oval, and those eyes and lips, so subtly coloured yet so imperious.

She's not your typical biscuit tin beauty at all. She's pure diva presence.'

He hadn't argued with Girl about whether it really showed the woman they both called Bing Fa. After all the pipa player in the painting on the front wall downstairs had the same face. And when Arno brought the picture up close to his face, he'd smelt very old Chanel No. 5. It was just too much of a coincidence. It had to be her.

Still, something held him back from taking the key Girl was pressing into his other hand. He had never thought to open the house, not once in all the eight years since he'd found his diva doll. Besides, hadn't Gran come to him in Guangzhou before she died and told him it was dangerous to open the doll house?

'I'm not sure it's going to do us any good, unlocking the house,' he said to Girl.

But Girl had come up with all the right arguments. 'We're not going to lose anything by opening the house,' she said. 'If nothing happens, we'll be the same as before. And if Bing Fa really has powers and can help us, we'll be better off. Either way, you can control her, can't you? Gran did tell you, didn't you say?'

Which Gran had, the night she'd come to Arno in Guangzhou. And which Arno had told Girl about. He didn't have an excuse not to do it. Not with Girl looking at him with such big wet eyes.

He pulled out the key hanging from the chain around his neck and, taking Girl's hand, walked with her towards the trunk like he'd tried to do once before. This time he didn't hold back. When they reached the trunk, he unlocked it without mishap and took the diva doll from her stage without misgivings. And then, he lifted the doll house from where it had been sitting since his seventeenth birthday and gave it to Girl.

Girl set the house on the floor, knelt in front of it, pulled Arno down beside her and handed him the other key.

'You open it,' she said. 'Open it and ask Bing Fa for help against your aunts, then promise to set her free. It's the only way. For both of us.'

In the moments before Girl uttered those words, Arno had been thinking how absurd it was for the two of them to be kneeling there in front of the doll house, hoping for a spirit to grant them a boon. It was just his imagination gone into hyperdrive. It was all a load of rubbish. But then Girl had said 'for the both of us'.

No, Arno had told himself, it was impossible that Girl felt the same way about him as he did about her. But what if . . .

'Alright. I'll open the house and we'll make our wishes,' he told Girl. 'But we won't burn the house. Instead, I'll do what Gran told me needs doing to keep Bing Fa under control. After which we'll close everything up. Okay?'

Girl had not disagreed, and Arno had taken the key and inserted it into the keyhole in the front door of the house. Despite its rust, the key slid in easily and turned without any trouble. And then the entire front wall of the house had swung open to the accompanying melody of *Qiu Shui Yi Ren*.

'That's your father's song,' Girl exclaimed.

'Mine, you mean,' Arno countered.

Girl had not bothered to argue with him. Reaching past him, she lifted the house, turned it over and emptied its contents onto his top sheet.

It had been disappointing, the stuff that fell out. An unmagical length of frizzled black hair binding an old bone button, a twist of pipe-cleaning wire, a bent metal ear pick tarnished almost black, a twist of string that looked like part of a shoelace, some old copper coins, and a rather scratched glass charm, the kind that might hang off a child's anklet or bracelet. Separately, there was also a lock of very fine baby hair, a wad of yellowed tissue stiff with dried mucus, a feather and scabs of matted hair—Arno's own eyebrow hairs.

'We're not going to get anything praying to that junk,' Arno said to Girl.

She'd disagreed. Picking up the string of objects from his bed, she let it fall slowly into her palm and examined each item in turn.

'There! There it is!' she exclaimed when at last she found what she was looking for.

It was the glass charm, moulded in the likeness of a pipa.

'This proves all the stories are true,' she said. 'There really is a Bing Fa who was a pipa player. This charm must be hers, tied to this string of hair because that's how you Tjoas have imprisoned her.' She dropped the string with the objects into Arno's palm and closed his fingers around everything. 'Can't you feel her inside?' she asked.

'A little buzz, maybe,' he answered, although in truth all he'd felt were the edges and corners of the objects poking into his palm.

'That's that then,' Girl said happily. 'We've got what we wanted. Now, let's burn the house and everything and free her.'

'That's a bit stupid if we're saying Bing Fa is in the glass charm,' Arno argued. 'Glass doesn't burn. It melts. She'll still be stuck inside.'

He hadn't liked Girl's pre-occupation with burning everything. But remembering Gran's instructions about pretending, he hadn't disagreed outright. 'Let's make our wishes to Bing Fa first,' he said. 'And then, since we need to see if she delivers, lets hold off on burning everything until our wishes are granted.'

It didn't occur to Arno that Girl could play the pretend game as well. She didn't say yes. She lowered her eyes. He took this for acquiescence and put the string of what he supposed should rightly be called talismans as well as the remaining loose objects back into the house. Then he closed it and placed the house back into its nook in the crocodile-skin trunk. Afterward he asked Girl to kneel beside him and make her wish too.

It didn't matter there were the two of them, he assumed. If there really was an all-powerful spirit called Bing Fa, she would be able to sort out their two wishes as easily as one.

Girl folded herself down next to Arno without objection, smooth as water. And then Arno made three kowtows, which Girl imitated. There they were, Arno thought, like the couples in the old wedding photos he used as source material, praying for blessings before an ancestral altar. The two of them, together, just as Girl had said.

It was a dream come true for Arno.

* * *

Of course, it was not a wedding. Girl and Arno had not, at the onset, wanted the same thing. Arno had intended to ask Bing Fa to destroy his aunts and give him back the ash house so he could build a doll museum for the diva. Which was to say, he wanted to keep Bing Fa's spirit inside the doll house, ossified, for another 100 years. Bing Fa had no intention of allowing that to happen. As Arno had knelt there in front of the doll house, she had given him the hint of a new idea. Why not have Girl beside him? Forever?

And that was what he ended up wishing for.

In return Arno promised to burn the doll house and everything in it, as Girl had said Bing Fa wanted. He did not lie and promise future children or songs as Gran had instructed. In his mind, if his wish was granted, it wasn't going to matter if everything else turned to dust. He would be entirely happy.

And perhaps, the wedding might have happened if Arno hadn't been so hung up on Gran's warnings. But he had.

25

Once Arno and Girl got off their knees, Girl had asked him to burn the doll house again.

'But you agreed to wait until both our wishes come true. We don't burn the house until she gives us what we want,' he said.

Girl hadn't understood the conditionality of the arrangement. She'd made a bargain, and now Arno was stopping her from paying for it. 'I promised,' she said, reaching past him to get at the house.

He pushed her away and she clawed at him. Which led to him slapping her and then a neck-scratching, arm-biting brawl that ended with the two of them on his bed, her whole body under his, and his weight pressing her into the softness of his mattress.

Her cloth was undone and tangled around her ankles. She could feel his leg hairs rough against her shins and the silky smoothness of his sheets on the backs of her bare legs, arms and neck. 'A wonder to lie on' Cook had said. And how right Cook had been, Girl realized. Washing and ironing them hadn't given her a hint how good it felt to be on them. How good it would feel to be between them.

Cook and Girl used ten-dollars-a-set sheets from the market which nubbled after the second wash and scratched at their

armpits and under their knees. Arno's sheets were an entirely
different matter. They supported Girl's back like water and
floated her back home into the stream where she and Buffalo
Boy had played. Back to the stream in which she'd pretended
to be a drowning princess whom Buffalo Boy had to kiss back
to life, a princess so near death Buffalo Boy often had to drag
the poor sodden thing to shore to kiss not only her face and lips
but her everything else with his everything else too. With his
lips and also with a tongue that could magically force hers into
exclaiming, 'There's a big fish growing between your legs!' As if
she hadn't been expecting it.

It had been too long, Girl sighed, as she sank more deeply
into the softness of Arno's bedding and gave herself over to that
watery feeling of the stream and of Buffalo Boy's body and hers
slip-sliding like fish. Buffalo Boy and herself, playing but never
going all the way. Because there was always the bride-price to
consider. Or rather, the lack of it.

The thought of the bride-price and its lack brought Girl
back to reality. Not an entirely unacceptable one, she realized.
She wouldn't have to save her stupid maidenhood for Buffalo
Boy if she was paying her own bride-price. He wouldn't care. He
wanted her anyway. And probably would want her even more,
if she came home rich. And here she was with Arno the Tjoa
heir on top of her, a fish growing between his legs. Arno, whom
she'd seen kneeling at Bing Fa's altar, apparently pleading to
keep a hold of his family's house and wealth.

Arno . . . Why not?

She pressed her body against his, brought a hand up to the
back of his neck and whispered into his chest, 'Please. We can
have everything if you'll burn the house and the charms and
set her free.' And then, keeping Buffalo Boy firmly in mind,

she opened her lips, brushed them against the side of Arno's fat neck and murmured, 'She'll give us everything once you burn the house. And I'll give you everything too.'

The entire weight of Arno yielded onto Girl, almost burying her. She'd won, she thought. But then he pushed himself up and swung his big hand across her face in a whacking slap.

'Gran said you'd try to trick me, but I won't let you,' he said, his breath coming out in gasps.

'No,' Girl protested. 'It's for our good.'

'I'll do it when she delivers, not before,' he wheezed, scrambling off his bed and toward the bathroom where he kept his nebulizer.

Girl stared after him, not quite believing that someone whom she'd helped grow a fish between his legs, had torn himself away.

'Be like water' Bing Fa had said to her. And she had been. But where had it gotten her?

She looked around the room ruefully, then smiled. She was where it mattered. Alone. Next to an open crocodile-skin trunk in which a doll house with a skein of talismans sat. Waiting for her.

She picked it up with one hand and hugged it close, wrapping her cloth back around herself with the other, and then she hurried out of the attic.

* * *

If Girl had gone all the way down the stairs right then, there'd be no role for B.K. Tjoa. But she'd forgotten her pouch and hank of hair. In the few minutes it took her to sprint up to the attic, cross into the sleeping area and pick up her things,

B.K. Tjoa arrived home and lurched into the lift. And as if
fated, the lift door opened at his floor just as Girl came back
down and stepped onto his landing.

He leaned against the staircase railing, blocking her way.
'Who do we have here wandering about in the middle of the
night?' he slurred.

Girl pulled her pouch and the doll house tighter against her
chest and tried to slide around him as she mumbled, 'I'm going
down to my room, B.K. Big Sir.'

He chuckled. 'But what were you doing up there that you
need to go down now?'

'Helping Arno Young Sir with some sewing B.K. Big Sir,'
she replied.

He winked, a soft drunken wink. 'I don't think so. Clothes
all mussed up. Slipping along so quietly,' he said, pushing
himself off the railings.

Girl feared he would fall on her. But he caught himself
against his door, steadied himself to a stand and reached a large
square index finger towards her reddened cheek. 'Been touched,
I'd say,' he mumbled. 'Definitely.'

She should have scuttled away quick as a cockroach then.
But fear had paralyzed her. Her feet were stuck fast. She could
only stand, caught in front of his hungry yellow eyes.

His finger traced down her neck and onto her shoulder,
towards the doll house she was clutching. His eyes narrowed.
'That's mine,' he said.

He pulled, one quick pluck. And then, it was indeed his.

'No!' she cried.

He smiled spitefully, put the house to his ear and began to
whistle that tune Girl recognized as Bing Fa's signature.

'Please,' she said, reaching for it.

'Ah-ah. Naughty,' he said, moving the house behind his head.

She took another step forward. That was a mistake. As soon as she got close, he folded his free arm around her shoulders and caught her.

'Now I've got the thief as well,' he said with a laugh.

B.K. Tjoa was much stronger than Arno. Even though he was drunk, it was impossible for Girl to wriggle out of his grip. Holding her like a hostage, he slid his back against his door and dragged her into his bedroom. She tried to scream, but fear had pushed stones down her throat. She couldn't even whimper.

B.K. Tjoa closed his bedroom door, pushed Girl against it and leaned into her body. Still holding the doll house above his head with one hand, he snaked his free arm down to the knot holding her cloth up. 'Don't I deserve what you gave my son?' he slurred into the top of her head.

His voice was heavy. His breath smelt of cigarette and liquor, smoky and sweet.

'Nothing,' Girl whispered. 'I didn't give Arno anything.'

He chuckled again, that soft gurgle Girl had once thought indicated kindness but now knew signalled he was preparing to eat. He said, 'I don't believe you. I saw what you did with my bird's nest earlier. I know what you're like.'

Still pinning her against the wall, he slid himself down the length of her body till he was kneeling on the floor with his face against her belly. Then, he set the doll house down by her heels.

'You must have done something for him, to get this house,' he said.

In answer, she kicked at his knees.

He slapped her feet. 'Naughty,' he said again, grinning and showing his big yellow crocodile teeth. 'But I like naughty.' And then, to Girl's horror, she felt a hand taking hold of her jaw and pushing it up and down in a parody of a nod.

'Are you saying you like naughty too?' he asked with a smile.

Girl could not answer, and B.K. Tjoa did not wait for her to. He pulled at her cloth.

She tried to shake her head, but only succeeded in pushing it against his hand.

'Be like water . . . Be like water . . .' Girl told herself as B.K. Tjoa's fingers, then his palms, ran over her skin.

And she did become water. Flowing water washing downhill, carrying away everything B.K. Tjoa was doing to her. Carrying with it the ashes of the doll house, the house she was earning with her body.

She let him pull her onto the floor near where he'd set the house down. She let him pull her thighs apart. Let him grope. All the while trying not to think of what he was doing. Trying only to shift her body towards the doll house, a hair's breadth at a time. Letting him do whatever he wanted. Submitting. Allowing. Like maybe her Ibu had, her first time. And maybe Gran too. And even Bing Fa.

He rammed himself into her. She stiffened, instinctively snapping her legs shut and clipping them together on the thing aimed at her. But to her surprise, there was nothing for her to catch. Nothing but a dead fish.

He snarled. Snatched his hands away from her and began to pull at himself. Without effect.

Girl tried to hold back the snort rising from the back of her throat. The Tjoa men were impotent, or almost. All of them, from Grandpa Tjoa who'd managed to father just the one son, to B.K. Tjoa who'd only produced maimed Arno, to Arno himself who'd pushed her out of his bed. It was funny really when she thought about it, how foolish she'd been to think she could be freed by them. Or any men for that matter. Even Buffalo boy, who was so beautiful, but so stupid. It was so pathetic she began to laugh and cry at the same time. There she was, praying to be in one of those block-buster TV serials where girls made good. And where had she ended up? In the kind of show where she had to run through muddy drains and fall into vats of syrup to get photographed with a chicken mascot and win an electric kettle or rice cooker. It was ridiculous!

But it was life, that's what her Ibu would have said. Sweet, sour and mostly bitter life. And it was true, Girl realized. Life was bitter. Especially the way her Ibu was always right, damn her!

Girl couldn't help braying at the truth of it, a big donkey bray that refused to stop. A bray so loud and mocking, B.K. Tjoa took offence. He bared his teeth and stretching out both his arms, pounced at Girl.

She kicked into his stomach, then reached for the dead fish between his legs and pulled. He doubled over, screaming. It was her chance. She gathered her cloth about her, scrambled up and stepped over B.K. Tjoa's writhing body, picked up the house, and ran with it.

26

Girl ran down the stairs, out the front door and into the night, pursued by the screeching security alarms she'd tripped. She ran between the pastel fronted houses whose flower plastered walls hid who knew what monsters, and towards the wailing music, clinking glasses and hushed laughter at the bottom of the hill. She ran until she was stopped by a sudden silence.

She was in the courtyard of a bar, a barefooted crying number two maid clutching a doll house against her ripped T-shirt, with her bare ass showing through her ripped cloth. A sight strange enough to stop the bar-room chatter, for a moment at any rate. Then a metal chair slid against the tiled floor and a kindly foreign voice came towards her from underneath the dimly lit palm trees, asking, 'Honey, what's the matter? Do you need help?'

Before she could answer, a muscled body stepped between her and the foreigner and said, 'We'll take care of this, Sir.'

The second voice belonged to a very large man with long brawny arms that ended in two noticeably beaten-up hands, the bouncer. He walked towards Girl with the soft feet and unblinking eyes of a snake catcher. But he was surprisingly gentle as he steered her out of the bar and then took off his jacket and tied it around her waist, over her exposed bottom.

'What happened?' he asked, in a variant of her village dialect.

'B.K. Big Sir,' she whimpered.

'The son of the old woman who died last week?' the bouncer asked. Then without waiting for Girl to answer, sucked on his back teeth, and spat, 'That one. Again!'

Again . . . The word hammered through Girl's bruised body. Now she understood why Gran had refused to tell her if her son had been naughty. Now she understood Arno's warnings and the reason for the precautions Cook had made her take.

'Again? I can't let it happen again. We need to go to the police. Help me. Take me to them,' she said to the bouncer.

'Are you sure? You know what the police are like,' he murmured.

Girl hesitated. At home, no one went to the police if they could help it. And if they couldn't, they'd only go if they had something to bargain with. She had almost nothing after B.K. Tjoa's clawing and poking. Even if they were willing to take the stained and scratched goods she offered, what would she gain allowing herself to be treated that way again? Not a marriage certificate. Not zeroes in a bank passbook. And if the police were truly different here in Kota Cahaya as people said, all she'd get then would be unsatisfying cold justice. Nothing.

She squared her shoulders and tilted up her chin. 'No,' she replied.

The man smiled, showing his gold-capped teeth. 'Clever girl,' he said. He brought his hand under Girl's elbow, cupped his fingers around it and rubbed his thumb slowly but surely against the inside of her arm. 'Why give more of it away for nothing, isn't that right?' he said.

The Administrative Officer at home had touched Girl in the same way when he gave her back her doctored passport and bade her farewell. But she couldn't allow any of that. Not any more. Not for nothing, certainly. She straightened her arm and pushed her elbow out. The bouncer let his hand drop without protest. It was then that she saw the heavy gold rings set with coloured stones on his misshapen hands and realized he wasn't merely a bouncer, he was also a broker.

She might have pulled herself up straight then, untied his jacket and flung it at him. She might have told him off the way her Ibu or Bing Fa would have. 'You're right, why give it away for nothing? Come back when you can find me someone who'll pay a virgin's bride-price. Then, we'll talk.' But she wasn't her Ibu or a pipa diva. Instead, she sank into her hips for a second, then turned on her heels and ran back the way she'd come, his jacket tied around her ripped cloth, the doll house clutched against her T-shirt, a breaker backwashing up the hill.

Halfway up the hill, she ran into Arno who'd come out looking for her. He shushed her, wrapped his shirt around her and walked her back to the now silenced house like a baby. With Cook, he carried her over the threshhold to the lift and took her up past B.K. Tjoa's quarters to his attic. As B.K. Tjoa lay passed out on his chaise lounge, Cook blew the air-mattress up in the work room and Arno lay her on it. Then Cook wiped her clean. And afterwards, Arno gave her some of his pills and hummed Bing Fa's song to calm her.

* * *

While Arno hummed, Girl dreamt she was running again, Bing Fa's song following after her. The song wound past the pastel walls of the Green Hill houses and the mouldy walls of Cini

shophouses and the click-clack of mahjong tiles and the tinkling
laughter of the girls in the bars at the bottom of the hill and
the tink-tonk-tonk of wedding gongs and the Administrative
Officer's 'shush' and B.K. Tjoa's chuckle and the bouncer's
falsely friendly voice warning her against the police. It wound
through the stones leading down to the riverbank and brushed
at her feet and calves and coiled around her right heel and sank
its fangs into both sides of her ankle and woke her, even as she
was dreaming.

'You,' she said accusingly.

She heard Bing Fa laugh, and then reply. 'It's good to know
you haven't given up and died after all.'

'How can you laugh?' Girl asked, incensed. 'It's all happened
because of you telling me to walk like water. It's all your fault.'
And then, still dreaming, she'd stamped her feet down, hard.

Her right foot clamped over something smooth and strong,
a snake which spoke with two voices.

'Don't you feel better after doing that?' the first said.

'So much more alive?' the second followed.

Girl looked down and saw a glowing yellow whip snake
with two heads, one resting on each side of her ankle.

'You bit me,' she said.

The snake nodded, first with its glowing yellow-eyed right
head, then with its red-eyed left head.

'Anger is powerful medicine,' the head with yellow eyes told
her.

'Better than hunger,' the red-eyed head said.

'Or fear,' yellow eyes added.

'Who's talking about fear,' Girl said. 'I'm not afraid.'

The two heads reared. 'We didn't ask. Are you sure?' they
mocked, their tongues darting in and out.

In her dream, Girl knew she had her foot firmly set over the snake's body. All she had to do was press down hard and the snake would be dead. She was in control, like Gran had told her to be. She had no reason to be afraid.

But if so, why was one of the heads hissing, 'That's what she thinks.'

And why was the other hissing back, 'Let her think what she likes, what she doesn't know won't hurt her.'

Girl knew snakes lied. And two-headed snakes were the greatest liars of all, the Cini in town used to say. This two-headed creature had come from Bing Fa, whom Girl was beginning to suspect was nothing more than a trickster. It had all been a waste of time, she thought angrily. She should kill the snake and get on with what she needed to do to earn her bride-price, the selling of her still intact maidenhood.

She pressed down with her foot. So there!

The snake's body squirmed. The two heads around her ankle laughed. Something flipped. Something else pulled. 'You didn't think you could, did you?' she heard red eyes and yellow eyes saying in unison as the yellow body whipped away.

It had been free to leave whenever it wanted, Girl realized. It had only allowed itself to be pinned under her foot to give her the impression it was trapped.

Still asleep, she watched as the single tail of the snake swished between the stones of the riverbank and retraced its path to the ash house and up the marble steps to the attic, where it slid through the locked doors of the crocodile-skin suitcase and into the doll house. The snake had come out from the trunk, followed her to the riverside and wrapped itself around her ankle, then gone back into the trunk as easily as Bing Fa's voice had entered her head. As easily as Bing Fa's strength had entered Gran's failing body. As easily as her stories had seeped from the diva doll's body into Arno's imagination. As if it was free to go wherever it liked.

Free . . . Understanding flooded through Girl's sleeping body.

Bing Fa didn't need letting out from the doll house. She was already able to go everywhere. It was all a smoke screen, her story about promising anything to anyone if only they'd free her. Whatever it was that Bing Fa wanted, Girl realized, it wasn't freedom.

'Don't believe her,' Girl tried to tell Arno. 'Don't think we can ever be in control!'

But the pills he'd given her were finally doing their work. She could not get out of her dream. She managed to form her mouth into an 'o' and kick her feet feebly. But that was all she could do. She could not make her body do anything else.

27

Arno shows Sister Mary Michael what Girl's body did manage to do.

It is the Saturday morning after the nun's first night in the house. She and Arno have woken, washed and dressed. They are in the basement, in the wash yard next to the servants' quarters, where Arno is giving the nun a graphic illustration of what eventually happened to Girl's body.

'That's what I saw when I came down here,' he says, laying his Girl doll flat on the cement floor, bending one of its legs at the knee so the foot goes almost all the way up to its hip, then lifting its arms out and up above its head and twisting its body around at the waist, so it is nothing but a tangle of parts. 'And it's my fault,' he says. 'Because I put those pills in her mouth.'

However, Sister Mary Michael has spent the night immersed in Girl's story and then all of pre-dawn Saturday being whispered at and sung to by Bing Fa. She has been shown what happened just before Girl fell. She knows, it wasn't just the pills.

* * *

As the night wore on, Girl had become more restless and begun to kick at the sheets and slap at Arno's hands. His humming now seemed to irritate her. He tried everything, unwinding the sheets from her, straightening them out and cocooning her back in them, wiping her face and brushing back her hair; giving her two more of his magic sedatives. But nothing helped.

It was then, when he was at the end of his tether, that Arno realized his Gran was right. Bing Fa had to be reined in.

The doll house with the talismans inside was on the pulled-out flap of Arno's worktable, where he'd placed it after prying it away from a hysterical Girl. As Arno went to pick it up, he could feel that it was buzzing with a frantic frightening energy that seemed to burn through his fingertips.

'Keep away!' he felt the house telling him.

He backed off.

He would need something that had belonged to Big Mother to subdue the spirit, he realized. But what?

There was a skein of blood red embroidery silk in his sewing box, he recalled. A remnant from Big Mother's own sewing kit, Gran had said. And then there were the remnants of Big Mother's Pekalongon batik sarongs, squares and squares of them. He'd be able to manage with the silk and those squares, he thought.

Wrapping his hands in two squares of batik, he opened the house, picked up the length of hair with the talismans attached and dropped it and the other loose objects onto a third batik square he'd laid on his lap. Afterward, he unwrapped his hands and, ignoring the prickling sensations against his bare skin, very carefully tied Big Mother's length of red silk to the length of hair. The prickling and buzzing stopped immediately. Arno gave himself a metaphorical pat on the back. 'The best is yet to be,' he muttered, unconsciously invoking the protective mantra from his school days. Then he began to knot the remaining loose objects to the red silk.

First was the baby hair that Arno guessed was probably his father's and which Gran must have deposited. Then the tissues and feather that must have come from his own lost mother. And finally, in lieu of the hair his mother should have left, the eyebrow hairs he'd deposited one diva story at a time.

Gran had said that the way to keep Bing Fa quiet was by promising her a few hairs and for any Tjoa children she might give to learn her song. Pipa players were always tempted by the chance to share their music but they didn't, on principle, give away their skills for free. Everyone had to give her something as a deposit. Well, Arno supposed, it must have been his lost mother's failure to leave some of his hair that resulted in the fiasco that was his young life. His bedwetting. His stuttering. The teasing and bullying that had resulted . . . It was Bing Fa's revenge, her reaching out from inside that doll house to afflict him with everything that had made his young life hell.

Things had been much better after he himself started making good on his mother's lapse. It was as Gran had told him. His eyebrow hair offerings hadn't meant anything to him, but Bing Fa must have viewed it differently. By giving her that bit of himself, he and Bing Fa had made an equal exchange. A part of himself for a part of her music and her stories. A sliver of his life for a sliver of hers.

* * *

'What drivel,' Sister Mary Michael hears Bing Fa's voice whispering in her head. 'As if anyone, let alone the Madams of pipa players, bring up their girls on offerings of hair and nails.'

'You must have wanted them there at some point,' Sister Mary Michael tells her silently. 'You're the one who put those ideas into everyone's heads. Arno's. His mother's. His grandmother's. It was only because of those stories that Arno was trying to put the talismans back into the doll house.'

'You don't know what I wanted and what I didn't want. Maybe I did want him to tie everything together and put it back in the house. Maybe I had to wait for him to go mad and for you to arrive to get what I wanted,' Bing Fa retorts.

'That's a lot of maybes,' the nun says. 'So many maybes it sounds to me like you were just making it up as you went along, one failure after another.'

What can Bing Fa say? She had been surprised by Arno's mother, who had possessed such a stone-cold heart she'd tried to kill her maimed baby before she ran home to her village. As for Arno's Gran, who would have guessed that love could have propelled her dying spirit all the way to Guangzhou to caution her grandson about exposing the talismans? And then there's the mystery of Big Mother and how that dour woman who could not win her husband's heart, managed to win all six of his daughters', Irene included. Sister Mary Michael is right. None of it has quite worked out as expected because those unfathomable things, hearts, kept getting in the way. And since Bing Fa can't make any kind of rebuttal to the nun's comment, she does what she always does when she gets the short end of the stick. She withdraws.

* * *

Bing Fa had not been reticent though, on that night when Arno was tying the length of hair to Big Mother's length of red silk and binding all the talismans together. Then, she'd made herself heard, loud and clear.

'Stop that,' she'd hissed. 'What are you doing? Are you thinking of backing out?' she'd accused him.

He answered, 'No. But, after that close call of Girl's with my father, I want to be sure. I want to see if you'll give me Girl before I do what I promised.'

'You Tjoas, none of you can be trusted,' she'd complained. 'If you want me to do anything, I'll need a deposit.'

'But you have my hair already, scads of it. You don't need any more.'

Arno had hit on the truth that Girl was trying to communicate from inside her drugged body. Bing Fa didn't need any more hair, not from Arno, nor from anyone else. Bing Fa didn't need either Arno or Girl to free her either. She just wanted to maintain the illusion that they owed her, so that she could keep them under her thumb.

'It's a trick,' Girl tried to call out to Arno. 'Don't listen to her.'

But Arno had not heard Girl.

Instead, Arno heard Bing Fa saying, 'Listen, when I gave your Grandmother a son, she gave me some of his hair, not hers. When I brought your father to your mother, she gave me something from his body. And when she exchanged you for her freedom, she left a feather from her marriage bed to seal the deal. You've asked me for what you want and I've done half the work already. There's the girl, right here, mere steps from you. Don't you think that as a sign of good faith, you should give me something of hers now? Go on, one little lock of hair, and then you'll see. You'll have the rest of her in no time. No time at all. Her name will be on a marriage license, her body in your bed and your child in her belly. You'll see.'

Arno had shifted his bottom against his heels and peered into the centre of the room where Girl lay, muttering and struggling, but still deep in sleep. She was at his disposal. He couldn't resist.

His wooden floor did not betray him. It had creaked a little when he tip-toed towards Girl and a little louder when he lowered his knees down next to her, but it was completely silent when he snipped the lock of blue-black hair from behind her left ear. And although the floor creaked again, a little, when he padded back to his worktable, it didn't make enough noise to wake Girl. She merely sighed as if she knew there was nothing she could do about any of it. She'd made a promise at Bing Fa's crocodile-skin altar too. This was part of the deal: Arno taking up the skein of talismans he'd lengthened with Big Mother's blood-red silk and weighted by the small bundle of loose objects he'd knotted onto it. Arno looping the red silk tightly around her own lock of hair, then coiling up the whole length of it, silk and frizzled hair and talismans and her good black hair, everything together. Arno sliding it into the doll house. Arno closing the house and shutting Bing Fa's music away.

* * *

In her sleep, Girl heard the music winding backward, going against time and pulling her along with it. It was as if she was being dragged by her hair, which had somehow grown long again. She was being taken up the riverbank and along the way the two-headed snake had gone, until she was back in Arno's attic, inside the crocodile-skin suitcase and locked in the doll house. She was underwater, submerged in a murky green cave beneath the seabed. Everything was running the other way. The rivers going uphill and collecting in a sea whose entire length and depth was contained inside a house no bigger than a saving box, where she, a full-grown girl, was trapped.

She opened her mouth to scream and choked on the water flooding in.

'Slowly, slowly, sip it slowly,' she heard Arno saying. He was kneeling beside her, holding a glass of water to her lips. The backward running water had returned her to safety. To the ash house and into Arno's soft fat unthreatening arms. Or so she thought.

But Arno had betrayed her.

He had not understood this. Although Girl hadn't said no to Arno that night, she had certainly not said yes. He should have realized of course, from the angry tears she cried when she heard what he'd done with her lock of hair. And from the way she turned her back to him. Instead, he chose not to understand. He soothed her into what looked like an uneasy slumber. And then, still clinging to the hope that she'd come around in the morning, he shambled to the other end of the room and climbed into bed.

Worn out by Girl's tears, Arno slept deeply. But Girl did not. She awoke.

We want what we want. And even if we don't know what that might be, our feet will take us there and our hands will know what to reach for when we've arrived. Girl's feet took her slip-sliding down the fish-bone staircase and past B.K. Tjoa's landing into the mirrored cave of the dining room and through the black tube of the kitchen to the shining red door and the back garden where the frangipani tree was and the mynahs roosted. Arno and Cook had forgotten to re-arm the security system after carrying Girl into the house, and all was quiet as

Girl's hands pulled her up the tree and reached through the thick long leaves and furled flower buds to settle her in a crook where two branches separated. It was there, in the still night, that she finally anchored her dizzy and disoriented body, and hung her two feet out into the open air.

In the after-midnight dark, Girl couldn't see those two feet and ten toes dangling over the wash lines drooping with washing. Nor could she see the basins and stones of the wash yard. But it didn't matter. She had risen above all that—the sick, the slop, the shit. She had become a ghost so weightless even the birds didn't know she was there among them. No wings rustled. No yellow eyes opened. No red bird throats screeched. Except for the fruit bats sending their high-pitched whistles into the night, all was quiet. Even the growling freeway beyond the back wall was still.

Girl waited. The tree branches bore her body easily. She could stay all night and no one would find her up there, she thought. But of course, morning would come. And then what? B.K. Tjoa would wake, walk out to his balcony for his morning cigarette and look down. Arno would peek out from his dormer window. And there she would be.

No, she couldn't stay. She had to be away.

We want what we want and our feet will take us wherever to find it. Girl's feet were pointed at the top of the back wall, a surface the width of ten toes. Beyond that wall, behind the divide of trees and bushes, was the freeway that connected everything to everywhere. A way for her feet to take her home to Buffalo Boy. If she could get to it.

She crawled further out along a branch until she could sense the top of the wall under her. Willing her hands to hold on, she slowly swung her body outwards and down. The branch creaked.

A bird called out in alarm. There was a flurry of beating wings and frantic screeching, followed by a swarm of beaks pecking at Girl's face and arms and hands. She let go.

She fell towards the staring headlights of the first lorry of the day. Its beams pierced up and through the trees on the slope, washing over her and lighting up the shards of glass on the top of the wall. And as she plummeted towards the shards, she wondered, who had shattered bottles and scattered them onto the wet cement of the wall way back when? How had they known then that girls would try to use this tree to escape?

28

Even if Girl regains consciousness, she is never going to say yes, Sister Mary Michael realizes. Girl had thought Arno was trustworthy and he'd disappointed her. She won't forgive him, ever, no matter how hard he tries to change her mind.

Arno and the nun have left the sad little wash yard and are sitting down to breakfast in the mirrored dining room. Sister Mary Michael is eating more porridge and pickles. Arno is tucking into a full English breakfast. Fortified by bacon, sausages, eggs and toast, his hopes that Girl will say yes have risen again.

'I'm not that interested in the money or the trust,' he shares with the nun. 'I'd be entirely happy if Girl would just agree to marry me.'

Going by how angry he'd been about his aunts' appropriation of control over the trust, the nun knows this can't be true. All she says though is, 'You want Girl to say yes as in go through with that proxy wedding you were trying to orchestrate yesterday?'

Arno giggles, embarrassed.

'Well, that was a bit OTT,' he admits. 'Where I am now, a simple yes will do. No ceremony or anything needed.'

'But she's in a coma. And even if she isn't, she's half-way across town. How do you think you'd manage to hear her?'

Arno picks up his never far away Girl doll. 'Her,' he says, patting the doll's hair, 'Girl speaks through her. That's how we communicate.'

'All the way from her bed in the nursing home?' the nun asks.

'Well, it would be better if I was right next to her. And if we had a go-between, like they have in her village,' Arno allows. He shoots Sister Mary Michael an expectant smile. 'Why don't you be my go-between and come with me to ask her,' he suggests.

And then, before the nun can answer, he drags her by the hand to Gran's room.

'This is why I think she'll say yes . . .' he says, bending down to retrieve the doll house from the carton the nun had deposited it in the previous night.

Unlocking it, he shows her the string of talismans for the first time and shares what he thinks each of them means.

When he's done, he says, 'We can take these to her with my Girl doll. And you can ask her for me. Okay?'

And because it is no more outlandish than many of the other requests Sister Mary Michael receives, she doesn't hesitate to say, 'Yes.'

* * *

They arrive at the nursing home with the Girl doll and the talismans nestled in a baby basket, and are shown to the far corner of ward that smells of old bodies, stale urine and diaper cream. There, on a bed with week old sheets, is Girl. Her eyes closed, seemingly dead to the world.

'There she is,' the nun says. 'Go to her.'

Arno approaches the bed and curves his big hands around Girl's waxy cheeks. Then he begins to pat the light sheet covering her prone body, starting at her shoulders and moving on to her chest, her belly, her legs and her feet before returning to her inert cheeks and half-closed flaccid lips. He pats and pats as if he's trying to wake the life in her. But she does not respond.

'I thought it would be different if I came personally and asked, but it's still a no,' he says to the nun. He tries to shrug it off. Then, rolling back his shoulders and puffing out his chest, he says to the nun, 'Could you try?'

The nun moves nearer and touches Girl's water-swelled hand. The girl is clinically alive, but she isn't present. 'It's the same kind of nothing you fell into last night,' she says to Arno.

'What nothing?' Arno asks.

It's a mistake mentioning that small fact, Sister Mary Michael realizes. They're only allowed to visit for thirty minutes. She'll be wasting time explaining how Girl's stillness feels exactly like the stillness on Arno's body when she touched him the previous night. How he'd been a breathing sweating shell temporarily vacated by the personalities that had spoken through him. Nothing but a body that exuded all kinds of human emissions and yet was devoid of any personal character.

Instead of answering, she traces her middle finger along the eyelashes peeking through Girl's taut eye sockets. They're prickly with dried tears and yet the nun feels no trace of grief. Girl's chest is rising and falling as she breaths, but her heart is neither laughing nor crying. She's like a guitar with broken strings. And if so, the nun wonders, how has she managed to enter the nun's dreams and join her comatose body to the nun's?

She puts her hand on Girl's head, shaved bald for hygiene's sake and as smooth as a porcelain doll's, and closes her eyes.

She brings her attention to her fingertips. Still, she feels nothing emanating from the girl.

'Because it wasn't just her, you know,' she hears Bing Fa's voice telling her. 'She had help.'

And indeed, the nun realizes, how could this helpless girl alone muster sufficient energy to reach out to her? The moving spirit behind Girl's appearances must have been Bing Fa.

She stares at the comatose girl with her swollen body, waxy skin and doll-bald head. She looks nothing like the teenage beauty Arno claims to love, nor the spirited young woman who attached herself to the nun in her sleep. There isn't even a resemblance to the dusty skinned village girl in the newspaper cuttings the Bishop had shown Sister Mary Michael. But the nun realizes, this is the real Girl. The one with a twenty-four-alphabet-long name on her passport and work permit. A barely alive mass of flesh wrapped around sluggishly coursing blood.

'Look at her,' she says to Arno. 'She's not in a fit state to marry anyone.'

'She could be in a better state if she said yes,' he replies. 'She'd wake up then.'

'But the way she is, how might she say yes?'

'She speaks to me,' Arno says. 'I hear her.' He taps his chest and his temple and explains, 'In here and here.' And then, he adds, 'As you do too.'

'But how does she do it?'

'We're joined, like this,' Arno says, twining his index and middle fingers together. 'I joined us with some of that red thread. That's why we can communicate. At least between this nursing home and the ash house.' He folds his arms then and smirks knowingly at the nun. 'That's why,' he tells her, 'That's why I know she entered you last night to tell you her story. She entered you all the way through, until you could feel what she was feeling. Feelings you never felt before.'

'Perhaps,' the nun says, trying to keep her response neutral. 'But it could just as well be a story you're making up.'

The boy is not fazed by her apparent disbelief.

'Well, if you don't buy that, how about this?' he says. And then he begins to tell her in a sing-song old-time story-teller's voice, 'Once upon a time there was a Tjoa heir who'd set his hopes on becoming a magician. And when it looked like that heir wasn't going to do too well at his PSLE's, his Gran decided to make those wishes come true. She threw a whole lot of money at courses on hypnotism, card tricks, sleight of hand and voice throwing. And it turned out, that Tjoa heir was a natural at it.'

He waves a hand towards an old woman in one of the beds adjoining Girl's. 'She looks enough like Gran. Ask her how I do it.'

As if pulled on strings, Sister Mary Michael finds her head turning towards the old woman. And out of the old woman's sagging mouth, she hears the by now familiar voice at once close yet distant, at once suggestive of the closest intimacies and the cruellest taunts.

'It's all an illusion,' the voice says. 'An illusion.'

This is the first manifestation Sister Mary Michael records in her official notes. That voice saying those words which couldn't possibly be coming from the unknown old woman nor from Arno either, because she'd heard the voice before she ever laid eyes on either of them, she writes by way of explanation. It's a voice which must belong to someone or something that's manifesting through the two of them and is penetrating her as well.

This is also when she makes her first official enquiry, which she also records. She crosses herself and pivots to face Arno squarely. And then she demands, 'In the name of our Lord Jesus Christ, tell me your name. Your true name.'

Arno flinches at the mention of the Lord, another sign of spiritual affliction, the nun records. 'You shouldn't make me do that you know, play jokes like that on you,' he complains. 'I'm me, Arno Tjoa, the useless guy with more than enough imagination to drive himself and all his aunts crazy. That's who I am.'

'Are you sure?' the nun pushes.

'Does it matter?' he replies. 'Whatever you see and hear, that's the way things are. There's nothing I can do about it.'

It's the perfect opening for the nun. 'Then let me help you,' she offers.

Arno pulls out the string of talismans. 'Can you make her forgive me for this?' he asks, pointing to the lock of black hair hanging from the end of the skein. 'Forgive me, then say yes.'

'What does it matter if she says yes? She's out of protective custody and the authorities are sending her home. Your aunt Irene called the Medevac on Friday morning. I hear Girl will be leaving this coming Thursday.'

'I don't care about her body. You're a Sister of Succour. You know that's not what matters. It's her soul I want. Once I have her soul, I'll be able to put it anywhere. Even in here,' Arno says, pointing to his Girl doll.

'Until someone dies, the body and the soul are a single unity,' the nun intones despite having seen far too many exceptions to be certain about that piece of doctrine.

'She's as good as dead. Half the time she isn't even in her body any more. Haven't you noticed how she's been wandering about, watching us and speaking to me and through me?'

'If she's so steadfastly refusing to marry you, why would she do that?' the nun asks.

'Because we're connected,' Arno declares. 'We're connected even beyond death.'

'When she dies, she'll enter another realm,' the nun tries to tell him patiently. 'A realm beyond human reach.'

'But you can do something about that,' Arno says, pulling at the crucifix pinned on the nun's blouse. 'You've come from the Bishop. You can ask him to do it. To conduct a wedding for me and Girl.'

'She isn't a Catholic.'

'But I am, and I'm the one doing the asking.'

'The Bishop won't say yes without Girl's consent. And look at her! She isn't capable of giving consent.'

'But he must,' Arno insists in a sibilant whisper. 'You have to ask him! You must! I want a wedding and he has to say yes. He has to!' He pushes against the nun with his enormous belly until he's backed her up against the edge of the girl's bed. 'You have to ask him.'

Sister Mary Michael is not intimidated. She brings her face to Arno's. 'Are you telling me you want to be like your Grandpa Tjoa then? Make another Bing Fa? Hold a woman captive until she turns into a spite-filled spirit?' she asks him, pushing gently against his belly. 'That's not what you want for your Girl, is it?'

Arno stands and strokes the Girl doll's hair. 'No,' he whispers finally. And then twisting on the skein of talismans, he adds, 'It's just that I don't know why she won't forgive me. I did it out of the kindness of my heart. Out of love. They can't hang a man for kindness. Nor for love either. Not even if it's love that a woman doesn't want. I offered a helping hand. It was up to Girl whether to take it or not. I didn't force anything on her, least of all my body. All I did was take a lock of her hair.'

'Without her permission,' the nun reminds him.

'All right. Okay. She didn't say I could take it. But there's no harm done. It's only a down-payment. If she doesn't say yes, I'll take the lock out from the doll house and give it back to her and let her go her way. And yes, that plait of hers too. I suppose that was a bit more than a lock, that plait. But that's not a problem. I've put it in a safe place. Not in the doll house. I know better. But I'll give that back to her too. For sure. I promise.'

So far, the nun has not seen the plait Girl mourned and Arno stole. Still, it's in her mind when she suggests, 'What about doing it right now?'

'But what will happen to me afterwards?' he asks.

'You'll be released from what's bound you since you were seventeen,' the nun replies. 'You'll be free and no longer beholden to any promises you made to Bing Fa.'

'But I don't need that. I've already seen through Bing Fa and so I'm already free of her,' Arno says. He clutches the Girl doll tighter. 'What's binding me is her, don't you see? And I don't want to be free of her. Not ever.'

'She hasn't said yes to you all this while. Why not let her go her way, as you say?'

Arno looks at the nun, bewildered. 'Why not? Can't you see why not? Gran's dead. The diva's thrown me aside. And no matter what I say about the house, my aunts will find a way to steal it from me. And then, what? If I don't hold on to Girl, what's left?'

The nun points to the Girl doll. 'You'll have a very nice doll. One of the thousands in your very valuable very famous collection,' she tells him. Then, she unpins the crucifix from her blouse and fastens it onto Arno's T-shirt. 'And you'll have this too,' she tells him softly. 'A new life. In Him.'

Arno looks down at the floor and then up at the ceiling.

'Have I told you before that god has never answered any of my prayers?' he says.

'Yes. Just yesterday in fact,' the nun replies. 'And what I'd said was, he always answers mine.'

'Ah, yes. I remember.'

He pauses to consider the matter, then says, 'Can you give me one last chance to convince Girl?'

It can't do any harm, the nun thinks. The boy might finally see how hopeless his obsession with the girl is. And perhaps the Lord might affect a renunciation then. And if not? Well, even though Sister Mary Michael's hasn't spent a full twenty-four hours with Arno, she has enough evidence to recommend a full deliverance. If he can't be convinced today, the Bishop will be unbinding him soon enough.

'All right. But you've to do it my way,' she tells him.

To her surprise, the boy nods. And when she opens her palm to take the skein of talismans from him, he hands them over without protest.

She prays over the objects tied to the hair and silk string and sprinkles them with Holy Water, then unties the girl's lock of hair and hands it to Arno.

'Just this,' she says. 'Give it back to her with your apologies. Then we'll see what happens next.'

Holding the lock of hair like a brush, Arno goes up to Girl and circles the swell of her closed eyelids and cheeks and the hollow of her throat with it, all the while pleading with her to marry him. This continues for about fifteen minutes, as Sister Mary Michael prays. Girl is stubbornly unresponsive throughout. And then, what the nun prays for comes to pass. Arno loses patience, flings the lock down on the girl's chest and tells her three times that he's done with her.

In Girl's culture, this is renunciation. Despite not having gone through the rite of unbinding, she is now free of Arno. And once she's free of Arno, she's also free of the ash house and the doings in it. A Miracle, come to pass in a most unexpected way, Sister Mary Michael realizes.

She murmurs a thanksgiving. She would like to have done more for Girl. But it has not been given her to change the world Girl was born into. As for saving Girl from the pitfalls of the flesh, even if she had come earlier, Bing Fa would have outplayed her at that game. In the circumstances, Arno's renunciation is the best that can happen, and for that, she must be grateful.

She leans over Girl and plants a kiss on her forehead.

'Go with providence,' she bids the girl.

Turning to Arno, she tells him, 'There, you've earned her forgiveness.'

But Arno, realizing what he's done unwittingly, can only look at her with stricken eyes.

* * *

In a daze, Arno allows Sister Mary Michael to take Girl's lock of hair from him, fold it in a piece of tissue and tuck it into the suitcase underneath her bed, the one she'd brought with her from her village. He does not protest when the nun tells him to bid Girl goodbye. Clutching the baby basket whose contents are now minus a lock of blue-black hair, he follows her out of the ward and into his aunt Irene's car without a word.

It is only when the car comes off the freeway and turns into the street running up the hill that he speaks.

Sister Mary Michael is expecting a tantrum, or at least an accusation. Instead, he asks quite calmly, 'That's it? That's how you free me?'

'Not quite,' the nun says. 'That was just to unbind you from Girl.'

'And then?'

'There's still all the curses and promises around the skein of talismans. The Bishop will need to go to the house to do a blessing and an unbinding for you and your family. That's going to take a few days. I've to write up my report. And we'll have to find a day that suits all your aunts.'

'My aunts! Why them?'

Sister Mary Michael doesn't want to go into the reasons with the driver sitting in front overhearing everything.

'Let's wait till we're back inside your Gran's room,' she says.

* * *

Bing Fa watches with her non-existent heart held in tight as Sister Mary Michael pulls the string of talismans from the baby basket, winds it into a coil and places it on the black toy table in Gran's room. Then she turns to the boy.

'You had things to ask me?' she says to Arno.

Arno nods. 'You said you had to wait on my aunts. Why them? I thought it was just me and Bing Fa, and maybe my diva doll and the doll house.'

'Based on everything you've said and everything else I've experienced in this house, that string of talismans contains promises and spells made over at least three generations,' the nun explains. 'There's a high probability it's not just Girl or you or your father or grandfather who were tied to these spells.

Your aunts probably are too. Big Mother must have offered something for your grandfather's return to sanity. Why not her daughters?'

'I guess,' Arno mutters.

'Well, I'm sure. Sure enough to put it in my report,' Sister Mary Michael replies, momentarily forgetting some of the last-minute retractions she's had to make in the past.

'Remember the six Barbies you hung over the door panels?' she reminds him. 'Those were your aunts, you said. So even if they weren't part of the old spells, you've involved them with that little tableau.'

'It was a bit of imagination, not a spell,' he protests.

'Perhaps you didn't cast it. But believe me, something reached out to them through that scene you enacted,' the nun insists.

Still, Arno argues. 'They won't believe you. They won't come.'

'They'll come, your aunt Irene at the very least,' the nun assures him. 'Your aunt Irene was the one who asked the Bishop for help. He'll persuade her. And as for believing me. She won't need to. She'll understand.' She points to the talismans on the table. 'She just has to look at these talismans, that's all.'

Sister Mary Michael hasn't really understood the purport of the words she's just uttered. But there they are as the nun turns the key of the doll house and Bing Fa's song broadcasts itself into the room once again. These are the words Bing Fa has waited almost 100 years to hear.

'It's going to happen,' Bing Fa feels her heart singing. 'It's surely going to happen.'

29

And there they are on Tuesday, three days later: the Tjoa sisters, arrived and standing in a row in the ash house foyer like they used to stand when they were young girls. The four younger girls, Eileen, and Irene.

Irene! Bing Fa feels her heart swell.

Irene has ensured they are all dressed appropriately. Not in their usual black, Bing Fa is pleased to see, but in a medley of happy jubilant colours that exactly match the diva's mood today. The younger sisters are in variations of pastels. Eileen is in white. And Irene? Irene is in red. Bright red. The colour of power. Bing Fa's colour.

* * *

An exorcism, of all things! Irene shifts uneasily as she waits in the line. She's going to be hard put to explain to anyone why she, Irene Tjoa, has spent her Monday rescheduling appointments and cajoling her sisters to gather here in the ash house on this Tuesday afternoon to wait for a cleric to arrive, to begin the necessary.

The Bishop was convincing, that's all she thinks she can say.

When His Grace called her on Sunday, he'd hemmed and hawed about what the necessary was. 'A deliverance for Arno.

An unbinding for the Tjoa ladies. A cleansing for the house,' he'd said. In short, an exorcism, Irene had concluded.

It goes without saying, Irene has told herself, one doesn't go around proclaiming a belief in the imponderables. But imponderables can't be simply dismissed either. The ash house is old and hasn't had a cleansing since Big Mother's legendary cleanout around the time Irene was born. Another one is long overdue. From the recent worsening in Arno's behavior it's clear they aren't simply dealing with a case of bad seed passing from father to son.

'It was remiss of me not to have arranged a cleansing sooner,' Irene had confessed to the Bishop. Late is better than never, though. And now they're here, even Eileen, the doubting one. They're here, all six of them, standing still and solemn, all doubts suspended for the duration of the exercise.

They'll be done before dinner Irene has promised. But His Grace is taking his graceful time. When he finally breezes in, it's ten past the hour and still he's walking easy as you please with his assistant in tow not at all abashed about being late.

Shepherding Irene and her sisters into Gran's room as if they're in his house and not the reverse, he announces, 'We're going to start the ritual proper in the attic, with Arno. Before that however, I thought I'd let Cook watch over him while we give you the whole story and get any questions you may have out of the way. And to do that . . .' he waves genially at the assistant who has followed him into the room, 'Here's Sister Mary Michael Chan who spent two days with Arno. She's the one who did the assessment and made the recommendation.'

The assistant is a shrivelled up old nun whom Irene suspects is on the verge of senility. Instead of going straight into the story, she begins to tell Irene and her sisters about her younger days when she'd been their schoolmate.

Irene doesn't remember her. Nor she senses do her sisters. However, it would be rude not to pretend otherwise given how warmly the little nun is greeting them. After all Big Mother did not train them up for nothing. And so, they all smile and make the required noises about how long it has been and how everyone has changed. They allow the little nun her reminiscences about Tjoa Ek Kia's Cadillac and the choir and their a cappella group.

'I was always carried away by your singing. It was like angels,' the nun gushes.

'We're more like toads now,' Eileen says.

'If we were to sing at all,' one of the others adds. 'Because, we haven't you know? Not in years. Not since Irene lost her voice.'

This nugget of information seems to affect the nun unduly. She turns to look at Irene with almost teary eyes. 'You lost your voice and stopped singing?'

There's nothing to be gained from Irene not telling the truth. 'I married a smoker and second-hand smoke does things to the vocal cords,' she says.

It had been no contest between a monied marriage and the prospect of audition after audition in faraway cold countries for the rest of her life. 'One has to make choices,' Big Mother used to say. 'One can be the wife with all the power or the mistress with all the love.' There was no need for Big Mother to explain more. One did the necessary.

'It doesn't matter,' she tries to comfort the nun who seems so unnaturally bereft. 'We've found other things to do together.'

Eileen chuckles. 'Yes. We lunch. And we complain about our husbands. And we plot how we can chuck our brother and nephew out of here.'

Irene sighs inwardly. Like their brother B.K., Eileen's mouth is prone to running off in a mean vinegarish way. It gives Eileen pleasure, Irene knows, to see how the nun cringes at her words.

'Moving on doesn't mean moving anybody out,' Irene says. 'We're just trying to find a good solution within all the constraints we have, that's all.'

This is her cue for everyone to get back to business—the items lying out on Gran's table. Six Barbie dolls wrapped in tissue, a black plastic doll box, a doll dressed in a red qipao, and a doll house Irene vaguely remembers playing with. And last, but not least, the problem upstairs in the attic—Arno lying on his bed pretending to be dead.

'Sister Mary Michael,' the Bishop prompts.

The nun straightens her shrivelled body then totters over to the table and unwraps the dolls.

Irene and her sisters have been told who the dolls represent. Nonetheless she hears one gasp then another as the dolls' half- and full-grown naked bodies are revealed.

'It's us,' Eileen says. 'Are you suggesting he's casting spells on us?'

'Not quite,' Sister Mary Michael explains. 'Arno couldn't remember hanging the dolls up. It's only later, upon consideration, that he gave the impression he'd put you all on trial and was sentencing you by proxy. There was probably a spell cast, but Arno was only a channel.'

'Like something possessed him and made him do it,' another sister comments.

'Whatever! However!' Eileen interrupts. 'Arno doesn't need to be possessed to do what he did. The fact is, if he believes this would harm us, he can't be in his right mind.'

Eileen is in denial, Irene realizes. The nun is right. Arno is only a channel. The stuttering fat boy she knows is not capable of the challenge she sees in those staring doll eyes, nor the malice gleaming from their naked plastic bodies.

'There's more, isn't there Sister?' she prompts the nun.

The nun nods, then hands around some photos.

'This is what the room looked like when I arrived at the house on Friday evening,' she tells them. 'There are the dolls. And there's the wedding tableau. Arno was preparing to marry Girl, with a doll as proxy. And all of you, or rather the dolls representing you, were to be witnesses.' And then, pointing to the fully-dressed doll in the Chinese costume that's also on the table, she adds, 'And this other doll too.'

The nun's big eyes, made larger by her reading glasses, pass slowly from Irene to Eileen to the others. 'Is there anything else I can tell you?' she asks.

Irene would have thought the images of the dolls hanging by their hair with their pointed feet desperately reaching for firm ground and the contrast with the pretty hopefulness of the wedding setting would be enough for everyone. If Arno is not mad, then clearly he's possessed. They should all be getting on with the exorcism, no further questions needed. Yet, it is she herself who asks, 'The Chinese doll, who does she represent?'

'It's your father's second wife, the pipa diva Bing Fa,' the nun answers. 'It seems this persona and Arno are intricately bound. I believe she appears to him and he sometimes channels her. The girl was in contact with her too. And there are indications she appeared to your father's youngest wife as well.'

'But we were told Bing Fa died before any of us were born,' Eileen protests. She turns to the Bishop. 'Doesn't the church say there are no such things as ghosts? Why is Sister saying she's haunting us?'

The Bishop repeats what he'd said to Irene on Sunday evening. 'According to doctrine, the spirits of the dead depart for heaven, hell or purgatory. What lingers are unclean spirits who are servants of the evil one. The entity we're talking about is unlikely to be the actual spirit or soul of your father's second wife, the pipa player Bing Fa. More probably it's something that manifests as her. That's what Sister means when she says Arno is channelling Bing Fa or speaking with her. It's simply a convenient way of naming the malign entity.'

'Such an entity would have its own name, wouldn't it?' Irene asks.

'Yes, it would, and that's what we are aiming to find out when we go upstairs for the rite with Arno.'

'And that will be soon?'

'Once Sister finishes telling you about this China doll,' he says, giving the nun another nod.

The nun continues, 'As you've all been informed, I took Arno to see the girl on Saturday and persuaded him to let her go. That closure with the girl encouraged him to break with this pipa doll too.'

Irene catches a small self-satisfied smile on the nun's face as she conveys that information. 'That's a significant step since he's seen this doll as a proxy for the Bing Fa persona for so many years,' she says.

'But what do you mean about breaking with this doll?' Irene asks.

In answer, the nun asks Irene, 'Are you familiar with the big crocodile-skin trunk in the attic?'

'Yes, it was my father's and used to be in his office. I had it moved into the attic after he died.'

'Your father's. I see . . .' The nun nods as if another loose end has been tied.

'Well, that trunk was where Arno kept his pipa doll as well as the doll house which serves as the repository for a string of talismans binding your father and his descendants to the persona called Bing Fa. It's as much a part of the binding as the skein of talismans,' the nun tells the sisters. 'Yet, when we got back from our visit to the girl, Arno decided to make a clean break with it and with the doll.'

She passes out another set of photos, this time of Arno marking verticals and horizontals on a steamer trunk's surface and then prising the squares of crocodile skin off the underlying cardboard. 'As you can see,' the nun says, 'Arno went straight to the trunk and began slicing through the skin with an X-Acto knife. He wasn't violent. Resigned would be more the word. He might as well, he said. He'd promised his grandfather to free the diva and since it was over with Girl, he thought he should cut away his other ties as well.'

The images remind Irene of a visit she'd made to a wholesale leather works to buy a crocodile-skin handbag. It's as if Arno is skinning an animal, except that there's no blood.

'What did Arno want to do with all the skin?' Irene asks.

The nun points to the black plastic box next to the doll house, which Irene now sees is lined with rust-red fragments of crocodile skin. 'He asked us to put the diva doll in there and take everything down to the back garden. We were to conduct a prayer of renunciation with him and then burn everything,' she informs them.

'And will you? Is that the proper thing to do?' Irene wants to know.

'I'll be doing it,' the Bishop answers. 'And yes, that's the proper thing to do to a malefice. We bless it. And then we burn it, on the stump of the frangipani tree you cut down.'

'And when will that be?' Irene asks

'As soon as we're done with Arno,' the Bishop replies.

* * *

Arno is sitting on the attic floor in his work area, facing his dolls, with his back to the landing. He is staring at the plastic fronts of his doll boxes with an expression as impassive as the dolls. His hands, though, are not impassive. Rather they're busily ripping away the clothing from a doll in his hands, his Girl doll, whom he's dressed again in her wedding kebaya.

Irene watches as Arno's thumbs dig under the rose border of the kebaya then poke through to split the lace. As his surprisingly delicate fingers pull at the waistband of the sarong, and as his big ham fists close, one around the doll's lower half, the other around the top. He twists, the way Irene had been taught to twist when pulling apart the thighs and drumsticks of chicken legs. Then like the chicken legs, the doll too falls apart.

'He woke up wheezing,' Irene hears Cook saying. 'I went to the bathroom to get his medicine. And when I came out, he was here. Doing this.'

She sees the nun kneel beside Arno and ask in a very quiet voice, 'Why?'

'I don't . . . I mean I didn't know . . . I forgot it only needed three words to let her go,' she hears Arno answer in a piteous mewl.

His hands twist the doll's arms from its torso and pull the doll's legs from the lower half of its body. He lays all four limbs out neatly in a row as if he's setting up a butcher's display. He places the giblet-sized chunk that used to be the doll's pelvis beside its limbs. And then, he snaps out the doll's head.

'Don't,' Irene hears the nun say.

And in the same instant she also hears the Bishop roar, 'I command you, in the Name of the Father and the-'

'Why not?' Arno asks. 'It's got nothing to do with Girl now. She's free. She won't feel any of this.'

'It's not nice,' the nun tells him.

'Nice?' Arno looks away from his doll shelves and towards the dusk-lit memory room beyond the French doors. 'Sunsets are nice. But heartbreak? Heartbreak isn't,' he murmurs as he picks up an X-Acto knife and starts to hack at the doll's hair.

Irene hears the Bishop whispering to the nun and sees the nun flitting behind her sisters to fetch the Bishop's surplice and purple stole and a wooden case from which she pulls a crucifix, a bottle of Holy Water, small containers of oil and salt, and finally prayer sheets, a prayer book and a rosary.

The Bishop moves to a corner to pray and dress himself. The nun hands Irene the rosary. 'I'll be assisting his Grace with the ritual. Can you lead your sisters to pray the Rosary to support us?'

'Of course,' Irene says, turning to stare hard at Eileen. The way Arno is, surely Eileen knows that even her doubting prayers are needed.

'Cook,' the Bishop calls. 'Can you squat down behind Arno and hold him?'

Cook obeys.

The Bishop signs a cross in the air.

It begins.

* * *

An exorcism! Of all things, the thought comes to Irene again. No doubt she has watched the movies and read the books. She has even attended a talk organized by her parish. But still, she's not ready.

Irene had expected drama—spitting and cursing, demonic voicings, exhibitions of inhuman strength. There's none of that. It's just gabbling, and more gabbling. The Bishop signing and sprinkling and asking for mercy. The nun echoing. The Bishop intoning the Litany of Saints. The Bishop saying an intercessory prayer beginning with 'We sinners' that makes Irene feel suddenly resentful. The Bishop commanding obedience from the 'unclean spirit' and its 'minions'. And then the nun signalling to Irene to start the rosary with her sisters, and the Bishop laying hands on Arno.

Irene holds her breath when this happens. Something dramatic should take place now, surely. But all Arno does is glance up briefly at the Bishop and brush the hands away.

Undaunted, the Bishop reads out a gospel account of an exorcism, and another, and then a third as Irene leads her sisters into the fourth decade of Hail Marys. And all the while, on the floor in front of them, Arno goes on with his business—the depilation of his doll, one hank of hair at a time.

Suddenly the memory of a much younger Arno superimposes itself over the mound of man-flesh at Irene's feet. Arno is seven or eight years old and Cook is squatting behind him as she's doing now. Irene is staring down at him, as she is now. They're at the beach and Arno is hacking the tentacles off a jellyfish. The wind is blowing in from the sea. A thunderstorm is coming in. She, Irene, is whispering a Hail Mary.

'Pray for us sinners . . .' Irene hears herself saying again. Now though, she isn't at the beach. She's in the ash house attic, praying with her sisters as the Bishop and nun go about their sprinkling and crossing and gabbling. The image of the young Arno is gone. But the recollection of how violent he had been, and how shocked she was, remains.

He had been bitten by a jelly fish and had decided to take revenge on one of its kin, unfortunately washed onto the beach by the oncoming storm.

'Leave them alone,' Cook had said, as she squatted behind him.

But he hadn't let them be. 'They hurt me. I'm hurting them back,' he'd replied.

'Jellyfish sting. You can't blame them. That's what they do,' Irene had told him.

'And this one's dead anyway. You're wasting your time taking revenge,' Cook had added.

And now, as Irene and her sisters continue to hail Mary and bless the fruit of her womb and the Bishop and nun finish up their readings, Cook tells Arno the same thing. 'It's only a doll, you're wasting your time trying to take revenge on it,' she says.

But as he'd done those many years ago, Arno ignores the advice.

By this time, he has reduced the doll to a mound of shredded plastic and wire strand fluffs of hair which he wraps in a square of jute cloth. 'Here. I'm done. Do whatever you want with it,' he says, handing the package to the Bishop. Then he collapses backwards into Cook's arms, in a dead faint.

Irene starts. Finally, here's a sign she's read about. This is it. Resistance. A definite symptom of possession.

The Bishop and nun seem to think so too. Sister Mary Michael hands the Bishop the crucifix, which he waves in front of Arno's unconscious form like a sword, all the while spitting out 'Behold the Cross' and 'Begone' and 'I cast you out' while the nun joins the sisters in their Hail Marys.

It takes ten more decades of the Rosary. Then, as suddenly as he's fallen into his faint, Arno opens his eyes and sits up, apparently returned to himself. But Irene wonders, which is Arno's true self? The socially inept fat boy she's so accustomed to disparaging, or the maniac she's just witnessed mutilating a plastic doll?

30

No one wants to linger in the attic after the ceremony. It's all too much, the incense hanging heavy and dank in the air, the floor slimy with Holy Water. The sisters are more than glad to leave Arno reading fashion magazines with a watchful Cook and crowd into the lift. They're quiet as mice, with only Eileen venturing a question.

'Are we sure he'll be fine from now on? Are we sure he won't have any more fits?' she asks the Bishop.

'Nothing's for certain,' he replies. 'Arno is attracted to that power and it may come back to tempt him again. Only regular attendance at Mass, Confession and Holy Communion, can protect him.'

'But he won't go, unless someone makes him,' Eileen says.

'And if he doesn't, all this would have been a waste of time,' another sister adds.

'I'll see to it,' Irene hears herself say.

She would have seen to it anyway, she supposes, even if Eileen hadn't raised the issue. It's what comes with being the eldest, the responsibility that goes with the privilege. That had been Big Mother's constant refrain when she lined the sisters up for their weekly accounting. One stroke of the rotan on Eileen's palm for being rude, another four strokes on each of the others' palms for infringements Irene has forgotten. And for Irene who hadn't done anything, five strokes, because she was the oldest sister and she'd failed in overseeing the rest of them.

The beatings weren't personal, Big Mother used to tell Irene. She was simply doing what she thought right by her oldest. And she'd proved it when she passed on. She'd left Irene her best jewellery, including the diamond belt buckle Eileen coveted.

If anyone should feel hard done by, Irene thinks, it's Eileen. Big Mother and Eileen never got along. No need to be a genius to understand why though. It's Eileen's mouth, as tactless now as when she was seven.

'Well, if you move him in with you, that solves a lot of things,' Eileen's tells everyone just right then. 'Moving on and moving out would be one and the same, regardless of what you said earlier. We'd be free to do what we want with this place. And hand over half of the spoils to the church. His Grace would commend that, I'm sure.'

The Bishop pretends he hasn't heard Eileen. Instead, he tells them, 'It's nearly five and I've been informed you all need to leave by seven. I'm thinking then that we go ahead with unbinding all of you first, after which Sister and I can do a cleansing for the house.'

There are no objections. The Tjoa sisters follow him back into Gran's room like dutiful schoolgirls. The Bishop motions them towards the blackwood chairs aligned on the long sides of the toy table, then seats himself in another one near the door panels. Sister Mary Michael comes into the room last and slides past everybody to take the chair nearest the doll house.

At a nod from the Bishop, the nun pushes the doll house towards the sisters. 'This is one of the malefices we're concerned about, the one that houses all the others,' she announces.

'Malefices are objects used to channel curses towards targets. And in this instance, the targets are the members of your family,' the Bishop adds.

He continues, 'Sister will be opening the doll house and will be showing the talismans inside to you and explaining their significance. This will give you more clarity about who has been or may be bound by the curses. And since everything's cursed, I'd like to ask that you don't touch them, no matter how tempted you are.'

His eyes scan the six sisters. 'This is crucial. So may I have your agreement please?'

Eileen strokes her jaw with her index finger, then flicks it suddenly against the back of her earring. 'You're the expert,' she says lightly, almost rudely.

The nun takes that as agreement and continues with her explanation. 'According to Arno, who claims to have heard part of the story from your father's youngest wife, Gran, and learnt the rest in dreams sent by Bing Fa, she was bound to this family and imprisoned inside the house by your Big Mother. The binding spell resides in a string of hair to which your father's personal belongings and some of Bing Fa's are tied. Over time, this spirit learnt to escape its prison and contact members of the household, whom she'd tempt with favours. In return for these favours, it would ask them to free it. As a deposit of good faith, it would also ask the supplicants for something personal, for example a lock of hair from the supplicants or a loved one. Apparently, it would waive outstanding debts if the supplicant or their loved one learnt the spirit's signature song.'

Sister Mary Michael pauses here and points to the front of the doll house. 'As we now know, none of the supplicants ever released the spirit. It is still in there, attached to the string of hair. As for the music . . .' She slots the key into the keyhole of the front door. The front façade of the house begins to swing open, and as it does, the jerking tinny tune sputters into the room.

'This is the melody Arno hums almost constantly,' the nun tells the sisters after the house is fully opened and the music has stopped. 'According to Cook, it's also a favourite tune of your brother B.K.. It was the first indication both Arno and his father were under the influence of the same spirit.'

'No, that's rubbish!' Eileen protests. 'How could anyone possibly be charmed by that music?' she asks, raising unbelieving eyebrows at both the Bishop and the nun.

'That's precisely it,' Sister Mary Michael replies. 'No one in their right mind would find this music enchanting. But they were caught. They were tricked into hearing something else by a preternatural force. A force in this house.'

'You're suggesting they were possessed,' Irene says.

'We're not just suggesting it,' the Bishop answers. 'In the case of Arno, we know it. His reaction during the ritual we completed shows it isn't a hypothesis.'

'But, as far as my brother B.K. is concerned, another hypothesis might be unholy spirits of the liquid variety,' Eileen says, to answering giggles from her younger sisters.

Irene glares at everyone.

The giggling stops.

'Please continue, Sister,' she says to the nun.

The nun reaches into the doll house and slowly draws out a skein of talismans.

'We believe that this string with the charms tied to it contains a series of spells that bind the whole family,' the Bishop explains pointing in turn to each of the charms and explaining them,

from the glass pipa trinket, to Tjoa Ek Kia's personal items, to
the wads of tissue coated with hair. When he's finally done, he
takes a long breath and looks around once more at Irene and her
sisters to ensure he has their attention. 'As you can understand,
this string represents a multi-generational family binding. That's
why we asked all of you to come. As directors of the family trust,
you represent the family line. As we unbind you, we will be
unbinding the whole family.'

'Big Mother never told us anything about this. It can't be
true. If that's what you heard from Arno, well!' Eileen protests,
while in the background, Irene hears her other sisters clicking
their tongues in disbelief, and mumbling 'mumbo-jumbo' and
'it's too fantastic' in disbelieving tones.

Although Irene does not say anything, she too shares her
sisters' doubts. The tangled length of hair and silk with the so-
called talismans knotted to it has the same sorry insignificant air
as the music that had jerked into the room. The grubby lump of
god-knows-what is particularly pathetic. It's all detritus, stuff shed
in the course of ordinary living. The pipe cleaner, the ear pick, the
shoelace, the coins . . . She had seen similar objects on her father's
desk in his trading room. Sometimes, there'd even been a short
hair or two, overgrowths pulled from the mole on his left cheek or
the inside of his ears. They're things one would sweep away into a
dustpan, then deposit in a rubbish heap for burning.

They are of no significance, Irene tells herself. But if so, why
is it that she finds herself reaching towards the string in spite of
the Bishop's admonitions? And why is her right index finger
dropping onto the scratched glass charm shaped like a pipa and
stroking it?

'I remember now,' she hears herself saying. 'I had one
exactly like this.'

And then, her mouth curves, her cheek bones lift and her face splits into the most enormous smile for no reason she can fathom.

* * *

Bing Fa hovers over the developing scene with bated breath. Finally, the charm is where it should be, below Irene's questioning index finger. And there are Tjoa Ek Kia's other daughters. Eileen waiting to pounce if Irene should make a mistake . . . And the others . . . One looking everywhere around the room but at Irene, another with eyebrows drawn together in worry, and two examining their nails. Not one of the five able to give Irene any guidance about what to do next.

Irene turns to the Bishop, who shakes his head. His answer is unambiguous. She is not to engage with whatever is calling to her. But that's not the answer Bing Fa wishes Irene to act on. She waits as Irene's eyes move towards Sister Mary Michael. Unchecked by the Bishop, the nun's frail fingers are picking at the knot attaching the pipa charm to the string of talismans. All the while, she's staring at Irene, her big black eyes hungry for something Irene can't give. Something Irene has lost. Her music.

But no . . . Bing Fa blows gently against Irene's throat. 'You could never lose that, precious. Not you,' she whispers into Irene's head.

The pipa charm now set free on the black surface of the table wobbles, catching a beam of the evening light reflecting off the koi pond. The beam bounces off the facets of glass and toward Irene. And just like that Irene remembers who Sister Mary Michael is—the underfed girl who used to hide behind the piano during Irene's and her sisters' private singing lessons.

The daughter of the very strict school nurse. Irene's most ardent admirer.

'I can't. I haven't sung in years,' Irene says to the nun.

The nun's eyes turn to the doll house. She nods almost imperceptibly. Irene has been given her answer. Reaching across the table, she pushes the front wall of the doll house shut, then turns the key to open the house again. The wall swings forward and the music begins to play once more, just as jerking and tinny as before. This time however a voice sings along to the music. Irene does not recognize whose voice it is at first. But as the singer gains confidence she realizes who it is. It's she, Irene, who's singing. '望断云山 . . . looking at the clouded mountains, 不见妈妈的慈颜 . . . my loving mother gone, 楼静羹残 . . . my passing the dying hours, 难对襟寝寒 . . . barely enduring the chilly quilt, 往日的欢乐 . . . the joy of bygone days, 方引出眼前的孤 . . . shows up my loneliness now, 梦魂无所 . . . while my soul dreams, 几时归来呦 . . . of your return, 妈妈呦 . . . O my mother.' It's she, Irene, who is filling Gran's room with unbearable longing.

'Oh, stop that!' Eileen says, slamming the doll house shut.

'Where on earth did that come from?' two of the others ask in unison.

'Madam, my grandmother used to sing it to me,' Irene says. She points at the glass charm. 'I had a glass pipa like this that grandmother tied around my wrist. She let me suck on it. It kept me quiet when she had guests. That and the song. I'd go to sleep when she hummed that song.'

'Our grandmother was dead by the time we were born,' Eileen reminds Irene.

'No, it was mother who died,' Irene replies. 'Or at least, I think . . .'

Irene stops here and finds herself looking again to the nun for answers.

The nun hesitates. Then, after raising questioning eyebrows into what seems like empty space, pronounces, 'You're right. It was your mother who died. And that's the charm she left you.'

But as Irene's youngest sister says when she lifts Irene's hand away from the charm, 'Mother couldn't have died then. Otherwise, there wouldn't have been the rest of us.'

None of it makes sense. And there is no time for Irene to ask the nun to untangle the puzzle. For all at once, all five of Irene's sisters are upon her.

'It's impossible,' they declare like a chorus. 'Big Mother didn't speak Chinese. She didn't even like music. Our grandmother couldn't have taught you that song. And not Big Mother either.'

And then, above the hubbub, Irene hears Eileen shouting, 'The Bishop's right. It is cursed.' And she watches, helpless, as Eileen sweeps her hand across the table and swipes the charm off it.

The charm arches through the sunlight before falling onto the white marble floor.

It breaks.

Irene closes her eyes and brings her hand up to her throat. It's sore. How could she have sung those high notes, she wonders? Yet, it did happen. And all because, unbelievable as it might seem, she allowed herself to be tempted, she succumbed, and she was entered.

It won't happen again, she knows. The music in the air is gone, dispelled by the sound of splintering glass. And it is Eileen who has saved her, Irene realizes. Another imponderable to digest.

She looks across the room to where the charm has fallen. The line between sunlight and shadow is now clearly drawn across the marble floor and the broken pieces of the pipa are lying where the shadows are darkest. It's as if some higher power has decided to consign it to oblivion, so it will never trouble anyone again. And Irene supposes later, that is what would have happened if not for Sister Mary Michael.

The nun gets up from her seat and goes to pick up the pieces and bring them back to Irene. The rounded body of the pipa has splintered from its neck and the neck itself is broken into two. All the life is gone from its faceted surfaces. It's a tragedy, it suddenly occurs to Irene. And yet, why should it be?

'And why not?' Irene hears the nun say.

She drops the glass pieces onto the table and turns to look at the nun, confused.

The nun gives her a quick sideways glance, then a nod, as if to tell Irene she understands what it feels like. That sense of disbelief upon discovering whom you have come from. Who you really belong to. That total bewilderment because you are so different from that other it can't possibly be true even if science can prove it incontrovertibly. But why should she understand such feelings, Irene wonders? These emotions may be what the music-starved child of an impecunious school nurse might have experienced, but certainly not herself, the first daughter of the Tjoa family.

It's the effect of the music, Irene tells herself. She's powerless against it. It's still holding on to her. And that's why she's also powerless to take back control of the proceedings.

Her middle sister is the one who ends up turning to the Bishop and asking, 'Shall we continue?'

And uncharacteristically, it is Eileen who echoes, 'Yes please. Can we go ahead?'

So they go ahead. All six of them, the Tjoa daughters, are freed and will remain free so long as they keep themselves protected.

'Regular attendance at Mass, Confession and Communion,' the Bishop reminds.

'Especially Irene and Arno,' Eileen, gone back to playing the sceptic, adds.

Irene should have shot a disciplining glare at Eileen for that. But she can't seem to pull herself together. All she can do is follow along as her sisters mouth the closing words and sign the cross. All she can do is take one 'Amen' at a time, fingers crossed that she can make it to the last with some semblance of dignity.

She does make it.

After what seems an eternity, it is finished. There is a flashing out of compact cases and lipsticks, a rush to freshen up and then hurried awkward goodbyes.

Irene understands. There had been something sickening about the rites they went through. The sprinklings that felt like some enormous creature was sneezing all over them. The repeated references to demons and sin in the prayers. The actual prayer of renunciation, where they had to use the first person 'I', as if they really were guilty of sins beyond the odd mass missed while on holiday and a careless curse word now and then.

There they were, Irene thinks, the six of them going about their business and taking care of their families. And then to learn they'd been subjected to an evil spirit's curse for over half a century and to be brought up close to that spirit. To be . . . Irene doesn't want to mince words. To be exorcised. She shudders.

But now the Bishop has committed the six dolls, the doll house, the diva doll, the remnants of the Girl doll and the threads and talismans to the mound of earth in the back garden. He's lighted a fire that roared and crackled like an Old Testament holocaust and reeked of hell. Now the six of them have been given leave to leave so the Bishop and the nun can continue with the rest of their disturbing rituals. Now it's over. Why wouldn't any reasonable person want to rush away?

Nonetheless. Irene still lingers.

* * *

Irene trails after the Bishop and Sister Mary Michael as they process through the house praying, following them from Cook's basement and through her brother B.K.'s rooms to the memory room and the attic.

Once in the attic, the Bishop begins to cleanse Arno's dolls, reciting the deliverance prayer and crossing each box row by row, from the left of the room to the right, and from the top of the shelves to the bottom. Sister Mary Michael, following behind him, sprinkles Holy Water onto the surface of the boxes, and kneels and stands and crosses herself then arches to sprinkle again, more than 1,000 times. It's an ordeal Irene almost does not expect the nun to survive. And yet she manages.

It's Arno, watching from the work chair by his sewing machine, who breaks down.

He had whimpered all through the proceedings as the drops of Holy Water falling on the plastic surfaces blurred the features of more and more of his dolls. And by the time the Bishop stands up from the very last box at the bottom of the farthest shelf, Arno's face is as wet as the fronts of his doll boxes.

'They didn't like that,' he says tearfully to the Bishop.

'No. They weren't meant to,' the Bishop replies.

Irene considers the dolls. Their expressions haven't altered. They're in no need of salvation, they're saying. But the Bishop's thumb smudges on the front of each box can't mean nothing, she thinks. Nor that water dripping down the front of the boxes and onto the wooden floor. If the dolls have indeed been appropriated by one or more malign spirits, certainly, they're cleansed now. If she is to believe anything then she must believe this, that the Bishop had done his job with the dolls. As surely, he has with her. Or with Arno.

But there is the Bishop, placing one end of his stole over Arno's left shoulder for what seems to Irene must be the umpteenth time. And there is Sister Mary Michael, lowering her head and starting to pray again. How effective are these rites if they must be repeated so frequently, she asks herself, feeling something akin to desperation.

Perhaps, even the Bishop can't be sure. Perhaps, that's why he's prescribed that continuing regiment of Contrition, Confession and Communion. Perhaps, Irene realizes, all anyone has is the power of prayer. And so, when the nun reaches her hands out to Irene and Arno and says, 'Let's pray together, we'll all feel better after it,' Irene allows hers to be taken without protest.

Arno though is less willing.

'Pray? I don't want to,' he says, tucking his hands under the bottom of his T-shirt. 'I want to marry Girl, that's what I want to do. I'll only pray if you perform a wedding ceremony. Will you do that?'

The Bishop reaches for Arno's hands, pulls them out very gently from the T-shirt and places one of them in the nun's free hand. 'I already prayed for a marriage for you Arno, during your deliverance earlier today,' he says. 'A wedding feast in heaven, with God.'

This time Arno does not mention his doubts about God. He merely tells the Bishop, 'Well I don't remember that. Why don't you do it again.'

The Bishop smiles. 'Yes. That would be a good idea. We'll close our evening with it then.'

He turns to the nun. 'The Canticle of Zachary with the antiphon and doxology please, Sister.'

This canticle giving thanks for unexpected sons and the blessing describing the heavenly wedding feast are not ones Irene knows by heart, but she is able to stumble along as the nun and Bishop recite it. Arno, who requested the prayers, merely watches. When they arrive at the blessing, though, Irene sees that Arno is smiling blissfully, soaking up the description of the wedding as if he, indeed, is the one being wedded. And whether it is truly divine power or just suggestion, his face glows when the Bishop sings, 'And you my little one, will be hailed . . . Hailed, Prophet of the Most High.' By the time the Bishop arrives at the closing antiphon, a repetition of the description of the heavenly wedding, Arno is swaying ecstatically. For better or worse, the Bishop seems to have given Arno a wedding ceremony that satisfies. When, at the end of the prayer following deliverance, Arno sighs, a huge contented out breath, Irene is in no doubt that Arno is unbound and cleansed. That he is, for the moment, free.

As for Irene, what can she say about herself?

Something had called to her and for a few seconds she had allowed herself to be entered. That has altered her in some inexplicable way. For the first time in her life, she feels a lack. As if something has been taken from her. She has discovered what seems to be a hole in her memories, a forgotten something she has left behind and whose existence she only now remembers. She is not herself. Or, she corrects herself, she is not the self she had believed herself to be. And yet, who she is, she can't say. She might be unbound, but she does not feel free, only befuddled.

Sister Mary Michael's parting words when they are finally done serve only to confuse her further.

'I don't know who's more wretched, the child who doesn't love the mother she knows, or the one who doesn't know her mother,' she says. And then, her big black eyes drilling into Irene's, she asks, 'What do you think?'

Irene looks away. 'It's not something I've thought about,' she answers.

'No. I suppose not,' the nun says as she squeezes Irene's forearm with unseemly intimacy. 'That's how brilliantly your Big Mother's plan worked.'

Irene has no idea what the nun means and tells her so before brushing the nun's fingers away and rushing out of the house toward her waiting driver and car.

The nun whispers something to Irene's retreating back. Something Irene pretends not to hear. Something Irene answers only when she's out of the house and in such a quiet under breath she's quite sure no one can hear her. Not even the seemingly evicted spirit who lingers alongside her on the five-foot-way.

31

It is noon the next day, a Wednesday, when Irene returns to the house. As always, the three musicians glower from the foyer wall. As always, at noon, the sun is shining directly into the air well and onto the koi swimming restlessly around their black-tiled prison. Indeed, if not for the string of talismans, the glass charm and Sister Mary Michael's parting remarks, Irene can almost imagine it's still the previous Friday.

But it is not Friday. There is no going back, Irene knows. She will have to move on. As Arno too needs to.

Arno's move is the reason for Irene's visit. She has discussed the matter further with the Bishop and her husband, and all have agreed it will be more convenient for Irene to supervise Arno's recuperation if he moves. It's only Arno who now needs convincing.

Irene doesn't go up to the attic immediately. Instead, she goes to look for Cook first, to check if Arno has been up to any more shenanigans.

Cook is in the basement bathroom. From the sounds Irene hears, her loyal retainer is indulging in a long splashy midday wash. And why not, Irene thinks? Cook has earned it after the troubles of the last few days. She'll let Cook take her time.

On a whim she steps into Cook's room to wait for her instead of going back upstairs to the kitchen.

The room is so heavy with the smell of old kitchen fat and over-sweet sweat Irene almost backs out. But Cook has left her passport and bank passbook lying on her bed, and tempted to see what is in the latter, Irene ventures further into the room.

She picks the bank book up and opens it at the last printed page.

Cook had managed to save quite a bit from her festival ang pows, mahjong game tips, skims off the marketing money and the top-ups Irene gives her to keep her brother B.K. in order, not to mention the commissions deducted from those in-and-out girls. The last row shows a number more than a third of the way to six figures.

That's not the actual amount in Cook's stash, Irene believes. The date on the last deposit is two days before Gran's funeral. There must be more somewhere. And when Irene lifts Cook's mattress, she finds it, the blue fifty-dollar bills from the funeral ang pow and the $5,000 worth of gold-coloured $100 notes Irene has given her.

Irene had told Cook the $5,000 was a legacy from Gran that she was paying out ahead. 'Because there might be delays and legal complications with the will,' she'd explained.

Cook, quite bedazzled by the largesse, had thanked Irene over and over. 'No worries that I'll squander it,' she said. 'I'll put it toward my retirement, just like I promised Gran.'

Irene still had need of Cook then, to look after B.K. and to manage Arno and the house. 'Surely you're not retiring yet,' she'd said to Cook.

But those needs of Irene are gone. B.K. has been at the hospice for nearly two months and soon Arno will be moving too. It's Cook's time as well.

'Twenty years is more than enough,' Cook tells Irene when she's queried about her plans after her shower. 'I've tried and tried with Arno, but nothing's going to change. Sure, he was a cute chubby boy. But then you know the difficulties. And all the nonsense these last few days. It's only going to get worse.'

Cook wraps a towel over her frizzed wet hair, taking her time now she and Irene are soon to sever their Ma'am and Cook ties. 'It's not Arno's fault. I understand. Those spirits the Bishop and that nun say are haunting the house, they're enough to send anyone who isn't quite right over the edge,' she says, digging her fists into the top of her hips and arching her back. 'But not me,' she declares. 'I want to be walking out of here a sane woman, in full possession of my senses and my body in good working order, not carried out on my back like Girl, or Big Sir, or Gran. I want to be gone before that happens.'

'But we've cleansed the house,' Irene reminds her. After all, she can't have an ex-cook saying things like this to her next employer, especially if that future employer is likely to be someone in her circle.

Cook sniffs. 'Clean! That's what I was told when I first came to work here. But that's not what my experience says now.'

The insolence of the woman surprises Irene. Who would have thought? Yes, it's best to move Arno out and put an end to things quickly before Cook climbs all over her.

'When are you planning to leave then?' she asks.

Cook walks to the bottom of the service staircase, arches her back again and begins to heave her heavy body up the steps. 'The sooner the better,' she replies, tossing her answer over her shoulder like so much rubbish.

Irene allows the insult to bounce over her own shoulder and down the steps into the wash yard where the girl crash-landed. Whatever relationship she and Cook had, it's over. There's no need any more to exert energy keeping Cook down. Yet, almost unconsciously, Irene clicks her heels faster to overtake Cook on the steps, and maintains her pace so she can keep a two-step lead on Cook all the way through the corridor to the lift.

'It's coming up to the end of your contract. In view of your service, I'll pay you to the end of the period. But I'll cancel your work permit tomorrow and you can leave on the same flight as Girl,' she announces to Cook at the front of the lift. And then as she presses the call button, she adds, 'Next week.'

Cook's bravado leaks away. She deflates like a punctured balloon. 'But Arno?'

'Arno will be moving in with me. That's why I'm here today, to tell him that,' Irene replies, stepping into the lift.

Cook follows her in.

Irene knows Cook has ridden in the lift exactly twice in the twenty years she lived in the house. There was the time fifteen months ago, when she carried the girl up in the lift after her brother B.K.'s supposed attack. And then there'd been yesterday, when Irene had asked her to follow after the Bishop and Sister Mary Michael to mop up their sprinkling. If this is how uppity Cook is going to get, it is definitely a good thing she's going pronto.

But apparently Cook has changed her mind. Planting herself firmly in front of Irene, she says, 'You can't make me go back on the same flight as Girl. I've given my life to this family. You can't do this to me.'

'Cook, it's precisely because you've been so long with us that I'm doing this,' Irene explains. 'You're going to get a rest before you decide on next steps. You'll have time to choose the colour of the walls in that house you told me you're building for yourself. You'll be able to walk in those rice fields you bought the last time you went home. You wouldn't even need to cook. You could take a walk down to the market and buy something from the girl's mother.'

'No,' Cook almost wails. 'I can't be taking Girl home the way she is, and me fat and alive. Everyone will be talking. And if not talking, there'll be raised eyebrows and sour looks. There's no way I'll be able to sit long or sleep easy. I wouldn't even be able to buy a bowl of goat soup or chicken stew from her Ibu or anyone else in the village. It's impossible. I need a lag for everyone to forget. Half a year at least.'

Half a year, Irene thinks. Well, she should have figured that out before burning her bridges.

Irene has seen the CCTV footage. If Cook had really been concerned about her place in that village, she should have kept a closer eye on the girl instead of letting her wander around the house unsupervised. Better yet she should have thought twice before offering the job to someone with that girl's temperament. After all she knew what B.K. was like and what he was apt to do to girls. Cook has made her bed and she will have to lie in it.

'It's up to you,' Irene tells Cook. 'I'm moving Arno and closing the house next week. You'll have to be out by then. You don't have to go home to your village. I can buy you a ticket to whatever town you want, or I can call around my friends. They've eaten your food. I'm sure at least one of them will be happy to have you.' She steps out of the lift. 'I'm going to talk to Arno now. You think about it and let me know by tomorrow morning.'

Cook stares at Irene, her eyes as defiantly blank as those on the faces of Arno's dolls. And then she punches the down button.

Irene lets her go. She could hardly have dragged Cook out and made her take the steps. Cook's far too heavy. The

important thing is, she's shown Cook she's the Ma'am, the one
with the upper hand.

Now for Arno . . .

* * *

Arno is rolled up in a cocoon under his duvet. Both his front
and back air conditioners are going full blast, Irene notices with
irritation. If Cook was doing her job and following the proper
protocols, she would have turned the air conditioning off at
nine, allowing the heat in the room to rise and drive Arno from
under his covers. But, Irene sighs, this is what happens when
one allows the reins to slacken. It's no wonder the electricity
bills are so high.

She turns off the air conditioning and pokes at Arno through
his covers.

'Come out from under there, please,' she says.

As Irene speaks, she realizes these are the same words she
used on Friday when Arno was backed up against the wall under
the table in Gran's room. But it's Wednesday now and he's been
delivered. Presumably, it won't be déjà vu. She and Arno should
be able to have a reasonable conversation today. She hopes.

She pokes at him again. 'Arno, get up this instant. We need
to talk about your future.'

He groans, pulls the duvet more tightly about himself and
mutters, 'No wife. No kids. What future?'

She draws apart his curtains and opens his dormer window.
The smell of frying meat wafts up from the kitchen. Good, she
thinks, Cook has gone back to work.

'Lunch is almost ready,' she says, dragging the duvet off
Arno's body. 'Don't you want to go down and have some?'

Arno can always be tempted by food. He sits up, screwing his eyes against the light, and says, 'If I behave, will you take me to see Girl later?'

The girl is off limits, the Bishop and Sister Mary Michael had emphasized. Although Arno did renounce her during his last visit and the nun did persuade him to leave the lock of hair with her, Arno would continue to hanker after the girl for some time, they'd said.

'Notwithstanding the fact we burnt the hacked-up Girl doll?' Irene had asked.

'Notwithstanding that,' the Bishop had replied. 'If Arno's to remain well, he's not, on any account, to see the girl again before she's sent home. You have to be gentle about denying him access to her, but quite firm about it.'

What Arno needs though, Irene decides, is a straight talking-to, not gentle denials. And now Gran is out of the way that will be what she gives him. She sits down in the rocking chair facing him, clasps her hands together, and prepares to give him the long and short of things.

'Didn't you say you were done with the girl?' she asks.

He moans. 'I fucked up. As usual. Back in the nursing home, when she wouldn't say yes, I told her I was done with her. Three times. You know what that means, where she comes from?'

Yes, Irene has seen enough girls from that part of the world to know.

'You've repudiated all your rights,' she replies. 'And you've cut the doll up so you can't have a proxy wedding either. It's over. It's over and it's time you accepted it.'

'You mean I've got to accept that I fucked up again.'

'I mean you haven't been well and there's no chance of you getting better if you keep thinking about the girl,' Irene tells

Arno. 'But if you stop and you get better, maybe there'll be someone else. A nice caring woman. Not a scheming second maid. And not a doll.'

She's speaking in a placating murmur, exactly the way Gran used to speak when Arno had meltdowns. What is possessing her? What happened to firmness and the truth given straight? Why can't she stop this soothe-the-baby babbling?

'You remember how happy you were when the Bishop said that closing prayer over you yesterday, the one about the marriage of the church to its heavenly bridegroom?' Irene hears herself continuing to babble. 'Well, if you come to live with me and we both go to daily Mass and to the Bishop for a blessing every month, you could feel happy like that all the time. And then you'd be in a better state to find a wife.'

'Move in with you! Go to daily Mass! Monthly blessings!' Arno's voice rises with each exclamation. The proposition is clearly preposterous to him. 'No. Over my dead body!' he expostulates. 'The idea! Living with you!'

From experience, Irene knows he's going to shout himself into an asthmatic fit.

She goes to the bathroom for his nebulizer, sets it on the denuded trunk beside his bed and sits back in the rocking chair. And as Arno rants and then begins to wheeze, she tries to anticipate the many ways their conversation might turn, playing it through in her head like she'd seen her father Tjoa Ek Kia do before his negotiations. She knows Arno will calm down eventually and she has set aside the whole afternoon. She has plenty of time.

It takes nearly an hour before Arno comes to his senses and she can engage him again.

'We're both too old for the kind of nonsense we had on Friday, Arno,' she starts. She nods toward his work room. 'Go get a chair and come sit down and talk.'

She's in the rocking chair and Arno is standing over her. It's a position of advantage she's allowing him to have, so he feels safe enough to shuffle over to the other side of the attic to pick up a stool.

He comes back with it, sits down and engages. 'I know what the court said. I've a right of residence,' he tells Irene.

'Yes,' she agrees. 'The trust can't make you leave. You need to want to.'

'Exactly,' he says.

'But who'll look after you?' she asks. 'Cook's leaving next week along with your girl,' she tells him as if it's already done and agreed on. 'You can't rattle about here alone.'

'I can do for myself,' he says.

Arno has never had to look after himself, not for one day in the whole of his twenty-five years, not even when Cook went on leave. Irene has always sent someone over. Despite his words, Irene hears doubt in his voice.

'I've the back part of my house free,' she tells him. 'It's the old servants' quarters, entirely redone, with enough space for a workroom. And there's a pantry too. I could have my cook put your meals there, so you don't have to come in. It won't be any trouble.'

No trouble at all, Irene thinks. A better than breakeven trade, all things considered, given how much it costs her to keep this old house running.

'I could learn to manage,' Arno says. 'We could get a new girl.'

'You're a single man. I'm not sure you'd get permission from the Ministry.'

'But my dolls . . .'

'You can bring the dolls. I've two other helpers besides my cook. It's no problem having one of them clean your quarters. The dolls are part of your business. The Bishop said you'll be fine with them if you treat them only as business,' she says.

Arno smiles. It's one point on his checklist ticked, Irene knows. But he isn't ready to give up all his delusions yet.

'I could have my business here. We could build a doll museum and charge visitors,' he proposes.

'No,' Irene cuts him off. It is time for 'the' talk.

'Arno,' she says, 'I'm not your Gran so I'm not going to hide the facts from you. The truth is the income from the financial assets in the trust hasn't been enough to pay allowances for you, your father and your Gran for years. For quite some time I've had to top up everything and pay the running expenses of the house including Cook's and the maids' salaries. But your uncle's retiring. It's not fair to ask your cousins to foot the bills. Moreover, your Gran had wanted to give something to the church. That's why we want to sell the house. To save on the household expenses, free up some cash for you and your father's allowances and make good on your Gran's wishes. Do you understand?'

He nods reluctantly.

Irene sees that his lower lip is stuck out. A sign of rebellion.

She gives him the bottom line. 'It's like this. If we don't sell the house and we rely on the assets in the trust to pay its running expenses and your allowance and your father's bills, we'll have to dip into capital. It will all be gone in about eighteen months. And then whether you like it or not, you'd have to sell the house and you'd be out on the street with almost nothing.'

'No!'

'Yes,' she says. She presses her advantage. 'If, however, you come and stay with me and allow us to sell the house, your allowance can continue indefinitely. Besides, the Bishop says there are nasty malign things lurking about in these walls. You'll feel much better staying with me. And when you're better, who knows? We can maybe go looking for a wife for you.'

'You think so?' he asks, pathetically ready to clutch at straws.

'We need to get there first,' she temporizes.

'You'll like the room,' she goes on. 'We kept most of the old features. It has red tile floors, a high ceiling with open rafters like here. And . . .' She dangles another incentive. 'I'll put in shelving for your dolls.'

'You'll let me bring all my things?' he asks again.

'Everything up here except for that.' Irene points to the denuded trunk. 'You've ruined it. We'll get you something else for a side table.'

'That's all right,' he agrees. But then he adds, 'I've one more thing. A secret thing.'

Irene isn't keen to bring a secret and presumably uncleansed something into her regularly-blessed and pristine home. But Arno can't continue living here either. She'll have to pretend to go along with him.

She smiles at Arno.

'Show me what it is first, and we can discuss it afterwards,' she tells him.

* * *

Arno takes Irene down to the kitchen, empty except for the flies buzzing around the lunch Cook has set out. Cook herself is nowhere to be seen. Irene can hear her bumping around in the basement but decides not to call for her. Neither she nor Arno are ready to eat yet. And Cook is packing, no doubt, which is as it should be. Cook is leaving. There's no need for her to see whatever Arno's going to share. No need to add more grist to the gossip mill.

Arno leads Irene out to the mound of earth in the back garden, now topped by the doused ashes from the previous evening's fire. Using the back of a broom handle, he begins to hack into the earth beneath the ashes. The secret he wants to show Irene emerges half an hour later. Hidden about a foot deep in the ground, between the dead roots of the tree, it is a flaking brown bag almost impossible to differentiate from the burnt plastic and leaves layering the top of the mound.

He pulls out a patchwork cloth pouch from the bag and opens it to show Irene what's inside.

Irene recognizes the black and shining 'something' in the pouch's depths immediately. It's the hank of hair she cut off the girl on her first morning in the house, seemingly alive despite the hours under the fire, the months it has been buried and the even longer time it has been separated from the girl's head.

Arno draws the plaited hank out of the pouch and drapes it over Irene's forearm. The plait, its two ends fastened with orange rubber bands, looks eerily like the banded pipe snakes that used to lurk in this very back garden when Irene was a girl. The bits of leather flaked off from the purse and clinging to the folds of the plait add to the impression. To Irene, it's as if a newly molted snake has settled on her, a shining black length pulsing against her as it readies itself to slither away onto the ground and into the remains of yesterday's fire.

'I'll come live with you if you let me bring this along,' Arno says.

Irene lets the plait slide off her arm and onto the top of the mound of earth. 'This' is not 'something' the Bishop would approve of, she's quite sure. 'We should leave this if we want to find you another bride,' she says to Arno.

Arno picks the coil of hair up, brings it to his belly and strokes it, shushing at it as if he's calming an animal. He looks up past the parapet of B.K. Tjoa's balcony, towards his dormer window, and then he begins to speak in a soft sing-song voice suggestive of the closest intimacies and the most unconditional love. A voice that does not sound like his at all.

'There are so many stories about hair,' he says. 'If you let me bring this with me, I could tell you some.'

'Why would I want to hear them?' Irene asks, quite unmoved by the voice.

'Because there are things you should know that you don't even know you don't know,' the voice that is not Arno's murmurs. He lifts one hand off the plait and points towards Irene's feet. 'Stories about that for example,' the voice says. 'That and how it relates to you'.

Irene looks down to where Arno is pointing. There's nothing there except the piles of ash and earth he's overturned, the crumbled layers of the diva doll's scorched clothes and the strips and clumps of melted plastic from yesterday's fire.

'That,' the voice says again as Arno nudges at a sooty lump of melted glass with the flat of a foot. 'That's your charm. Don't you want to know more about it?'

Irene stares at what's left of the pipa charm, it's three pieces diabolically fused together again. This is the charm her birth mother tied around her baby wrist with a plaited skein of her hair. It's a version of the pipa her mother used to play, while singing that song she'd sung yesterday.

'Recognition, that's what she wants,' Sister Mary Michael had tried to tell Irene as she was walking away the previous evening. 'That's what she gave her soul to the devil for.'

Irene's reply, said so softly only she herself heard, had been, 'It was Big Mother who gave me my position and Gran who soothed my hurts. I don't owe anyone else any other kind of recognition.'

It's the dead woman's choice, Irene justifies to herself. Her birth mother had made her bed and she would have to lie in it; for eternity, if need be. Furthermore, Irene reminds herself, it's best not to meddle with imponderables or allow oneself to be beholden to them. After all, she doesn't want to turn into someone like poor besotted Arno, someone hanging on to a girl's hank of hair in the belief it will save his life.

She kicks the glass nugget away and brushes dirt over it with her shoe. She doesn't need to bury it deeper. It will be buried under bricks and plaster before the year is out, when the demolition gang comes to tear the house down. And then it will be gone. For good.

'I've never felt a lack, not knowing what I didn't know,' she says to the voice that is not Arno's. 'Why should I want to find out now, near the end of my life?'

Arno winces and clutches even harder at the hank of hair. 'Does that mean, you're not letting me take this along to your house?' he asks in his own voice.

Irene considers her options. The Bishop will be displeased. But it's only a hank of the girl's hair. Nothing to do with spirits or demons. First things first. Her priority is to get Arno out of the ash house. She'll simply have to ask the Bishop to take that hank of hair away from Arno later. And if that takes another donation. Well, there'll be surplus after the house is sold.

'You can bring that along with you if you like,' she tells Arno.

After all. There's only so much time in a life. No one should have to waste it pondering what could have been and should have been. One can only do what one can. And then one must move on.

32

It has all been about Irene, Sister Mary Michael knows now. Bing Fa's daughter had been the reason for everything she did. And what an utter disappointment that daughter had proved to be. It was heartbreaking.

One can only do what one can, and then one must move on, Irene had said to Sister Mary Michael after the deliverance. Now that months have passed and Sister Mary Michael has the benefit of distance, she understands how wise Irene was.

She was not heartless, as Bing Fa had hissed into the nun's head after the deliverance. She'd just been clear. Clear enough to know what she could carry and what she could not. Sadly, for Bing Fa, Irene had decided the pipa diva and her story were too heavy a burden.

Still . . . If only . . . the nun muses. There must be something she can do to ease Bing Fa's pain.

* * *

She should not be back here in front of the ash house, Sister Mary Michael knows. It's been more than half a year since the deliverance. The family has been liberated. B.K. Tjoa is dead. Cook has moved on to a new job with an even more illustrious family. Girl, who did not survive her Medevac flight, is truly in the arms of providence. And Arno and Irene are bearing with each other as best they can. She and the church are done with this matter. But still, as if called by some unearthly music, she has taken the bus across town and labouriously climbed to the top of Green Hill to stand once more in front of the Tjoa ash house.

Unlike her first visit, there is no longer a door guarding the house. There isn't a foyer with a painting of three disdainful musicians either. The koi pond and glass lift shaft in the air well behind the foyer are gone, as is the mirror-lined dining room beyond the air well and the slickly surfaced tube of a kitchen with the red lacquer door that led to the back garden and the frangipani tree from which Girl had fallen. The whole incongruously crazy modern interior of the century old house is no more. As Big Mother and Gran had warned, everything has turned to dust. All that's left is the façade, looking as forlorn as it had the first night Sister Mary Michael set eyes on it.

Ah, but dust can speak, the nun knows. And so, despite her assignment being officially over, she walks her creaking body through the faded front façade and steps across the threshold into the rubble.

Chips of red clay cling to Sister Mary Michael's sandals as she makes her careful way through the foyer. They're fragments from the bricks that formed the foundation of the house. If this had been the beginning of the case the nun would have bent down, dislodged whatever had attached itself to the soles of her shoes, and wrapped her hands about it to enquire of the house's history. But she has heard more than enough stories. And the case is over.

She walks on more quickly into the depths of the property. The sun is almost setting. Soon it will be impossible to see anything. And then sure as death, she'll stumble and there'll be dire consequences for her brittle bones.

Before that happens though, the nun sees it, that nugget of melted glass she doesn't even know she's looking for. It's not meant for her of course. But she bends down to pick it up anyway. She won't keep it for long, she tells herself as her fingers wrap around the nugget. No. She'll be casting it into the cleansing salt of the sea as soon as she can. Perhaps even tonight, before she goes home to the convent. But then, she hears it again. A voice, laughing. The sound of it like water, trilling down a hill of stones.

'You just can't help it Sister, can you?' it says.

秋水伊人 - The Autumn Water

望穿秋水	gazing into autumn water
不见伊人的倩影	searching for the shade of my beloved
羹残楼静	passing the dying hours
孤燕两三声	as a lone crane whoops
往日的温情	of bygone passion
只换得眼前的凄情	replaced by forlorn tears
梦魂无所寄	while my soul stripped of attachment
空有泪满襟	dreams
几时归来呦	and I can only wet my collar in vain
伊人呦	wondering when you'll come back
	my beloved

几时你会穿过那边地丛林	when you'll pass that grove yonder
那亭亭的踏印	that pagoda's shadow on the pavilion
点点地压真	your tinkling footsteps
依旧是当年的情景	pressing the ground
只有你的女儿呦	towards that scene from bygone days
已长的活泼天真	to see your daughter
只有你留下的女儿呦	lively and innocent
在安慰我这破碎的心	your only daughter whom you left behind
	to console my broken heart

望断云山	looking at the clouded mountains
不见妈妈的慈颜	my loving mother gone
楼静羹残	passing the dying hours
难对襟寝寒	enduring the chilly quilt
往日的欢乐	comparing the joy of bygone days
方引出眼前的孤单	to my loneliness now
梦魂无所依	as my soul stripped of attachment
几时归来呦	dreams
妈妈呦	and I can only wet the railings in vain
	o my mother

几时你会穿过故乡的家园	o my mother
这里边的橱具	when will you pass our family gardens
空弃的落叶	the kitchen tools in our sideyard
依旧是当年的庭院	the fallen leaves abandoned
只有你的女儿呦	into these courtyards of bygone days
以堕入绝望的深渊	to see your only daughter
只有你背弃的女儿呦	fallen into a deep abyss
在忍受无尽的摧残	your only daughter whom you left
	suffering endless cruelties

Music and lyrics - He Luting, Shanghai, early 20th century.

Acknowledgements

Thanks must first go to Nora Abu Bakar Nazarene at Penguin Random House South East Asia for taking this project on. Thank you also to Thatchaayanie Renganathan and Sai Prasanna for your thoughtful editorial inputs and to Pallavi Narayan and Ishani Battacharya for shepherding the book through to print and market.

Stories have sources. The inspiration for *The Ash House* came from the lingering presences in my childhood home built above the Hakka Cemetery near Holland Village, and the Peranakan house on Emerald Hill that I lived in at the turn of this century. The experience of other women, often invisible in our city state and taking refuge at the shelter for foreign domestic workers managed by HOME (Humanitarian Organization for Migration Economics), provided the living breath of the story.

As for those who helped midwife the whispers I heard into words on paper, thanks must go first to Regina May, who pushed me to 'out' myself as a believer in 'the imponderables', and to Raymus Chang who offered 'music' and 'strings' as plot devices to link everything together. Thanks also to Amy Tan and Kenny Leck, who slogged through the first rough drafts of the story and responded with tough love.

The manuscript would not have attained its final form without the careful reading and critique delivered by The Literary Consultancy under the Manuscript Assessment Scheme initiated by the National Arts Council Singapore and managed by Sing Lit Station; and three months of focused writing at the 2017 International Writers Program at the University of Iowa.

I am grateful to fellow IWP writers Yvonne Adhiambo Owuor and Antoinette Alou Tidjani for advance reviews, as well as Suffian Hakim, Stephen Carver and Verena Tay.

Karien Van Ditzhuijzen, you've been with me on this book from the very beginning. Thank you for introducing me to HOME and for your honest Dutch inputs, from the first draft to the nth.

Raelee Chapman, extraordinary short story writer and reader par excellence, you have been a support through all this and everything else. Know how valued and loved you are. I could not have done it without you.

Melanie Lee, thank you for holding my hand as this story goes into the world and for setting me up on social media. I'd still be dithering offline otherwise.

And family—Minh, Claire, Stuart, Sean, Tim and baby Kian—writers need head space and distraction. You gave me both and more.